MORE THAN HUMAN

"What are you, Falcon?" When he did not answer her, Steve prodded, "Are you human, or something else? Your eyes are so different." Her fear returned. "Oh, God. You even asked me if you seemed human to me." She tried to pull her hand out of his, but he held it tighter. "Let me go."

"Please let me explain. I am half human. My father was a human, from the planet Norona. My mother is felan, from the planet Emiron. Therefore, I am human *and* something else."

Steve's hand was cold and clammy, and she swallowed several times, as if attempting to control a rebellious stomach. Falcon opened his hand and let her pull away.

None of this is real, Steve told herself. *It's more of the dream, and I'll wake up in a minute, and everything will be normal. And I will never have hungered for love from an alien life form....*

RAVES FOR *TOPAZ DREAMS:*

Other *Leisure Books* by Marilyn Campbell:

PYRAMID OF DREAMS

Topaz Dreams

MARILYN CAMPBELL

LEISURE BOOKS **NEW YORK CITY**

To my soul sister, Roni Lee Chadick Sullivan Russo Buzzi for recognizing Falcon's capabilities even before I did. May you always have romance in your life.

A LEISURE BOOK®

December 1992

Published by

Dorchester Publishing Co., Inc.
276 Fifth Avenue
New York, NY 10001

Chapter One

Innerworld, Planet Terra (Earth)
*It is easier to suppress the first desire than to
satisfy all that follow it.—Benjamin Franklin.*

Clang! Governor Romulus's heavy broadsword
crashed against Falcon's shield for the hundredth
time. At least it felt like the hundredth as Romulus's
arms strained and the muscles in his legs burned
from the energy required to remain standing, but
Falcon gave him no quarter, no chance to catch his
breath.

"Uncle!" Romulus shouted at his tireless opponent.

Falcon lowered his weapon and angled his head
slightly to signify his lack of understanding. Romulus
laughed when he realized he had automatically used
the Terran expression Aster had taught him. "I
mean, I give up before you kill me. *Drek*, Falcon,
what did you have for breakfast this morning?"
Rom dropped his sword and shield and peeled off
his protective helmet and gloves.

Falcon pulled off his own headgear and, with a quick shake of his head, his thick mane of gold-streaked hair fell to his shoulders in waves. "You have become soft, my friend. I remember a time when you beat *me*, and barely took a deep breath. Perhaps being governor has made an old man of you," Falcon quipped in a rare show of humor. "Then again, perhaps having Aster as a mate has more to do with your loss of strength!"

Romulus laughed again, both at the memory of his first meeting with Falcon and his reference to Aster. Between her and his work, Romulus no longer felt the need to purge the primitive beasts within his civilized mind. As he and Falcon headed for the Arena's refreshing room for showers, he recalled that he had not known during a joust eight months ago that the Black Knight he faced was Falcon, a superb trainer of ancient sports in the Arena as well as a highly skilled tracker.

A special law enforcer with highly developed extra-sensory powers, Falcon rarely used his unique abilities for much more than finding lost items in the peaceful, law-abiding Innerworld culture. But by the time Rom learned the identity of the knight, Falcon had twice exercised his tracker talents for Rom's benefit. The first time was to rescue Aster from another Terran, the criminal, Victor Rodriguez, when he tried using her to force Romulus to return him to his home on Outerworld, as the Noronians called the Earth's surface. The second time, Falcon had journeyed to the United States to find Romulus when he had been abducted by the billionaire industrialist, Gordon Underwood.

Since his first game with Falcon in which Rom had been the victor, he had achieved his life-long career goal of becoming governor of Innerworld. More important, however, was that he had found his *shalla*, his soul's mate, and had joined with Aster, in spite of all the obstacles, including the law forbidding mating between their races.

As he undressed and stepped into the shower, Rom reflected on the circumstances which had brought his people to Earth ten thousand years ago. Volterrin, a dustlike substance, was discovered in abundance in the Earth's core, and the Noronians had settled a mining colony there. The Noronians had considered the native Terrans being humanoid like themselves as an advantage and to protect the colony, it was decided that some Noronians would inhabit Earth's surface and integrate with the primitive Outerworlders. But Terrans were not allowed in Innerworld.

To travel by ship between the two worlds, the Noronians bored tunnels through Earth's twelve magnetic fields, but as Earth's population grew, accidents occurred. Occasionally, an undetected Terran vessel moved into a tunnel doorway just as it was opening for a Noronian ship, and the Terrans on board were transported into Innerworld. The Noronians considered these Terrans dangerous and inferior, but they could not risk revealing their presence inside the Earth by sending the Terrans back to Outerworld.

Aster Mackenzie had come to Innerworld that way. Despite her determination to return to her world, the Noronian prejudice against her, and the near certainty that mating with Aster could destroy his political career, Rom had made her a part of him.

He smiled at that thought as he turned off the water and dried himself off. After dressing, he exited the refreshing room to join Falcon. He studied his friend's face as they walked, and realized that his own poor performance in the game was not entirely his fault.

"Would you care to talk about whatever is bothering you, Falcon?"

"I beg your pardon?"

"Something is obviously wrong. You normally have the strength of two men. Today you fought like ten. Besides that, every time Aster and I have seen you lately you've been as nervous as a cat in . . . Sorry, no pun intended." Rom was relieved to note Falcon had not been offended by his unconscious reference to Falcon's leonine characteristics. "Aster's worried."

Falcon smiled and nodded. "You are right, my friend, but it is not a matter easily discussed. I am not sure you could relate to the problem as a human any more than a felan from my home on Emiron could."

"Is that what this is all about—your mixed blood? Come on, Falcon, you've seen me at my worst. You've been inside my head and Aster's as well. If there's something we can do for you now, we certainly owe you."

Falcon considered the offer for a moment. Knowing that Romulus's and Aster's minds had been permanently bonded during the formal Joining Ceremony, and remembering how easily she was embarrassed, he suggested, "Perhaps if you could assure me that Aster is not listening, I would not find it so difficult to explain. I would not wish to cause her discomfort."

"She's busy. She won't notice if I block my thoughts from her mind for a short time."

"It does concern the fact that I am the offspring of a Noronian male and an Emironian female." He did not elaborate since the circumstances of his conception were still a well-guarded secret among the Emironian felans. "After so many years I thought I had adjusted to being half human and half felan. Now something quite unexpected has begun, and I am struggling between fighting and accepting it." When Romulus simply raised one eyebrow at him, Falcon decided to share his dilemma.

"I believe my body has entered the human stage of puberty."

"*What?*" Rom asked with a cough. "I figured you were about my age, not that fifty-four is so far from adolescence."

"To be precise, I have attained forty human years, but for a felan that age would signify the end of childhood. Since my physical body was formed almost entirely from my father's genes, I had always assumed my life span would be determined by my human half. Now I am of the belief that if I have only now reached this physical stage, I may live far beyond that."

"You shouldn't let the possibility of longevity bother you. Many of our people live well over two hundred years."

"It is not that. I will live each day to the fullest, regardless of how many of those days are granted

13

to me. What is happening to me now has made me aware of the possibility that there may be more changes in store for me. You see, as I matured on Emiron I never knew which half would control my development. I inherited many of the mental powers associated with the felans, including empathy, but my appearance is much more human, with the exception of my eyes, of course."

Rom was accustomed to Falcon's unusual catlike eyes, but he automatically recalled how their luminous topaz color and black, marquis-shaped pupils had fascinated Aster. He ignored the familiar twinge of irrational jealousy, and thought back to his first encounter with the Emironians.

Once during his academy years in Innerworld, Rom had journeyed to Emiron to attend an astrophysical exposition. Although the felans there walked upright, their spines were curved and their extremely thin bodies were covered with a fine down in shades of brown and blond. Their rounded faces, flat noses, and slanted eyes confirmed their relationship, however distant, to the feline family. The males could be easily distinguished from the females by the huge mane of wild hair, which not only covered the male's head but continued down his spine. Rom also remembered how the human women had been intrigued by them.

Falcon, on the other hand, possessed a totally human, masculine appearance. Besides Falcon's features being humanoid, he stood erect, about six feet tall, and his lean body was solid muscle. The other major difference between him and his felan parent was that, with the exception of Falcon's full head of blond, light brown, and golden hair, and straight brown eyebrows, the rest of his body was almost void of hair.

Realizing his attention had rudely wandered, Rom gestured to Falcon to continue.

"I never felt that I belonged on Emiron, but neither did I feel truly comfortable on Norona. There was a restlessness within me that drove me to find a place of compromise. After many years of travel, I settled in Innerworld shortly before I met you. Here I am tolerated and appreciated for my skills. I have been content with my life—until now." Falcon took a deep breath and lowered his eyelids.

Romulus was confused by the blush that appeared on his friend's cheekbones.

"I had always assumed I inherited the felan's inability to experience personal emotions, including sexual desire. Suddenly I find myself craving a female, regardless of the species. I walk around in a state of discomfort a good portion of the day. Excuse me, Romulus, but the incredulous expression on your face is making it rather difficult for me to continue in a serious manner."

"I'm sorry, Falcon. As I recall, the physical state you're describing is most certainly common in adolescence. I don't see that it's such a problem, though. *Drek*, man. Let me treat you to a night, no, make that a week, at the Indulgence Center. You've got a lot of catching up to do, and I can assure you none of it is painful. Put it on my account. Since I met Aster, I've only been there for my monthly beard removal and hair trim."

When Falcon continued to frown, Rom thought perhaps the man didn't understand what could be purchased at the center. "Besides the personal grooming services, restaurants, and entertainments, the Indulgence Center here in Car-Tem has one of the most extensive menus of sexual gratifications, not to mention some of the most beautiful and talented pleasure females you'll ever find. And if it's lack of experience that's putting you off, you could even select a responsive android to teach you whatever you don't already know."

"I fear it is not that simple. I am not ignorant of the physical activity involved in satisfying this need. It is the desire itself that presents the problem. If I give in to desire, a decidedly human emotion, what will be next? Hate? Fear? Anger? How could I cope with such strong feelings when I already absorb those of anyone who comes near me? Surely you remember when Victor Rodriguez tortured Aster and you saw her mutilated body. Your violent fury blocked my ability to perform my job until you controlled yourself. If I open myself to human emotions, will that mean the end of my felan mental powers, or will I be in constant turmoil because of a struggle between the two? I do not wish to decide my fate at all, yet my physical body is making demands I am not prepared to satisfy at the risk of losing a part of myself."

Romulus could not help but notice that Falcon's speech sounded strongly emotional for one who denied having personal feelings. The man had just said more in the last five minutes than he had spoken since they met. It occurred to Rom that the final choice would not be up to

Falcon. He was already changing, prepared or not.

"Falcon, you are Aster's and my friend, whether you are felan, Noronian, or a blend of the two. Remember, we are always here if you need us." Rom reached out and grasped Falcon's hand, then gave a small chuckle. "Seriously, you never, ever—"

"Never," Falcon replied with a narrowing of his brows. "I am, what you call, a virgin."

The emergency message reached Romulus as he and Falcon were leaving the Arena. In less than ten minutes Rom was back in his office concentrating intently on the details of the disaster that had just occurred. One thousand people dead, a ship destroyed, the tunnel collapsed, all in a split second, with no viable explanation of how or why it had happened. Because the passengers and crew were instantly disintegrated, there was no way Medical could restore any of their lives, as they would be able to do if the victim's bodies were relatively intact. Never since the first Noronian colonists' arrival and the Great Flood's drowning a major portion of Outerworld's civilization had Innerworld known such a tragedy.

The Innerworld ship had departed through the tunnel on schedule, and the doorway in the Atlantic Ocean opened smoothly. Suddenly outside interference jammed the signal, causing the doorway to close just before the ship soared through.

Romulus's instincts told him this catastrophe was connected with other recent unexplained events. About a month ago, Outerworld Monitor Control,

Innerworld's agency responsible for keeping tabs on everyone and everything on the planet's surface, had reported dozens of odd messages which no one could decipher. They *were* able to determine that the jumbled letters, numbers, and symbols were originating somewhere in the northwestern quartersphere of the surface. They also knew that only someone in possession of an Innerworld ring would have direct access to their central computer system. The elaborate opal and gold ring, easily recognized by most Innerworlders, was worn only by a select few since it was more than a means of identifying a fellow Noronian. The special ring was a micro-computer that could give a properly trained user the key to vast power.

Every Innerworld emissary wore one. As agents placed in strategic locations throughout Outerworld, the emissaries assisted OMC by blending into the various cultures, observing, but never interfering with, the normal advancement of Outerworld civilization, unless the future of the planet was threatened. Every emissary could be trusted implicitly, and it had been verified that none of their rings were malfunctioning.

Until now, Romulus had not been certain that those messages had anything to do with the mysterious disappearance of the pleasure female Delphina. Two weeks ago, following a routine reassignment from the Indulgence Center to the remote Gladly volterrin mining camp, Delphina stepped into the glass transmigrator cell and vanished. The technician testified that he hadn't yet programmed the control panel to send Delphina to her destination, but she definitely transmigrated out of the departure cell.

Delphina never arrived at Gladly, and no one had uncovered a single clue as to her whereabouts. But it was known that someone with an Innerworld ring could have brought her to them. If it could be assumed that this someone was the same person transmitting the messages, then Delphina had been migrated to the source of the interference on Outerworld. The problem of the missing female was made more difficult by her limited intelligence. She would have no way of knowing who or where the nearest emissary was to help get her home.

Romulus had put off sending any trackers out to search for her, hoping another message would come in that could be traced to a more specific area within the northwestern quartersphere of Outerworld, but the transmissions stopped abruptly following Delphina's disappearance.

This day's disaster proved he had waited too long. Only one possible explanation remained. A ring was in the hands of a novice, one who had not been trained to use it properly, but was attempting to do so anyway. There was only one ring unaccounted for, Romulus's, and he knew who had it: Gordon Underwood, the unscrupulous man who had abducted Romulus when he and Aster were on their secret mission in California six months ago.

Because of his background in astrophysics and his diplomatic accomplishments, Romulus had been chosen to contact Doctor Katherine Houston, a scientist at the Palomar Observatory, with a solution to prevent an enormous asteroid from destroying the

Earth. Aster, more familiar with Outerworld and its people, had accompanied him. All would have gone well except Dr. Houston's secretary had eavesdropped on their conversation and had relayed to Gordon Underwood the fact that an alien was in California.

At times Rom was almost grateful to Underwood for kidnapping him. Aster's subsequent show of bravery and loyalty to Innerworld had weighed heavily in the Ruling Tribunal's momentous decision to permit Aster to join with him and be named co-governor of Norona's most valuable colony.

It had to be assumed that Underwood still possessed the ring he had stolen from Romulus, decided it was not merely jewelry, and was trying to learn its secrets.

Until the ring and Delphina were found, all transportation using either the transmigrator or the doorways would be limited to emergency use only. Norona would not be happy with the temporary suspension of trade with its mining colony, but Romulus had no choice. He would not risk any further loss of life.

Rom called to his assistant in the outer office. "Page Falcon in his quarters. Tell him to come immediately. We have another job for him."

Falcon frowned at the stack of books and files on Outerworld he had brought home following his meeting with Romulus. He was to review them as a supplement to the information he would find in the computer files. Learn only the bare essentials, Rom had said to him, enough to get around in the United States without attracting attention. Fortunately Falcon did not have to learn the language or wear a translator to communicate with the natives.

Falcon had journeyed to Outerworld twice—once to help Aster locate and rescue Romulus, and once as her guardian when she had returned to meet with Dr. Houston to complete the mission she and Romulus had begun. Both trips took place on the same day, and each had only taken a matter of hours. This time he would not have Aster to guide him or his behavior in that strange place, so he had no option but to familiarize himself with the country and its culture.

Aster. Would he ever be able to hear her name without recalling the private moments he had shared with her? Falcon would not have revealed it to Romulus, but he was certain that his current personal problem began during his encounter with Aster in Outerworld.

Separated from Romulus and deep in the throes of the mating fever that bound her to Romulus, Aster's emotions had suffocated Falcon. She had disproved the belief that only Noronians experienced the tormenting fever which two true soul mates experienced. Sexual release could temporarily cool the burning and desensitize the flesh, but only joining could cure the mating fever.

Falcon had not been able to use his powers to find Romulus until he had helped Aster alleviate her pain. By touching her mind, he had planted a very realistic, erotic fantasy which had relieved her sexual tension. But Falcon had found himself surprisingly captivated by the passionate hallucination she had experienced.

From time to time Falcon would discover that he possessed some new ability, and that had been one of those times. His own sexual desire had been awakened and it was becoming increasingly distracting, in spite of the mental control he exercised to suppress it. At least he had a complex assignment to occupy him for a while. Perhaps all he really needed was a sufficient diversion for him to get back to normal.

In order to fulfill this mission, he had to locate the missing ring and the female, Delphina. The only way he would find her, it seemed to him, was if she was already where he was going. At least he should recognize her. He knew she was almost as tall as he was, with a slender body, straight waist-length auburn hair, and bright green eyes. What little evidence they had suggested Gordon Underwood was the most likely starting point.

He picked up the dossier on Underwood. Aster had related some facts and hearsay about the man after it was determined that he had been behind Romulus's capture. Knowing that any small detail might help him locate and outsmart his adversary, and assuming Underwood still had the ring *and* the female, Falcon settled into his most comfortable chair to begin memorizing the contents of the first file.

Falcon studied the cover photo that accompanied the *Time* magazine article on Underwood. He was not only extraordinary in his accomplishments but in appearance as well. Although a large man at six foot four inches and 280 pounds, his massive shaven head still appeared oversized. It was implied that the large skull was necessary to accommodate his enormous brain. His features were sharp, his eyes narrowed as if in deep concentration.

The article noted that Underwood's parents had recognized his genius when he was a mere toddler, and with the help of a few special teachers, he soon surpassed all their expectations. He completed graduate school and obtained his first patent by the age of twenty in the young field of computer science. Besides his propensity for learning he seemed to be gifted with the Midas touch. He exhibited great foresight when investing his earnings, first in real estate and stocks and later in oil, with each venture being more profitable than the last.

There seemed to be continual speculation about his lack of interest in the opposite sex, because no one could give evidence of a close sexual relationship with *any* other human, male or female.

The journalist had written that the man seemed to be both selfless and selfish, a generous employer and a cruel taskmaster; a philanthropist who regularly made huge donations to various charities and nonprofit organizations and a ruthless egomaniac who allowed nothing to stop him from obtaining a desired goal.

One of his philanthropic enterprises, the Underwood Foundation, was established to offer support to groups, colleges, and agencies that focused on scientific achievements and space exploration. Through this foundation, Underwood kept his finger on the pulse of the future.

From their adventure, Falcon and Aster had surmised that the billionaire had a network of his own agents within the organizations he supported. Those well-paid individuals kept their antennae tuned to everything their superiors and coworkers did, then reported to Underwood when anything of interest occurred. At least that had been the circumstances regarding Walter Adams, Dr. Houston's devoted secretary at Palomar Observatory. Adams had revealed Romulus's presence to Underwood in repayment of some sort of debt. They were not able to uncover the exact circumstances since Adams had died suddenly of a heart attack.

The article then went on to report that the Underwood Foundation was located in an enormous complex beneath the desert in central Nevada. It was purported to be the size of a small city, with hundreds of people living and working there, but its existence was well guarded from prying eyes by an elaborate and sophisticated security system. Underwood had planned the development as a child, during the nuclear bomb scares of the fifties. The fortune he later amassed made the dream a reality.

Falcon could not verify how large the facility was since he and Aster had entered only one small room in the private hospital there, and had taken Romulus out with them in a matter of seconds. That time, however, Falcon had been tracking Romulus through the homing device implanted in his ear. Delphina had no such device as no one had expected her to leave Innerworld. Without the homing device and because of the size of the Nevada complex, searching for Delphina would be made more difficult because of the security system. The place was a veritable fortress.

Delphina's aura was unknown to Falcon so he could not hope to track her that way, either. He remembered that Underwood's aura radiated a very black presence, but he had never come close enough to the man to recognize the negative emanations through the thirty feet of sand and metal which covered the facility. No, even though he knew of the existence of the compound, Falcon could not easily begin his search in the desert.

When he had tracked Romulus to the foundation, Falcon had been able to rely on his ability to *see* events that occurred in a particular place during the previous twenty-four hours. But Delphina's trail was too cold for him to depend on that sense. He would have to track down Underwood the way an ungifted Outerworld detective would, or at least get to a location where the man had been very recently.

The article stated that Underwood had offices all over the world, but his headquarters were in San Francisco, California. To Falcon, that sounded like as good a place as any to begin. If Falcon was very fortunate, Underwood would be there when he arrived. If he was only moderately fortunate, he might sense where his prey actually was.

Falcon had been assured by Aster that his long hair with its multiple shades of blond would be considered quite normal in California. His eyes would not. Before leaving the Administration Building he had been fitted with special lenses which would mask his own spindle-shaped pupils with circular ones and dull the brightness in his irises. Unfortunately, the lenses also diminished his night vision because they shielded the reflective membrane in the back of his eyes, and his ability to see through lightweight materials was completely forsaken. Falcon rationalized if either of those talents were required, he would simply have to remove the lenses. His other extra-keen senses would have to make up for the deficiency.

For his journey he had been given an Innerworld ring which, among other things, he would use to tap into the transmigrator's computer to move from place to place, eliminating the need to depend on inferior Outerworld transportation, and the risks associated with such vehicles. Due to the ban on using the transmigrator unit, he would not be able to return to Innerworld until he had completed his assignment. Romulus had not liked the idea of Falcon using the transmigrator at all, because they could not be sure when the next accidental interference might occur. But there was no other way for him to get out of Innerworld since the tunnels were off limits until the missing ring was found.

Falcon reviewed the data regarding the identity he would be assuming, on the off chance he was forced to deal with someone in a position of authority. He was to be A. Falcon, an Interpol agent, originally from Wales. An Innerworld emissary employed in that agency had orders to enter a file on Falcon into their computers. His place of birth was meant to explain his pattern of speech. Apparently, there were so many accents and dialects in the United States that his clipped pronunciation would barely be noticed. Money had been supplied to him along with various pieces of identification.

One thing Falcon did not care for was the bag he needed to carry. Outerworld did not have supply stations that provided fresh, disposable clothing by making a verbal request, and Romulus assured him he would not enjoy the experience of shopping out there. He would have to take along clean clothing and grooming aids if he wished to be comfortable during his search.

It appeared that he had everything he needed with the exception of a working knowledge of Outerworld. He intended to spend the rest of that day and the next steeping himself in Americana. Then he would depart, ready or not.

Falcon allowed himself a moment to analyze something that he had set aside earlier. When Romulus relayed the facts of the ship's disaster, Falcon felt his friend's grief, but he himself was strangely affected by the news. Moisture accumulated in the corners of his eyes, and an unfamiliar tightening occurred in his stomach before he reestablished his usual firm control. Perhaps desire was not the only emotion simmering within him these days. He would have to maintain a very tight rein if he was to complete this job successfully. His personal problems would have to be put on hold.

Chapter Two

San Francisco, California
  The great fault in women is to desire to be like
  men.—Joseph Marie, Comte de Maistre

"Well, if it isn't *Lady Stephanie!*"

"Ooh, *Stephanie*, we missed your pretty face so–o–o, my dear."

"Hey, *Stephanie*, we all have to attend a *kung fu* seminar this afternoon. I hear you're the instructor!"

She held back the usual retort and let their raucous shouts and laughter wash over her. She hated the prissy name she was given at birth, and these guys knew it. Her father had always called her Steve, and that was the only name she answered to, that or Barbanell, her ex-husband's surname.

If her coworkers did not like her, however, they would not tease her, so she let them get it out of their systems. After all, it was she who insisted that they treat her as an equal rather than their employer, or worse, a woman. It would never do to let them see they could get to her. Nose in the air, shoulders back, Steve marched past them to her office as if she was six feet five instead of twelve inches shorter. Her private office was the only concession she made to her position in the firm.

Stopping in the doorway, she turned and looked each of them in the eye—Harris, Pollock, and Wang: a black, a gay, and an Oriental. No one could say the Dokes-O'Hara Private Investigative Agency was not an equal opportunity employer. Out of respect for her father and disrespect for her ex-husband, she had not changed the agency's name after she inherited her father's half of the business. Steve batted her eyelashes and smiled innocently. "By the way, *gentlemen*, I'm replacing all three of you with superwomen just like me!"

Her low sultry voice remained another source of teasing, but at times like this she used it to her advantage. The men broke out in another round of laughter. The bad thing about her voice was that she never sounded very convincing when she meant to be. The last dirtbag who thought she did not mean what she said was still in the hospital. Of course, that was also part of what got her an unplanned week's vacation.

"Barbanell!" Lou Dokes's stern voice preceded him into the bullpen.

Steve smiled quickly at the gray-haired, big bear of a man, knowing he had little resistance to the familiar gesture. "Good morning, Lou. Glad to be back."

"My office," he said curtly, turning away before he gave in to the urge to return her smile.

Steve settled into the chair on the opposite side of his desk and waited for the lecture to begin. He had been too angry with her to deliver it in its entirety when he insisted she take a week off to unwind.

"You may be interested to hear that your latest victim has regained consciousness and has agreed not to press charges against you for assault if you will do the same. Now, if he can be persuaded not to sue the agency—"

"*What?*" Steve's voice went up an entire octave from the beginning to the end of the word. "That bastard pulled a knife on me!"

"And *you* had a gun. Why the hell didn't you just point the damned thing at him and say, 'Drop it, scumball,' like anyone else would would have?" With a wave of his hand, he referred to the men sitting beyond the closed door of his office.

"I did."

"And?"

"He laughed and made a graphically explicit suggestion of how we could better spend our time together. Actually, I *was* considering the agency's public image, as you're always reminding me to. I figured disarming and subduing the subject was preferable to blowing his brains out."

"Disarming him? You undoubtedly accomplished that with your first highkick. I suppose you're going to tell me that subduing him required your administering a concussion, three broken ribs, a smashed kneecap, and an arm fractured in two places. And this has nothing to do with our precarious public image dammit!

"The man pulled a deadly weapon on you. If he refused to drop it, you could have shot him, according to the book. You have been preached at before about putting yourself at risk unnecessarily. When your father died, he left you his half of this agency because he believed you could take his place. I need a partner I can count on to stay alive until I get ready to retire. Hell, Steve, I've seen you pull the trigger when you had to and you're not squeamish about it. So it has to be that you get some kind of perverted pleasure out of beating a man senseless. Don't you *dare* smirk at me, girl!"

Steve worked the muscles of her face into a semblance of seriousness. Lou was the only person alive who could get away with talking to her like this without getting a taste of her temper in return. She respected and loved him as much as she had her father.

Her inheritance of the partnership did not alter the fact that Lou was technically her superior, but she managed to remind him of their lifelong acquaintance whenever she felt the need to soften him up. "C'mon, Uncle Lou. The guy was a real lowlife."

Lou's ears turned a bright shade of red. "When you are in this office, you address me as sir. What do you think your father would do to you if he knew about the kinds of scrapes his precious daughter gets herself into all the time?" Dokes shook his head slowly and let out a frustrated sigh.

Steve tried to look contrite and decided staring at her lap was as respectful as she could manage. Lou was wrong about her father, but only because he chose to raise the dead man to sainthood rather than remember him as he truly was. Actually it was her dad who had taught her how to cuss, and who had remained a maverick until the day he was killed.

He would not have been ashamed of her. She had turned out just the way he had raised her, to follow in his impressive footsteps as the meanest, son-of-a-bitchin' private investigator on the West Coast.

Dad had also taught her to keep quiet once Uncle Lou started reminiscing about the good old days, when the two men had begun their careers together in the Federal Bureau of Investigation.

One thing Steve could count on: once Lou got going about her father and some case they had worked on together, he dropped all pretense of lecturing her for her unprofessional behavior and other misdeeds. She only needed to listen with one ear; she had heard all the stories a hundred times. They had replaced the bedtime stories other kids heard when they got tucked in at night. And Steve cherished every one of them.

She had always been more than just Daddy's little girl; she had been his protégée. Her mother had been the calming influence between the two explosive tempers and had always taken equally loving care of them and her quiet son.

Because her father told her it was necessary, Steve had kept her nose in her school books, and when the other little girls were learning ballet and tap, she was learning the disciplines of *tae kwon do* and *jujitsu*. By the time Lou and her father had left the Bureau to open their own agency, Steve had a B.S. in criminology and was headed for law school at Georgetown, because that was the way her old man had done it.

Occasionally she had felt a touch of envy for the pretty, popular sorority girls, but she had accepted the fact that she was a brainy Plain Jane, with her straight, short-cropped brown hair, dark hazel eyes, and freckles on her ordinary nose. At any rate she had been too busy studying and turning her firmly muscled body into a weapon to be bothered about a few silly school dances. The irony was that she almost fit in now that it was the style to have a hard body and a boy's haircut.

In her last year at Georgetown, Vinnie Barbanell had turned her quiet life around. Inexperienced as she was, he had easily dazzled her with his footwork and passionate kisses. Steve had been so overwhelmed that such a handsome young man wanted to marry her that she hadn't really listened to his reasons for choosing her. She had agreed to remain in Virginia with him and to put off her career until they started their family. Thank God she had retained enough sense to finish school before succumbing completely to his charm.

Though he had never admitted it, her father was terribly disappointed when she had not returned to San Francisco to take her place in the Dokes-O'Hara Agency. But Steve had never stopped trying to reassure him that all their plans were not forgotten, only postponed, until she gave Vinnie the family he wanted so badly. Her husband had promised they would move west in a few more years.

Steve had never had the chance to back up her promises and to set things right between her and her father. The man she had always considered invincible died in a car accident during a high-speed chase one month after her second child was born.

A second devastating blow had followed immediately after the first. Each time Steve had tried to talk to Vinnie about beginning her career it had ended in a screaming battle. During one of their fights he had stated that no wife of his was going to work outside the home and leave his children with strangers, and especially not at a job where she would endanger her life. Steve had then realized that he had married her assuming that she would be so grateful to him she would always remain a dutiful wife. Well, she had certainly been the perfect candidate—shy, plain, and a virgin, with a healthy body that would bear the brood of children he had anticipated having.

By the time their son was six months old, Vinnie had found someone who understood him better than his disagreeable wife. He had even managed to forget that he was the father of two small children. The divorce had been ugly, but Steve had survived—for her baby, Vince, Jr., his two-year-old sister, Mary Ann, and the promise she had made to her father.

Three and a half years had passed since then. Sometimes it felt like a lifetime, sometimes like it was only yesterday.

Lou finally wound up his tale. "Michael O'Hara was one of the best there ever was, and don't you forget it, little girl." He paused a moment and rubbed his eyelids with his forefinger and thumb, as if it was a strain to remember that the child who had worshipped him and her father was now a thirty-three-year-old woman and his business partner.

"Listen, Steve, you don't have to prove anything anymore. No one doubts that you're a good investigator, and we all know you can hold your own in a bad situation. Hell, you probably could without all that karate shit. But if you keep up the cowboy, or perhaps the correct term is cowperson, routine, your luck is bound to run out one of these days just like your dad's did. You have *got* to put a leash on that Irish temper of yours. I know you've got a good brain. Use it! No more stupid heroics. Got it?"

Steve's suspicious nature came alert. She had expected at least another half-hour of haranguing before he let her off the hot seat. "Yes, sir."

"Good, because we've taken on a new client, and the investigator on this case is going to have to use more diplomacy than muscle. It's kid gloves all the way."

"Are you going to lay it out or do I have to cross my heart and hope to die if I don't behave first?"

Lou ignored her sarcasm. "Remember Bob Crandall?"

"Sure. He and his wife visited Dad and Mom a few times. He was in the Bureau with you, right?"

"Right. But he left it years before we did. Now he's president of QRT, Inc., a think tank in Silicon Valley. They're our new client."

"What happened? Someone steal an idea?" It sounded funny to Steve, but Lou frowned.

"Worse. One of the thinkers is missing."

"How long?"

"A little over six weeks ago. The man's name is Karl Nesterman. Bob said he's one of the top computer scientists in the world. They felt privileged to have him working at QRT.

"Nesterman had been working in his study in his home in San Jose when his wife, Evelyn, went out to go shopping. Two hours later she returned and found that he and all his clothing were gone. She immediately called the police and was told she'd have to wait the usual twenty-four hours."

"What made her call the police? Was there a note? Any evidence of foul play? Or was it just that she couldn't believe her husband would leave her?"

Dokes gave her a shake of his forefinger to remind her to hold her questions. "There was only one thing which would seem insignificant to someone who didn't know Nesterman. He had left the power on for his computer system and a floppy disk in the disk drive. His wife insisted he would never go farther than the bathroom without shutting down and putting everything neatly back in its proper place.

"I had the new kid do the preliminary legwork for you while you were out last week. She talked to Mrs. Nesterman, then checked out his neighbors and coworkers. Nesterman was a real straight arrow, no hanky-panky in his personal or professional life, and just as fastidious as his wife claimed. You can review those interviews yourself.

"There was no hint of mid-life crisis, financial problems, or anything else that would indicate he had a reason to walk out. Everyone questioned was positive he would not have been involved in anything illegal, and he never touched drugs or alcohol.

"Although his clothing and some luggage were gone, no mementos, reading material, not even his portable computer were removed. For that matter, not a single item anywhere else in the house was tampered with. No fingerprints except the residents'. No forced entry or indications of a struggle. The doors and windows were all still locked when Mrs. Nesterman returned home. He left no note, and there has been no ransom demand. So what the authorities had was a big zero."

"*Had*?" Steve interrupted. By now she knew it was Lou's way to eliminate methodically everything a case was *not* before describing what it *was*. She described him as a plodder. It worked for him, but it usually drove her up the wall.

This time Dokes smiled indulgently at her impatience. "QRT has a lot of government contracts. At the time he disappeared, Nesterman was working on a top secret Defense Department project—something involving the development of a series of microchips for a new weapons system. When the local police didn't immediately come up with anything, Bob contacted Defense.

"Based on the assumption that it was a professional kidnapping and Nesterman's current project could be the real target, the FBI was called in. They didn't do any better than the locals. Since there was no ransom demand after a month had gone by, it seemed apparent that the perpetrators wanted to keep Nesterman. That meant that a foreign government or industrial espionage, U.S. or otherwise, could be involved. But from what we know now it looks like one of QRT's American competitors might be behind it."

Steve leaned forward in her seat, but kept her lips clamped against the next set of questions she would have fired.

"Mrs. Nesterman is no dummy. She wasn't going to sit back and watch everyone else get nowhere fast.

Although her husband never gave her any specifics about confidential projects, she knew he worked on them from time to time. She was not exactly in his class computer-wise, I gather, but she was no slouch on the keyboard, either.

"Instead of worrying, she spent her time reviewing the working disks he kept at home in hopes of finding a clue about who could have wanted him or his knowledge so much they would commit a crime as serious as kidnapping. It paid off. Nesterman kept a private journal in which he reviewed his daily activities. Even his wife hadn't known about it until she found it. Considering who his notes implicated, she decided to turn the information over to Bob Crandall instead of the law. The two of them decided to hire us. They were no longer confident the government could get Nesterman back."

"You're dragging this out on purpose, aren't you? So, who's our number-one pick for bad guy?"

"Gordon Underwood."

Steve's face lit up as her mind automatically rolled through everything she knew about Underwood. "Good grief. What was in that journal?"

"Two entries of particular interest. Here." Dokes handed Steve the sheet. "The first part is an excerpt from about eight weeks ago. The second entry was made two days before Nesterman disappeared."

Steve began reading.

. . . Gordon Underwood shocked us all today when he deigned to attend the association's luncheon. He's even more imposing than his pictures. To my greater shock, he walked right up to me and offered me a job for a ridiculous sum of money and a chance to "touch the heavens." I might have been tempted if it hadn't been he who made the offer. Everyone in the Valley knows the man's dealings are not always on the square, and if it wasn't illegal, or impossible, why would he have offered me $5,000,000 to solve a computer problem? He did not gracefully accept my refusal. After repeating that he wanted me for the job and no one else was good enough, he informed me I had exactly two weeks to change my mind. I can't forget the strange feeling I got when I looked in his cold eyes.

(Two weeks later) I don't know whether to report the incident. Evelyn would be so worried. If they only meant to frighten me, they did a good job of it, but I can't believe anyone would do me serious harm just because I don't want to work for them. Of course the two thugs who accosted me this afternoon didn't actually say who sent them—only that my two weeks were up and I would call a certain person in his San Francisco office tomorrow and accept his offer—or else. I can't believe they were serious!

When Steve finished reading, she let out a soft whistle. "Sounds like more than enough to sic the law on the big shot. Why did Crandall decide to give this to us instead?"

"If Underwood is behind Nesterman's disappearance, he's going to be even harder than usual to locate. As it is, he only grants telephone interviews to the media, and those only when it involves some new development he wants publicized. He's also on his guard against potential lawsuits and being served subpoenas since he's hounded by so many different Federal agencies. And when something like that comes up, I swear he has a kind of sixth sense about who's looking for him and vanishes into thin air.

"Crandall's afraid if Underwood sniffs a lawman he'll go further underground and Nesterman may never be found. His and Mrs. Nesterman's only concern is to get Karl Nesterman back and they think that the government might use Nesterman to get something solid on Underwood and not care what happened to the scientist in the process. Crandall's idea is to get someone in contact with Underwood to offer a deal, even promising not to press charges if necessary. The hope is that once he hears about Nesterman's journal, he'll be willing to negotiate."

"Underwood must be pretty desperate for something to go out on the limb this far."

"I'm not so sure. I think Underwood guessed Nesterman was not the type to brag about the offer or to report a threat supposedly from someone as powerful as Underwood. Up to a point he was right. He just hadn't counted on a smart wife getting into the picture. But then he's never been married, so what does he know?

"You'll get a clear picture of just how good Underwood is at evasion from the reports in the file on him." Dokes placed another file on top of the Nesterman case file. "You might want to call John to see if he's got anything else you might use."

Steve's brother, John, had never been interested in their father's adventures. Eight years her junior, John was the passive one, perfectly happy to sit behind a desk at the Internal Revenue Service, shuffling papers all day long. The IRS would definitely be one of those agencies thrilled to get something dirty on Underwood and to hell with anybody who got stepped on while they went after him. John hated it when she asked him for information, but he usually came through for her.

"Whatever cover you decide on, it had better be pretty convincing. You've got to get past a corps of secretaries and bodyguards before you can get near Underwood. He's got offices all over the country. Go where you have to go. QRT's picking up the expenses, but keep an eye on them anyway. We still have to justify what it costs, especially if we come up empty-handed. Well, what are you waiting for? You have a lot of reading to do before you get started."

"Yes, sir." Steve quickly stood up and picked up the files.

"Steve?"

"Yes, sir?" She stopped in his doorway and turned back to him.

"Regular check-ins, right?" He used his Uncle Lou voice.

"Yes, sir." Steve began to leave when he stopped her again.

"Barbanell!" He switched to his senior partner voice. "By the book!"

"Aye, aye, *sir*!" Steve saluted and headed for her office.

41

Reviewing the files did not take as long as Steve had anticipated. The trainee had done an excellent job of collating the information, and Steve promptly wrote a memo to Lou stating her opinion of the young woman's work. She never wanted to forget what it was like to be a rookie, or how important a few strokes could be.

She spent the afternoon in San Jose talking to Nesterman's wife and his coworkers at QRT. It was not that she had additional questions; she simply wanted to get a personal feel for the missing man.

There were no surprises at the office. Karl Nesterman was well liked and trusted. Bob Crandall was torn between concern for his employee and sweating bullets over the fate of the project on which Nesterman was working.

Evelyn Nesterman was warmly receptive to Steve's questions, even though it was probably the tenth time she had answered them. Her frustration and nervous fatigue poked through a strained veil of optimism. Steve reinforced the woman's rationale that her husband was alive. Whoever kidnapped him most certainly wanted his intelligence and knowledge, and they would have to keep him healthy to take advantage of them.

Satisfied with the interviews, Steve was doubly pleased to be heading home to Kensington ahead of rush-hour traffic. She decided to surprise her mom and the kids by taking them out for pizza and a movie when it wasn't even Saturday night.

Staying home with them last week had been an eye-opening experience. Unlike previous vacations, there were no structured plans or hectic racing from one activity to another. With no school for the children, there was nothing but time together, time to play, time to love, time to get on each other's nerves. Although her mother insisted Steve and her brother had behaved exactly the same way, Steve had not realized her five- and-seven-year-olds fought *constantly* about *everything*. Nor had she ever noticed just how many times her mother repeated the same bit of news or advice. Steve knew she was not alone with her mixed feelings of love, disappointment, and guilt, and she tried to be as honest with herself as possible about all of it.

She loved her family, but she would never have been happy being a full-time mother. She loved her work, and would never have been satisfied if she had not followed her dream, but she also would have had an enormous void in her life if she had never given birth to Mary Ann and Vince. As long as she needed to work to support her family, at least she was one of the fortunate ones, doing something she enjoyed and having the support of a kindhearted mother.

When Steve had returned to northern California after her divorce, she had happily accepted her mother's invitation to move into the big empty house where Steve and John had grown up. Ann O'Hara had deeply loved her husband and had taken care of him all their married life. She needed to be needed, and Steve needed a responsible, live-in caretaker if she was going to make her dream come true. Steve automatically stepped into her father's shoes as the family breadwinner and, along with her children, the recipient of her mother's abundant attentions.

43

She pulled her vintage Mustang into the driveway of the split-level home that she still thought of as her father's. It was an older home with small bathrooms and smaller closets, but it was paid for, with only taxes to worry about each year. Even though it was worth a small fortune today, there was no place in the San Francisco area they could move without incurring a huge mortgage. Her mother would never be as comfortable anywhere else anyway.

After Vinnie had left her, Steve had wondered if she would ever meet anyone else who would want to marry her with or without two babies. She had fretted over the idea of leaving her mother alone again. But there had been no reason for her concern. Vinnie had been right. No other man had shown her more than a passing interest since the divorce.

Steve could hear the German shepherd, Mr. Spock, barking the second she closed her car door. By the time she reached the front door, little arms circled her thighs and waist and two paws landed heavily on her chest. All three got the customary hug, kiss, and knuckle rub on the top of the head. Then normal chaos returned.

"Ma–a–w–m–e–e! Vince took one of my Barbie dolls and ripped its head off, and Mr. Spock picked it up in his mouth and now I can't find it anywhere! I think he *ate* it!" Mary Ann whined in a voice that threatened the safety of every glass window on the block. She squeezed a tear out of one eye to show how devastated she was.

Not to be outdone, Vince screamed, "I did not!" repeatedly throughout her speech, backed up by the dog's barking. It was impossible to tell whose side

Mr. Spock was on, or if he was simply defending himself against Mary Ann's accusations.

"It was her fault," Vince added when Steve raised an eyebrow at him. "She called me a baby, and—"

Steve cut off the rest of his excuse and restored order with a tried and true method—distraction and bribery. "How about pizza and a movie tonight?" It almost worked, until they discovered they could now fight about which movie they would see.

"You're home early, honey. You're not in trouble with Lou again are you?" Ann did not wait for an answer before going on. "Would you like a glass of wine? The Krebbs's cat got in our yard again today. Poor Mr. Spock almost went right through the window trying to get at it. I don't see why they can't keep that thing tied up."

Steve smiled and gave her mom a hug and kiss on the cheek. "No wine, thanks. I'm going to change into jeans. After a week in comfortable clothes, this suit felt like a straitjacket all day."

Heading down the hall, Steve could hear her mother's voice rising above the children's in an attempt to get them to behave. Just as there was a lot of love in their house, there was an awful lot of noise. Except late at night—after baths and prayers and excuses to stay up longer, after tea and a replay of the day with Mom, after the newscasters said good night. Alone in her small bedroom, it was very, very quiet.

Chapter Three

A stranger in a strange land.—Exodus II

From the Underwood Financial Center Steve had an excellent view of the Transamerica Pyramid. She could not help but speculate if Gordon Underwood felt a prick of jealousy when he stood at the entrance of his older, more conservative building, or if he pretended the architectural attraction did not exist. In reviewing the information gathered on Underwood, Steve learned he spent more time in his San Francisco office than any of the others. Its proximity made her decision to start there inevitable.

In order to bluff her way in to see him without raising anyone's suspicions, she picked a cover that had worked well for her before and might draw on the man's big ego at the same time. Dressed in a pair of worn designer jeans, a loose tee shirt under a large cotton shirt, baggy socks, and well-used sneakers, Steve looked ten years younger than her age. A lot of mousse to spike her hair, black eyeliner to enlarge her eyes, but no other makeup, and big, black plastic ear hoops completed her ensemble. A professional Nikon camera hung from a strap around her neck, and a scarred leather photographer's case was slung over her left shoulder.

The directory in the lobby listed the floor for the executive offices. In the elevator Steve remembered to stick a big wad of bubble gum into her mouth. The receptionist on that floor listened to Steve's explanation, made a brief phone call, and told her how to find the office of Mr. Underwood's executive secretary.

Steve's heart beat a little faster, but her palms remained dry. No way could it be this easy.

A woman in her fifties, with flaming red hair, bifocal glasses, and a no-nonsense expression greeted Steve as she opened the door and shut it behind her. "May I help you?" The woman took in Steve's appearance over her glasses and clearly disapproved.

"Yeah. I'm lookin' for Mr. Underwood. I'm here to do the photo layout for the article in *I*." Steve blew a medium-sized bubble and let it pop as she looked around the office with open curiosity.

"I'm sorry. We weren't expecting any photographer. At any rate, I have never heard of anything called *I*," she stated smugly.

Steve quickly dug a smudged card out of her shirt pocket which identified her as Zena, Freelance Photographer, with an address and phone number of an Oakland telephone booth. Handing it to the redhead, she identified herself in between bubble-gum cracks. "That's me, (crack) Zena. *I* is a new magazine (crack) like *People*, ya know? They gave

47

me this assignment yesterday. Said Mr. Underwood would be expectin' me. (crack) Look, maybe his secretary knows somethin' about it."

Before the woman could respond, the office door opened again. Steve automatically shifted to protect her back and get a glimpse of the person entering. The detective in her instantly sized up the man from a statistical viewpoint; the woman in her added a few extra details.

Male caucasian, age twenty-five to thirty, six feet tall, approximately 175 pounds, looks pretty solid, shoulder-length, stylized hair, honey-blond with streaks of light brown and gold, brown-topaz eyes which seemed to flash when the light hit them.

He had to be the most intriguing man she had ever seen. Not exactly handsome. Beautiful might have been more accurate—like a caged lion, a beautiful, wild animal, strictly controlled. Or was it just that gorgeous head of sun-streaked hair that made her think of a lion? No, it was also the way he prowled into the office outwardly at ease, but the close fit of his black slacks and open-collared shirt revealed a tightly muscled body that contradicted a relaxed attitude. He wore comfortable-looking loafers, made for walking, and carried a leather bag. She frowned as her perusal stopped on the ring finger of his left hand. He was wearing a gaudy opal ring. Not only was it ugly, it didn't match the wearer. A definite incongruity.

In one smooth scan, his gaze recorded every inch of the room, not stopping until it met Steve's bold stare. That action, combined with the way he seemed poised for action, told Steve his profession might have some similarity to hers.

Steve turned back to the secretary, who had also stopped to give the man the once-over. "I'll be with you in just a moment," she said to him. "Now, Miss . . ."—she glanced at the card in her hand again—"Zena. *I* am Mr. Underwood's secretary, Miss Preston. I do not have you listed as having an appointment. I suggest you recheck with whomever gave you the assignment."

The lion had moved out of Steve's line of peripheral vision, and she could only guess that he stood directly behind her. Suddenly she was certain. She tensed, ready to defend herself, but hoped she would not have to show her hand so soon. At first she actually felt his body heat, then the hair on her neck lifted slightly then settled again as he exhaled. He was . . . *smelling* her! Steve stepped quickly to her left and glared at him. Of all the perverted . . . .

Jolting herself back into character, Steve pleaded, "Ah, Miss Preston, I *really* need this job. Won't you *please* ask your boss to see me? I'll just take a few candid shots. Five minutes, tops, I promise." She sniffed and dabbed at her eyes on the last word, just in case Miss Preston had a soft spot for desperate kids.

The stern secretary relented a little. "Look, Zena. I'd like to help you, but it's impossible. Mr. Underwood is in the Los Angeles office all this week, but even if he were here, he would refuse to see you without an appointment. If you'd like though, I'll be glad to call L.A. for you and see if he has any openings." She reached for the phone.

"L.A.! Damn! They didn't pay me in advance for this gig, and they sure as hell didn't offer to pick up travel expenses. I've got too many other things going to waste time on this one. Thanks anyway. Can I have my card back?" Steve snatched it from the secretary's hand before she could object. "Thanks again. See ya." Steve swiveled clockwise fast enough to cause her heavy case to swing out to the side and catch the pervert squarely in his lower abdomen. "Oh, 'scuse me," she said with a smirk as she noted his pained expression.

As she drove to the airport, Steve tried to put the strange man out of her mind. She wished she had an excuse to hang around long enough to find out what he was doing in Underwood's office. He made her think of a half-finished jigsaw puzzle. Having seen just enough of him to get interested, she wanted to see the whole picture. Her first assumption was that he was a professional, maybe with another agency or police department, but a pro would not have crowded her that way without good reason, and what in the world was that smelling business about? By the time she parked her car, she gave it up as an unsolved mystery.

She could not be certain that Miss Preston would not alert the L.A. office about a flaky photographer looking for Underwood, but she planned to switch covers regardless. The photographer's case and camera went in the trunk and a huge black shoulder bag came out.

At the ticket counter she purchased a seat on the commuter flight to L.A. that left in an hour, and headed for the nearest ladies' room.

The guys called her big purse her "bag of tricks," and with good reason. First Steve wet her hair and blew it dry into a fluffy pixie-style, brushed toward her face. A full makeup job came next. In five minutes flat she put on foundation to tone down her freckles, three-color eye shadow, mascara, and complementary raspberry blush and lipstick. She knew how to make herself more attractive; she just didn't see much point to the fuss most of the time. But this was different. This was business.

Steve pulled a purple knit ball out of the magic bag. A few shakes turned it into a snug-fitting, mini-length, low-necked sweater dress. The black earrings were exchanged for silver ones, and a silver necklace and bracelet were added. Last of all, Steve donned sheer taupe pantyhose and black high heels. The discarded disguise went into the oversized bag and the new Steve hurried to catch her plane.

The first thing Steve noticed when the taxi dropped her off was that Underwood's Los Angeles office building looked exactly like the one she had just left. She quickly realized the interior design and layout were identical as well. Apparently Underwood's passion for power extended to controlling his environments. She had read that he was rather inflexible in his business decisions, but she got the impression he was downright weird.

Steve put on a pair of big, dark sunglasses and pulled a small notebook and pen out of her bag. As she stepped out of the elevator, she halted, made a quick note in the book, tapped the pen on her chin while she inspected the lobby of the executive floor, and wrote a few more scribbles. Without pausing at the receptionist's desk, she strode directly down the marble hallway toward her destination.

"Excuse me!" The young girl called after Steve. "You can't go down there without being announced!"

Steve never broke her stride as she waved the notebook in the air and called back over her shoulder. "It's okay. She's expecting me!" Heels clicking purposefully along, Steve tried to reach the executive secretary's office before the receptionist could warn her on the intercom. Timing and extreme self-confidence made up her new character's style.

As she placed her hand on the doorknob, it was pulled away from her grasp, causing her to stumble into the room. She was brought up short as her nose touched a small snap on a black shirt. Stepping back, she saw the shoes, the leather bag, the custom-fit black slacks over his thighs and hips. Steve barely suppressed a surprised gasp.

It couldn't be! Be cool, Steve. There's no way he could recognize you the way you look now. Leave the shades on, head down. How the hell did he get here ahead of me?

Steve heard his sharp intake of breath at the same time as his chest expanded in front of her. *God help me, he's smelling me again!* Steve made a mental note to change perfumes along with her disguises in the future. Normally, like today, she wore no scent at all.

"Excuse me, please," she said in a brusque tone as she pressed her palm against his chest. He didn't budge. Behind him, she could hear the secretary telling someone, probably the outside receptionist, that she would handle it, obviously meaning her. Who was this guy? Was he going to blow her cover or not? Until he did, she had every intention of going ahead with her charade. Using her own body as a wedge, Steve pushed her way past him into the office.

Nodding briefly to the secretary who had risen to deal with the intruder, Steve turned to one side then the other, made a few notes, then addressed the young woman. "Hi. Ronnie Howser. '60 Minutes.' This will only take a few minutes." Steve noted that this secretary was also a redhead, more strawberry than the first. Her nameplate on the desk read MISS PRESTON. Another example of company regimentation, Underwood-style, Steve supposed. Identical buildings, identical office layouts, why not identical secretaries?

"What will take a few minutes? I was not expecting anyone today, ma'am." The wary voice let Steve know this Miss Preston was not quite as sure of herself or her position as the one in San Francisco.

"Not today, hon. The shooting's tomorrow. I'm just getting the layout and lighting requirements." As Steve pretended to inspect the ceiling fixtures, she realized the man had left without saying a word. Her shoulders relaxed a little and she got on with her charade. "Is this his office here?" Before the woman could move, Steve pulled open one of the two doors in the back wall. A storage room. Swiftly, she moved to the other door.

"You can't go in there!" the redhead cried, beginning to show her distress. She had obviously been impressed by Steve's introduction, but not to the point of being bull-dozed.

Steve yanked the door open and marched into the next room. It was large, expensively appointed with dark woods and leathers. Built-in bookshelves lined two walls and another consisted of floor-to-ceiling tinted glass windows displaying the city of Los Angeles below.

"Perfect!" Steve announced as she paced off the room. "The camera can set up here. Great natural lighting. Probably won't need to bring in more than two spots. Say, where is he? It would help if I could line up a few of the Q's and A's ahead of time." Steve continued looking around as if she was not holding her breath waiting for the answer to her question.

Finally the secretary seemed to remember to whom she owed allegiance. "I'm afraid you've made a mistake, Miss Howser. There is no shooting tomorrow, at least not in this office."

"Certainly there is. I made the arrangements with Gordon, er, Mr. Underwood, myself at the Silicon Valley Association luncheon a couple of weeks ago. It was all decided. Go get him. He'll confirm it." Steve waved her little book at her to send her on her way. That was the final act to push *this* Miss Preston over the edge.

"Listen, I don't know who you think you made an appointment with, but it was certainly not *our* Mr. Underwood. He *never* makes plans without informing his secretaries, and his schedules are worked out at least four weeks in advance at all times. Never anything less and rarely does he make any last-minute changes. There were never any plans for him to be in this office at all this week. This entire week was set aside months ago for foundation business. I can assure you if he had agreed to any media coverage, I would have been duly informed, and I was not."

Steve calculated it was time to revert to being friendly. "I guess I should have known it was too good to be true. How am I going to live this one down back at the station? God, I've been bragging about my coup for weeks. What am I going to do now?" Steve took off her sunglasses and looked mournfully at the younger woman, whose ruffled feathers were slowly settling down. "I'm sorry, this isn't your problem. I feel like such a fool. I don't suppose there's any chance Mr. Underwood would be doing any of this foundation business here?"

Miss Preston took pity. "No. Everything has its proper place. Foundation business is conducted only at the Underwood Foundation . . . in Nevada. Now, I really have a lot of work to do, so . . ."

"Yes, of course. Again, I'm sorry for the interruption." Steve stopped at the door and turned. "By the way, the man I bumped into on the way in here . . . The camera would *love* his face. Any chance he works around here?"

"Oh, he certainly was nice to look at. No, I don't know him. Wish I did. You know, he probably would like to get an offer from you, though. He came in here because someone had told him Mr. Underwood would help him get a job. I sent him down to Personnel. If he filled out an application, they might be willing to contact him for you."

"Thanks. I might just go down and see them. Maybe the day won't be a total loss!" A quick side trip to Personnel confirmed what Steve already suspected. The man never showed up there.

55

* * *

Steve had a lot to consider during her trip back to San Francisco. Although she had not had high expectations for success when she started out this morning, she had remained optimistic. Miss Preston One had clearly lied. She was too efficient to have made a mistake about her boss's whereabouts. Miss Preston Two, on the other hand, did not seem shrewd enough to mouth a lie while flustered over something else. Of course, it was possible Underwood actually was in Nevada. He could even be hiding Karl Nesterman there.

There really were no alternatives yet. She would have to follow the trail wherever it led until she came up with something better. Tomorrow would be soon enough for a trip into the desert.

Tonight she intended to satisfy her curiosity on another matter. Walking into the lion in the L.A. office had practically done her in. The bag he carried indicated that he had been prepared for a trip, but he had to have used private transportation to get there ahead of her. She had taken the first flight out and he had not been on it. Steve was certain the man had seen through her disguise, yet he had not given her away. Why not?

The only logical answer was that, like her, he was after Underwood. It was unlikely he was working undercover for the FBI. Both Bob Crandall and Evelyn Nesterman assured her no one else knew about the contents of the journal that connected Nesterman with Underwood. She could not take it for granted that the lion-man was even on the right side of the law. Underwood was known to deal with some shady characters from time to time.

When Steve checked in with Lou later that night, he promised to make a few calls and get back to her before she left in the morning. All Steve could give him was the man's description, but at least he could try to find out if anyone official was dogging Underwood. The old-boy network was alive and well, and Lou always gave as good as he got.

Because of the information on Underwood's underground facility, Steve knew gaining access would require more than a simple disguise and a little acting. Although she turned down Lou's offer to send someone with her, she requested his assistance with some props and subterfuge. Sometimes the simplest plans worked the best, even when they had been used hundreds of times. And this one never failed.

In the town of Glendora, on the outskirts of Los Angeles, Falcon stretched out on a motel-room bed. The television monotonously murmured the day's news, but he barely heard the details. Things had not gone smoothly so far.

From Innerworld he had had no problem migrating directly to Underwood's San Francisco office, but when he had attempted to go to Los Angeles, he had discovered it was not as simple as he had anticipated. Street addresses in crowded metropolitan areas did not neatly translate into correlating coordinates that the transmigrator could adapt to.

He could get close to his destination using his ring, but the only way he could hit it precisely was to go back to Innerworld for recalculation each time he wanted to relocate. The temporary ban on using the main transmigrator prevented his doing that, and the strain of repeated migration through the dense layers of the planet in a brief time span would weaken his body considerably. He had no choice but to use his ring to get as close as possible then rely on Outerworld transportation for the remainder of the trip.

A vehicle called a taxi had taken him on a nightmarish ride through the city of Los Angeles which included a very slow progression on an expressway that seemed to be misnamed. He still had the calculation for the exact location of Underwood's desert facility, so he would not have to waste a lot of time traveling tomorrow.

For tonight he needed to rest and clear his head. His second journey to Outerworld with Aster had taken him to New York City, and he had been very glad to leave there. Los Angeles reminded him of New York. Millions of people congregated in such a small area, combined with the proximity and abundance of buildings and vehicles, created a noise level Falcon could barely tolerate. His hearing was too keen. He picked up sounds others did not hear— as he had heard the woman's gasp when she saw him the second time today. He forced himself not to think about how he had felt at that moment . . . how his body responded even now.

San Francisco had not been nearly as unbearable as Los Angeles. The outdoor temperature in San Francisco had been somewhat similar to Innerworld, and the city itself had been very pleasant to look at, unlike Los Angeles where the view was tedious and the weather was sweltering. The air itself was disgusting. How could people live in a place that poisoned their lungs and burned their eyes? Perhaps he was too sensitive in this regard as well. He could smell things others did not—as he had smelled the tangy fragrance that identified the woman for him despite the disguises she had worn.

Why had he never noticed that a female could smell that way? It was almost as if her scent had lured him, personally invited him to . . . He ordered himself to put her out of his mind and ignore the need rising within him. He needed to concentrate on the problem of controlling his reactions to this strange environment.

Worst of all was the emotional stress level. As an empath, he regularly absorbed the feelings and emotional responses of people nearby into his conscious mind, without those emotions directly affecting him in any way. He occasionally had slight problems blocking one person's extreme fear or anger from his mind. Today in Outerworld, the multitude of conflicting, strong emotions bombarding him from every direction had distracted him beyond measure. When he had left the second office, he had asked the taxi driver to take him out of the city and he had not let the man stop driving until he had felt the noise and stress abate. That was how he had gotten to Glendora. It was not the perfect place, but it was good enough for him to regroup.

The moment he began to relax thoughts of the woman intruded again. She had been nervous and a little afraid. He had absorbed it immediately. Who was she? What was she doing that he should see her twice in the same day in two very different disguises? She had also been interested in him as a male. Even if he had not picked up on it, he had seen it in her eyes when she had first looked at him. Could it be her desire he had felt and not his own? He was certain it was not, as much as he wished it was.

Falcon tried to redirect his thoughts by considering the falsehoods he had related in the past twelve hours. Living among Noronians he was accustomed to handling their code of honesty, although he did not feel bound by it. As a native Emironian, he pledged to help others whenever possible by relieving their emotional pain. Occasionally, it was not feasible to do that and still remain totally honest. Falcon knew his current circumstances might require considerable fabrications, which would require careful, premeditated responses if he was to be convincing. The less contact he had with the Terrans the better.

He switched off the television. It might have been helpful, but he had not listened enough to learn anything.

Carefully, he removed the lenses from his eyes. He had found them somewhat irritating before the dirt of the city turned them to sandpaper. They were not making this job any easier. After shedding his clothing, he showered then turned off the light and ordered himself to sleep.

He reminded himself one more time what giving in to *any* human emotion might mean. The possibility of trading his felan powers for a collection of uncontrollable reactions made his chest tighten with what he would call fear, if he wasn't positive that the discomfort was caused by the greasy food he had for dinner. If he could explain that away, why was it so hard to find an excuse for his response to that woman?

It was impossible. His body was tense, his manhood so rigid it was painful. Perhaps his mind was too overloaded to perform its usual function of controlling his body. If he did not find a way to deal with everything going on around him and within him, he would never get through this assignment.

He needed to relax. His body needed a release, and he was a world away from the Arena, where he could burn off the excess tension in a game. This was not giving in to an emotion, he reasoned. This was biological, and he did not seem to have any other option. Perhaps, just this once, it would be all right, and then he would be able to function normally again. Slowly, vaguely aware that he was making a choice, Falcon's hand moved to his thigh and higher. His fingers curled around the hard, pulsing muscle that begged for attention.

Just this once.

Steve searched the flat desert for landmarks as she drove the telephone company van along the barely recognizable road. Her brother, John, had come through for her, as expected, by supplying her with a copy of a report prepared by the Treasury Department during one of their investigations of Gordon Underwood some years ago. In the report were directions to Underwood's underground Nevada facility. She had attached a reliable compass to the dashboard as a precaution. At least she could find her way back to Las Vegas if she had to.

Lou had tapped one of his "friends" to arrange for the temporary use of the van, and that person had made sure that Underwood's private phone line had been sabotaged during the night, so that someone would call for service first thing in the morning. The guards would be expecting a repairman any time now. Steve laughed to herself. It seemed that no matter how much money or power a man or a company had, the phone company still had the upper hand.

The puzzle of the lion remained unsolved. Lou's contacts were not aware of any federal agency investigating Underwood at the present time. So, if he wasn't an agent, was he working independently? And which side of the law was he on?

When Steve recognized the beginning of a well-used airstrip to her right, she came to a stop and raised her binoculars. There, a considerable distance away, beyond the end of the runway, she could see the shack which hid the elevator that would take her down to the small city. Somewhere down there the Underwood Foundation was headquartered, and, she hoped, so was Gordon Underwood.

As she lowered the binoculars, she thought she caught a movement off to her left. Squinting against the glare of the sun, she could make out a figure, about a quarter of a mile away, moving in one direction for a while, turning, and heading in another just as methodically. Curious now, Steve picked up the glasses again. It was *him*! He turned toward the van and stopped. His gaze seemed to bore directly into her lenses. But that was impossible! He probably heard the van's engine and looked for the source of the sound. It only *looked* like he recognized her.

There wasn't a car or plane in sight. How could he have gotten out here? For her peace of mind she decided to resolve that question before she did anything else. She put the van into drive, turned to the left, and headed straight to where he was standing.

As she climbed out, he began walking toward her. Automatically, her fingers brushed the grip of her gun tucked in the back of her jeans and hidden by her loose shirt. The Glock was there, right beside the cuffs.

Like a tarantula and a rattlesnake, they halted an arm's length from each other and checked out the competition for this square of the desert. Her feet apart, her hands poised in front of her, Steve waited for him to speak or to move. Either way she was prepared to defend herself with words or actions. He did neither.

"Who the hell are you?" Steve finally asked. "What are you doing here?"

The man's right hand was moving toward her. Steve sensed the movement and reacted before she knew she saw it. With practiced ease, she grasped his wrist before he could strike, shifted her body into position next to his, and flipped his weight over her, using a simple hip throw. The next instant she prepared to drop her knee onto his chest and secure him on the ground, but he did not fall where she expected. As if he had taken off from a trampoline instead of her hip, he went farther into the air than she had ever seen anyone flip. He then landed smoothly on the balls of his feet.

Marilyn Campbell

Somewhere in the recesses of her mind she noticed that when his hand came toward her, he had extended the first two fingers instead of all five. It seemed wrong, somehow, but she was still not taking any chances. The flip had not worked. Surely her next move would put her in a superior position. She did not want to maim him; she merely wanted some answers.

Again he stepped toward her and began to raise his arm. Grabbing his wrist from a different angle, Steve swivelled his arm down and up against his back. Her heel caught his ankle to trip him a split second later. Before he could make any attempt to protect himself, she had him face down in the sand. Straddling his waist, she maintained a tight hold on his bent arm with her one hand while the other latched onto his free wrist and held it firmly on the ground to the side of his head.

Breathing heavily, but feeling somewhat cocky, Steve leaned forward and spoke close to his ear, knowing her movement would pull his straining shoulder to the limit. "I believe I asked you who you are. I want your answer now!" No one had ever gotten away once she had them in this hold.

At first he only countered her pressure on his outstretched arm, lifting it a few inches, almost as if he were testing her strength. Then in a move so fast Steve could not understand how he had done it, he jerked his body, twisted out of her grasp, and flipped her onto her back, rolling with her until she was pinned securely beneath his weight with her wrists held firmly over her head.

"You bastard! How the hell did you do that?" He had overpowered her without hurting her, except for her pride, but now she knew he could do that, too, if that was what he intended. His body seemed to be made of forged steel as it imprisoned hers, but a moment ago it had been as difficult to hold onto as liquid mercury. She squirmed, but the only part of her she could move was her head. Her gun and cuffs created uncomfortable indentations in her back. "Dammit! Say *something*!"

Still, he did not speak . . . with words. His eyes were relaying a message, but she could not understand the language until his hips shifted slowly, and his mouth came down on hers with an animal hunger.

Chapter Four

Illusion is the first of all pleasures.—Voltaire

Gordon Underwood savored the tender veal his man-servant, King, had prepared for lunch. He smiled at his beautiful guest as she nibbled on her own meal and received a contented smile in return. The eight-room log "cabin" around them comforted Underwood with its warmth and simplicity. Even the weather in this northern frontier pleased him now. July in Alaska was far preferable to California, and he was certain they would not have to spend another winter there.

Surely Karl Nesterman would stumble onto the answer soon. His thoughts drifted to the computer scientist in his secure quarters at the other end of the house.

Underwood would have preferred it if Nesterman had accepted his five-million-dollar offer. He did not particularly like getting his hands dirty unless there was absolutely no alternative. For some ridiculous reason the man had turned him down, and Underwood resented the fact that he had been forced to kidnap Nesterman to get his assistance. He would have gladly shared the glory with the scientist, but not now. Now, he was not certain he would even pay him if he *did* complete his assignment.

When the alien had mysteriously vanished from the hospital bed in the underground complex in Nevada six months earlier, Underwood had salved his wounded ego with the conviction that the alien's people would return for the gaudy opal ring Underwood had retained. He had immediately made plans to deal with such a visitor, so that he or she would not be able to escape so easily the next time.

As he chewed a succulent piece of meat, he thought about the way he had set out to make his scheme a reality. His first order of business had been to find the right location to set his trap. It had to be a place where secrecy could be maintained for a time. It had to be remote enough not to attract unwanted attention, yet close to civilization so Underwood could run his business with as little interruption in his normal routine as possible.

When he had learned of a five-thousand-acre parcel in central Alaska, he had snatched it up, using the customary trail of brokers and false corporations to carry out the deception. Located in one of the forests that had not already been claimed as a wildlife refuge, national park, or preserve, it was close enough to Fairbanks to satisfy his needs.

It had also met another essential criterion. It possessed a lake large enough for a medium-sized seaplane to land. Underwood had wanted the simple house built immediately and refused to be dependent on the Alaska Railroad and the vagaries of winter travel overland to get the construction materials and workmen to the area.

Once again he had proven the fact that if one had sufficient capital and clout, any obstacle, including Mother Nature, could be overcome. The totally self-sufficient house was completed to his specifications within four weeks, the final touches in the next four after he and King had moved in. He had placed the ring in a curio cabinet, along with other genuine artifacts, in a very specially equipped room.

As he looked at his dinner companion, he prided himself on his cleverness. His business had run uninterrupted as many years ago he had created a system which funnelled all information through his primary secretary in the San Francisco office, so no one ever questioned not hearing from him personally for weeks at a time. He could be anywhere in the world, but one phone number could be called and he would be tracked down minutes later if she deemed it necessary. Only she and King knew of his Alaskan retreat.

No matter how busy he was, Underwood was always available for her calls. After all, her loyalty was guaranteed, and she was also the most efficient of his army of secretaries. She was his mother, although he had not called her anything remotely personal since he was a child. Such sentiment was a weakness and Gordon detested weakness of any kind. She was also the first woman he had dubbed Miss Preston, after the original one was out of his life. Her name had been legally changed to further satisfy his whim. No one but the two of them knew her true identity or why Underwood trusted her with his empire, but no one dared cross her any more than they would him.

Underwood savored his meal as he leisurely tasted the lightly grilled vegetables and sipped at the full-bodied burgundy. His thoughts reverted to the instructions he had given King while they waited for someone to come for the ring.

Underwood remained convinced that the ring had a specific function, and even if its owner could afford to leave it behind, he wanted to know what that function was. But he could not devote the time it would take to find out as he could not ignore his business for that long. Only one man had the expertise to rival his own, and he had gone after Nesterman, certain if the money could not lure him, the promise of conquering the unknown would.

For once Underwood had misread his intended conquest. The computer genius was younger, shorter, slighter, and, unfortunately, much less ambitious than Underwood. His refusal had hurt Underwood's pride enough for him to take drastic measures. Thus Nesterman's freedom of choice was taken away. If he failed to cooperate, his wife would be killed. It was that simple. Most things in life were—when you had money and power.

When he had first told Nesterman about the alien, Underwood had been disappointed with the man's lack of interest. Eventually, however, Nesterman began studying the ring, whether out of curiosity or boredom, Underwood didn't care. Underwood

Marilyn Campbell

had brought in the most sophisticated equipment his company had, and set it up in one of the two windowless rooms that made up Nesterman's apartment. The man may have been a prisoner, but Underwood made certain he was provided with all the comforts of home, with the exception of his wife, of course, and a way to contact the outside world. Even if he could, Nesterman had no idea where in the world he was, since he had never been permitted to look outside and he had been kept unconscious for the duration of the trip there.

For the first two weeks of his captivity, Nesterman's findings had been limited to calculating the number of combinations that could be achieved by pressing the nodules on the sides of the gold band and/or moving the opal in its setting. The number was astronomical. Unfortunately, no matter how many combinations he had tried, nothing seemed to happen. Underwood had ordered him to keep working and to record every combination as he went along.

Now that Nesterman had had some success, Underwood hoped Nesterman solved the ring's entire puzzle soon. He could not know with absolute certainty that Nesterman's disappearance would never be connected to him. Given more time and a nervous wife, anything was possible.

"King, lunch was superb, as usual," Gordon complimented his manservant as he cleared the table.

Born of a Vietnamese mother and a Caucasian father, King was as tall and broad-shouldered as Underwood, with Oriental features and straight black hair. Ten years ago when King was twelve,

Underwood accidentally interrupted a gang of hoodlums from beating the youngster to death in a Hong Kong alley. The orphan attached himself to Underwood who educated and trained the boy in a variety of ways. King was an expert in the martial arts, a gourmet cook, an excellent valet, housekeeper, a licensed pilot, and Underwood's bodyguard.

At first Underwood had considered him little more than a pet project, or perhaps more like a pet. In a moment of perverse humor, Underwood named him King, and made him his personal servant because he liked the idea of being waited on by royalty. In spite of everything, King remained loyal and devoted to the man who was responsible for his life. Their lives intermingled in a way that was convenient and comfortable for each of them. To the outside world, King was merely an employee, but in private he was an integral part of Underwood's life.

Underwood pushed his chair back from the table, and walked to where his guest sat. "I believe we will have another cup of coffee before I get back to work—in the drawing room please, King. Delphina, after such a fine meal, only your lovely voice could be sweet enough to be dessert. I would like to hear that song again, the one about the Noronians' trip across the universe to the planet Earth." He held her chair as she rose, and waited patiently as she smoothed the gathers of her long chiffon gown. When she placed her fingertips on his forearm, he escorted her to the drawing room, which had been called the den before her arrival.

Underwood approvingly noted the crackling fire and the silver tray of liqueur decanters on the low table. He walked Delphina to her favorite seat by the fire, a large, tapestry-covered armchair. A few minutes later King entered the room carrying the coffee service and placed it on the table. After preparing their beverages, King slipped quietly from the room.

Underwood smiled at the elegant picture they created: he in his velvet smoking jacket, she in her pale lime Empire gown, a lord and his lady.

It had been well worth the trip to New York this week to purchase a new wardrobe for his house guest. The few things Miss Preston had flown up from San Francisco for the lovely young woman were entirely unsuitable. Delphina needed to be dressed like an empress. He found it impossible to explain it to anyone else, and had finally decided to choose the gowns himself.

After attending to other pressing matters in New York, he had invited several designers' representatives to bring some samples to his office. The power of his name was enough to bring them scurrying like ants. He had accepted the fact that a fresh flow of rumors would follow such purchases, but they would be impossible to confirm under the circumstances. He had piloted the plane to and from New York himself since King had to remain behind to attend to Underwood's special guests.

To compliment the gown, Delphina's beautiful hair was crowned by a wreath of baby's breath that trembled with each movement of her regal head. He marvelled at her loveliness every time he looked at her. No woman had ever had such expressive emerald-green eyes, or hair that perfect blend of red and light brown. Her cheekbones were a work of art as was her form.

He had not been stirred by a woman in so many years that he was genuinely surprised to find himself wanting to taste her lips and stroke her small breasts, to feel her narrow hips settle on his lap.

She was much too young. Oh, yes, she had answered that she was neither young nor old when he had asked her age. It was her pure innocence and delicate beauty rather than her actual age that discouraged his seducing her. He had avoided any sexual relationship, even with prostitutes, for most of his adult life because he had no desire for anyone to learn his secret.

A normal sexual experience was not enough, had not been since he was thirteen. He required something more to achieve gratification, and a man in his position could not risk such a weakness being used against him. So he suppressed his need and diverted his energies into accumulating money and power. Until Delphina appeared, he had not given his sexual desires a passing thought in years.

"Will you sing for me now, Delphina?" Her sweet feminine voice enveloped and warmed him more than the fire. He was glad Alaska's summer remained cool enough to allow lighting the fireplace. It seemed necessary to the scene, and it also pleased his guest.

The moment when Delphina first appeared, she had made him think of Napolean's Empress Josephine, and he found it impossible to treat her otherwise. She had responded in kind, as if they had rehearsed their lines in advance of their meeting. She fit the role so perfectly he could easily forget it was an act. He wondered if he had treated her like a whore instead, would she have accepted that as well and also acted accordingly? No, he could not imagine her as anything so crude.

Gordon tried to pinpoint the moment this fantasy replaced his previous life. The two of them had never discussed it; it more or less fabricated itself, and each hour, each day, it became more real and less make-believe.

Although he felt as if Delphina had always been with him, she had actually arrived less than three weeks ago. He remembered the exact moment because he had finally acquired the additional two percent he needed to have controlling interest of a British shipping firm that had dared to refuse to conduct business with one of his concerns. King had interrupted his phone call—which was absolutely forbidden—to tell him Karl Nesterman was demanding to see him. Since the computer scientist had been barely cooperative and completely unproductive so far, Underwood hadn't known what to expect.

As Delphina sang her ballad, Underwood recalled each detail of the scene that had set the stage for their relationship . . .

King unlocked the door to Nesterman's apartment as soon as Underwood approached, then blocked the lone exit with his body as his employer entered the windowless room.

"Well, Underwood, I was beginning to think you'd lost interest in your little project," Nesterman said sarcastically. He swept his arm in front of him. "You can see for yourself why I summoned you, *your Majesty!* Actually I'm glad you took your sweet time getting here. It gave me a chance to collect my wits again."

Underwood could not stop staring at the auburn-haired vision. The flutter in his stomach was not strictly caused by the possibility that this incredible woman-child was an alien. "How did she get here?" he asked in a choked whisper without taking his eyes off the woman.

"I'd like to say I wished for her, but I don't think you'd be seeing her too, if she were *my* dream girl." When Nesterman got no reaction from Underwood, he sighed and went on, "I believe I brought her here, or rather this ring did with the last combination I tried. I hate to admit it, but I think you might have been right. She's not from around here. She speaks English by the way."

Underwood stepped forward. Intending to remove quickly any ring she might be wearing, he reached for her hand. As he did, she curved her fingertips into his palm and he found himself bending at the waist to brush the back of her hand with his lips. "Welcome to my home, lovely lady. I am your host, Gordon Underwood. May I put a name to my good fortune?" He suddenly felt like a young boy, playing at some long-forgotten game.

She bowed into a deep curtsy before him, and when she rose, her emerald eyes met his with open friendliness. "My name is Delphina, your Grace. I do not believe I am where I was supposed to be. Might I be so bold as to ask my location?"

"You may ask as many questions as you like, as I will of you. But first, I believe some refreshment is in order. King, champagne and *pâté* in the drawing room, please. Oh, and bring some here for Mr. Nesterman as well. I believe he also deserves to celebrate." When Underwood offered her his arm, she gracefully placed her hand on it and smiled her willingness to follow his lead.

And follow his lead, she had.

When he had questioned her upon her arrival, her candidness had disarmed Underwood. It was almost as if she could not have lied even if her life had depended on it. This should have been an incredible stroke of luck to help him carry out his plans. With her, he would need no tricks, no chemicals, no deceptions or coercions. She had made no attempt to evade his questions. The problem was she did not seem to have many answers, and he had known instinctively that she was being completely truthful every time she answered, "I do not know."

Underwood had immediately noted she wore no ring. In fact, her only jewelry was a thin gold choker which she had explained was a universal translator. She could have responded in any language he spoke. She had shown no fear, no confusion over her situation, and only mild curiosity as to her future. Delphina had accepted her circumstances with surprising ease.

Delphina had also made no objections to the fact that she was not permitted to leave the house or to speak to anyone other than Gordon. When she was not secured in her room, King was always close by, but she had made no mention of her lack of freedom or the fact that the man she had met upon her arrival had even stricter confinement than she did. It was almost as if she had expected it to be that way.

Their lives had quickly taken on a certain pattern, a mixture of reality and fantasy. Underwood worked all day, but stopped to share each meal with her. She had no preferences herself, always choosing exactly what he selected to eat and drink.

Afterward they sat together in the drawing room over coffee or crystal snifters of warmed brandy, talking or playing games. Sometimes she would sing for him. From her ballads, he had learned the history of Norona and Innerworld, where she had been born. When he had questioned how much of the song was truth and how much folklore, she had not seemed to know that there was a difference.

Delphina also entertained him with her stories, another of her creative skills. Like Scheherezade she could weave a spell about him with her imaginative tales of faraway places and wild adventures.

At first Gordon had done most of the talking without being aware of how that had happened. He would begin asking her a question about her life, and he would end up talking about his own. She was the perfect listener, turning questions back on him, never interrupting with her own story, always making eye contact with him, hanging on every word he said.

Eventually, he had controlled the effect she had on him enough to learn about Innerworld. She had created vivid pictures for him of cities where crystal prism buildings stretched up to a lavender sky, and the barren deserts of the far provinces where the large orange sun with its white ring seemed even bigger because of the emptiness. Instead of attracting an astrophysicist or chemist to his lair, he had a very creative, stimulating sociologist. Delphina was well versed in the culture and lifestyle of her world.

Now, after she finished her song, he asked her to tell him about the laws of her people.

As always, she was more than happy to please. "The Noronian people, whether on their home planet or in Innerworld, are subject to a handful of basic laws: One must work at something productive, enjoy the work one chooses, and maintain one's body in a good and healthy manner. Violence and dishonesty are not tolerated."

Underwood thought it sounded like paradise until she said that. "It sounds like a workaholic's idea of heaven, as long as he's honest and nonviolent. But what if he's not such a perfect specimen?"

"If someone cannot abide by these laws, there are different methods of handling the problem. In the most extreme case, one might be reprogrammed to help one become a useful citizen."

"*Reprogrammed*?" Underwood said in disbelief. He did not need a terribly active imagination to have an idea of what that meant. He knew without asking that Delphina would not know how that was done, either, so he merely encouraged her to go on.

"As important as our work is, though, so is our leisure time. It is divided almost equally, unlike Outerworlders who have a difficult time balancing the two."

"Oh? And how do you know about Outerworlders' habits?" Gordon asked with a chuckle.

"I have met a few in Innerworld. Since there are many who live in my world, particularly at the mining camps, I was required to learn about your culture and history."

Underwood learned that was how she had been able to step into her role as empress so easily, right down to her archaic speech. She had studied his world, not knowing she would ever be whisked into it. "But Delphina, how did Outerworlders get into Innerworld in the first place?"

"Through the doorways, of course."

He pressed her for more information, but she knew very little about how it was done, only that they were referred to as accidents, and there were many doorways on the surface of the Earth. Immediately, he vowed to find one of these doorways and to see her world for himself.

It was not only a matter of curiosity, it was also because of something else she had told him. The average life span there was at least one hundred fifty years, and often much longer. Doubling his lifetime would be more valuable than any high-tech secrets he could glean from her people. What good would all his money do him if he was stricken with cancer? According to Delphina, they had a cure for that and most other diseases common to Terrans, as she called his kind. They had the ability to replace defective body parts successfully, even restore life within a limited time period. It was better than he could have dreamed. But how could he locate one of these doorways?

Gradually over the past three weeks he had realized one of the major pieces to the ring's puzzle.

If Delphina could be brought out by something Nesterman had done to the ring, then someone could go in as well, back and forth between two worlds at will. It had occurred to him that if Nesterman accidentally transported himself into Innerworld, that would certainly convince the scientist once and for all that Underwood had been right about the alien civilization.

Delphina had explained to him that the ring could be used for many purposes, such as moving a person from place to place in seconds, and she had told him that the Noronians had ships in which they could travel to distant galaxies in relatively short spans of time. How these things were done did not interest her. They just were. A person's behavorial motivation was much more interesting to her.

The only subject close to science or industry he had discovered that she was familiar with was mining. She had told him she had expected to arrive at one of the mining camps where she was to begin work as an entertainer. The Noronians mined for volterrin, a dustlike substance located in the inner core of the Earth. It was the source of energy used in Innerworld as well as shipped back to their home planet. That was the extent of what she knew about it, but it had been enough for Gordon to realize that the man who could introduce volterrin to his world would have wealth and power beyond anything he had heretofore imagined. All he needed was a way in and out of Innerworld.

As much as Underwood enjoyed Delphina's company, he had also thought of her as a lure, better than the ring that was obviously not one of a kind or even worth its owner's time to retrieve. In her, he had something much better. As the Innerworld had done before when he had held one of their people captive, someone would come to rescue her. And when that happened, he would force them to reveal the key to the ring's operation. Unlike the first time he had captured an alien, he was now prepared to keep him or her.

"Delphina?"

"Yes, Gordon?" She smiled and leaned forward in her chair, eager to answer his question.

"Do you like it here? With me?"

"Yes, Gordon, very much."

"You know that someone will come for you one day, to take you back to Innerworld, don't you?"

Delphina considered his words for a moment. "I suppose that would be a reasonable assumption, but no one has come yet, and it has been almost three weeks. Perhaps they have no desire to find me, or are unable to locate your home, and I do not know how to contact them."

He did not believe they would abandon her so easily. If they did, his plans would all be for nothing, and failure was not part of his destiny. Perhaps the fact that she had not been wearing a ring made it more difficult for her people to find her. They would still come . . . eventually. They had to.

Gordon began again. "At any rate, I want you to know something. Whatever happens, having you here with me has been the most wonderful time of my life."

"I please you well then?"

Her words surprised him. They insinuated that

she had been making an effort to please him and was not confident that she had. It seemed to come so naturally to her that he had never questioned why she behaved as she did. There could only be one reason that made sense to him now. Delphina was as fascinated with him as he was with her. Love at first sight. The little wheels in his brain spun a bit faster.

"Yes, Delphina, you please me very well. I don't care to think of how painful it will be when you leave."

"Painful? But I would not wish to cause you pain, Gordon. It is not permitted. If I am taken from here, you must find another to be your companion."

"I have never needed anyone before and I would not attempt to replace you. Any other woman would pale before my memories of you. No, there will be no other, and it will be *extremely* painful for me, but I would not keep you from your people."

"Then I will stay with you, Gordon, for as long as you need me." It was a statement of fact. She belonged to him now.

"Thank you, Delphina," he replied sincerely. "I would like that very much." What he actually had in mind was more along the lines of his returning with her to her world.

He might have continued such a promising conversation if King had not appeared in the doorway at that moment.

"Yes?" Underwood said without shifting his adoring gaze from Delphina.

"Miss Preston is calling from San Francisco, sir."

"Thank you, King. Delphina, please excuse me, my

dear. Miss Preston would not be calling unless it was very important. I must get back to work now anyway. I shouldn't allow you to distract me so, but I can't seem to help it. I will see you later this evening."

At the last moment he gave in to a small temptation, a gesture to seal the beginning of a more substantial relationship between them. Bending forward, he placed a light kiss on her parted lips. He wondered fleetingly if there was any way it could be different for him with her, or would he only succeed in turning her look of love into a sneer of disgust? As he left her, he decided there was too much at stake to take such a risk.

"Yes?" he said into the phone without any preliminaries.

"Something very odd occurred yesterday, so I followed it up. I think you'll be interested in my findings," Miss Preston replied quickly.

"I'll be the judge of that. Go on."

"Yesterday morning a young punk photographer showed up here, and tried to bluff her way into getting some pictures of you for a magazine I never heard of. *I*, she called it. Before I got rid of her a man came in, long hair, looked like a model, but there was something about him that was not quite right. After she left, he decided he was in the wrong office and excused himself.

"I wouldn't have given either one of them a second thought except for the call I got from the Los Angeles office this morning. A woman had been there, yesterday afternoon, claiming to be getting ready for a '60 Minutes' segment you had agreed to appear on. She apparently bullied your secretary there quite successfully. I do believe I warned you that she might be a bit too young for that position."

"Continue!" Underwood barked at her.

"Yes, well, I thought it was a strange coincidence that two women would be trying to see you in two different offices on the same day. I had told the photographer you would be in Los Angeles all week, but the woman who turned up there a few hours later did not match the description of the one I had met, except in a very general way. The man, however, was unmistakably the same. Just before the alleged television woman got there, the long-haired man had shown up, looking for employment of all things.

"Naturally I instructed Los Angeles to pull the videotape from her office surveillance camera, do a freeze-frame on the man and the woman, and wire it to me immediately. I'll have the whole tape by this evening, but I wanted to compare the faces right away, the woman's in particular. I'm looking at the pictures right now, and I have no doubt. It's the same two people. I'm not at all sure they know each other, though." She quickly relayed their behavior in her office, and that the woman had questioned the L.A. secretary about the man's identity.

Over the years, Miss Preston's mental radar had been sensitized to detect anyone projecting more than normal curiosity about Mr. Underwood. He had been investigated by enough government agencies to make alphabet soup: IRS, SEC, FDA, CIA, FBI, and HUD, to name only a few. Recently, even the Escondido Police Department had tried to link him to some little man's death. It was from that kind of badgering that she had to protect him. Gordon

Underwood was a genius. Her duty was to keep him from being annoyed by all the jealous people who constantly tried to find a way to lower him to their cretinous level.

The end of Miss Preston's allotted time approached. "Would you like me to run their pictures through the computer and see if I can come up with anything?"

"No. Transmit all four of the freeze-frames to me right now. I want to run the check myself. Put both of the video tapes in my safe for the moment. I'll have King fly down to pick them up tomorrow. What did L.A. tell the woman?"

"What she believes to be the truth. That you're in Nevada on foundation business this week."

"Good. Has Nevada been contacted?"

"No one unexpected has shown up yet today, but I told your girl there someone may turn up with or without a legitimate excuse to see you. Either way, I instructed her to say you got called back to San Francisco on an emergency last night."

"Fine. Let me know as soon as you hear anything from her. If they both show up there, I'll have to figure out what to do about them."

Underwood started to hang up when he had an afterthought. "Oh. Miss Preston. Good work." He pushed the disconnect button, cutting off what he supposed were her words of appreciation for his praise. Occasionally, one had to pay compliments, but one should not have to be subjected to the gushing foolishness that followed.

Chapter Five

Even a sheet of paper is lighter when two people lift it.—Korean proverb

Steve forced her eyes to remain open, staring at the face too close to hers to make out any features except the tightly closed eyelids. This was much worse than if he had hit her. The lips crushing hers held her face as immobile as the rest of her trapped body. What was most humiliating about her position was not that she had lost the struggle so quickly, but that he was prompting a response from her that she had no intention of giving. She could *not* give in to the temptation to close her own eyes and let the warmth spread through her. She would *not* part her trembling lips to give him the entry he was silently demanding.

As suddenly as the kiss began it ended. The man on top of her continued to hold her in place, but he lifted his head far enough away for her to see him clearly. He had the oddest look on his handsome face, like surprise. Was he surprised that she had not welcomed and returned his kiss, or surprised at his own actions? Steve did not get a chance to analyze the expression before it was wiped clean. This time she forced herself to hold her tongue until he spoke first. When he finally did, however, she wished he had remained silent.

"I trust I did not hurt you. That was not my intention," he said.

That voice! It was like nothing she had ever heard before, perhaps because it was more a matter of feeling than hearing. The deep masculine sound had a resonant quality to it that reminded her of the physical vibration she felt when the bass on the stereo was turned up too high. His speech had a hint of a brogue, but not quite Irish. Steve was unable to stop the shiver that passed through her when he spoke again.

"I was concerned that if you continued your attack you might injure yourself. If you promise to remain calm, I will release you."

Steve recovered sufficiently from the humming affect his voice had on her to be furious with his words. Who the hell was he? How dare he kiss her like that and not offer an apology or an explanation? She opened her mouth to vent her anger and lost her chance.

His mouth covered hers again, gentler than before, but just as domineering. Steve felt his tongue push between her teeth and was about to clamp down on it when astonishment stopped her. If his voice had been unusual, the feel of his tongue in her mouth was completely unreal. Rather than the smooth, slick appendage she expected, it was rough against the sensitive roof of her mouth, firm as it slid along her own tongue.

He did not invade but stroked and tasted every part of her mouth, as if it were a totally new experience for him and he did not want to miss any of it. Suddenly he emitted a groan that she felt all the way to her toes. No, it was not quite a groan she realized through a fog of sensation. It was like a . . . a *purr*.

"You were angry. You are not angry any longer," he analyzed aloud. "I leave it to you to decide whether we have a conversation or more kissing. The kissing seems to calm your anger and you do taste very . . . interesting."

He cocked his head a little and gave her the briefest excuse for a smile, one that displayed his straight pearly whites for only an instant. This man was harder to read than most. His eyes gave away nothing of what he was thinking.

"Why, you—" Steve cut herself off as his face closed in on her again. "No, wait, *please*." She had to figure a way out of this and his kisses seemed to drain her brain. He had just taught her an entirely new way of subduing an opponent. "Look, this may all be very entertaining to you, but I—I landed on something hard. My back is killing me. Please let me up now."

In another quicksilver move he rolled over, reversing their positions. Steve found her arms trapped between them as he held her firmly against him, using only one arm. Her legs were spread wide and locked in place by his. She felt like she had been placed in a vise, an extremely embarrassing one at that. This position was even worse. She was centered so intimately against him that she could feel the pulse of his hardened manhood. A frustrated whimper escaped her before she could stop it.

His free hand slipped beneath the back of her shirt and a moment later both her gun and handcuffs were tossed out of her reach. Steve started to object when his hand returned to the small of her back where the tools of her trade had made bruising indentations. Lightly, his fingertips touched the spots then moved in small circles, leaving tiny trails of heat that made the desert sun seem cool.

Steve's mind and body were at war. She should be struggling, fighting, doing something other than permitting this stranger to touch her. But her natural honesty made her admit that being completely at this man's mercy was possibly the most pleasurable thing that had happened to her in some time.

His hand abandoned her back for a moment and moved to her face. Ever so softly he stroked her hair. When his fingertips applied a gentle pressure against her temple, Steve felt her eyelids lower of their own accord. The next moment she gave up the fight; her mind surrendered along with her body. The little voice in her head had never failed her before, and now it was insisting that this man posed no threat to her.

She relaxed a little more and tried not to flinch when his fingers moved from her face to slip into the back pocket of her jeans. The weight of his hand in her pocket thrust her harder against him, but as Steve watched him, she had the impression he was either ignoring his aroused condition or completely oblivious to it. She, on the other hand, was finding it exceedingly difficult to think of much else. The only evidence he gave that he was not totally at ease was a slight catch in his throat when he spoke again—or did she imagine it?

Smoothly, he removed her ID folder from her pocket and read, "Stephanie Barbanell, Private Investigator. You are a law enforcement officer?" She made no response. He studied her ID, quickly comparing her picture with her face.

Steve felt the leather being slipped back into her pocket, and determined not to notice that his hand remained there.

"Look, I have no gun. You've already proven you're faster and stronger than I am. I'm obviously not in any position to take advantage of you. You know who and what I am now, so how about letting me up for a little reciprocal show and tell?"

"Show and tell?"

He actually sounded like he did not understand the expression, but then he must be teasing her. Considering what they already knew about each other's bodies, there may have been something to show, but not much left to tell.

Her close-mouthed adversary hesitated a moment before slowly releasing the iron grip he had on her upper body and untangling their legs. With a ridiculous amount of chivalry, he helped her to her feet, retaining her hand as he bowed slightly. "My name is Falcon. At your service."

Steve could not hold back the silly bubble of laughter. Was she supposed to pretend they had not been rolling around on the ground for the last five minutes? Well, to hell with him! She could act like all that touchy-feely stuff meant nothing to her, too.

"You find my name humorous, Stephanie?" Falcon continued to hold her hand, obviously not ready to give her complete freedom yet.

"First of all, nobody calls me Stephanie. I'm Steve. What's Falcon? Some sort of code name? Let's see some ID now, okay?" When he started to pull her along with him, away from the van, she rebelled. "Hey! Hold on! My gun!"

"We are only walking over there. My identification is in my bag. You said you wanted to see it."

Reluctantly, Steve went along, automatically calculating how many seconds it would take her to run back, grab her gun, and jump in the van. He would have to let go of her hand when he reached inside his bag. If she was balanced and ready to bolt, she might make it. Suddenly another thought intruded. What if this was only a ploy to get her further from the van while he retrieved a weapon from his bag? She would be turned away, running, her back an easy target. If that was the case, though, why wouldn't he have already . . . .

Too late! He tightened the grip on her hand, as if he sensed her intention, and opened his bag with his other hand. Steve's breath came out in a soft puff of relief as he handed her his wallet and released her at the same time.

The ID looked real enough. He was the man in the photo: A. Falcon, Interpol. Steve studied it for a long moment. It was certainly possible. He had made her think he was a pro from the beginning, but Lou's assurance that he was not a Fed had left her wondering.

"What does the *A* stand for, Falcon?"

"I prefer to be called Falcon, *Steve*."

"*Touché*. Where are you from? I haven't been able to place the accent."

"Wales," he answered without hesitation.

That explained the almost Irish brogue. "Okay, say I believe you are with Interpol. Why are we tripping over each other? What are you doing here in the States?"

"I am here to retrieve a valuable item stolen from my . . . country. Also, we believe an abduction has occurred by the same person who has the item."

"You're working on the Nesterman case, too?" Steve wanted to bite her tongue. Where was her head? She could hardly withdraw her admission, but perhaps it would encourage some openness on his part. "So, you *are* after Underwood. Whatever Nesterman was working on must be pretty high-powered to get Interpol involved. Or was it the item you mentioned? An antique or artifact maybe?"

Falcon nodded. "The man named Underwood has a ring that does not belong to him. If I can track him, I will find the ring. And you? You are looking for Underwood in hopes of finding . . .Nesterman." It was more of a conclusion than a question.

"Yeah. Well, the bottom line is, we're after the same man, and the way Underwood's operation works, it won't take him long to figure out something's up. When he does, he'll crawl further under his rock. Why the hell did you have to show up in two different places at the same time as me? Why didn't you do something about your appearance?"

"What is wrong with my appearance?"

"If you're fishing for compliments, forget it! You've got to realize two women working for the same man, even in different offices, might just talk to each other! If so, they would be abnormal if they didn't mention seeing a man who took their breath away. Geez! You're even wearing all black again! Doesn't Interpol teach their agents anything about low profile? Meanwhile, since we showed up at the same time, you probably blew my cover as well, intentionally or not. Damn! Those were two of my best routines, too. Well, I suppose we can always hope those secretaries don't have daily conversations and no one's expecting us here."

Steve relaxed her stance, paced for a moment, and turned back to Falcon. "I'm not giving up yet. Maybe I can get away with one more disguise since my agency has already arranged to mess up Underwood's phones." The Interpol agent had stood quite still for her lecture, not arguing, not defending himself in any way. She figured he would comply with her orders now that he understood.

Using her most authoritative voice, she finally said, "Okay. Listen up. I'll go in as planned since I've got the cover. You stay here. I'll let you know when I come back if Underwood's in there and you can go right ahead with whatever you were planning before I interrupted you—whatever that was you were doing out here. They have a camera outside the shack, but they couldn't possibly have seen our little dance from this distance."

"No."

His refusal stopped her just as she started back for the van. She spun around to face him again with her hands on her hips, and braced herself for a different kind of fight with this insufferable man. "*No*? You're *not* going in there ahead of me, and I'm sure as hell not planning on showing up with you in tow again! You're too easy to spot."

"I do not object if you come along with *me*, but I will not remain here. I must get as close as possible to do what I do best."

Steve sighed loudly. "And what, pray tell, do you do best?" She held on to her superior attitude, but her thoughts flew back to the way his kisses had momentarily scrambled her common sense. The blush that warmed her cheeks must have given her away because he flashed her another half-smile before replying in a serious tone.

"I track. Since you are trying to locate Underwood as well, would it not be reasonable to combine our efforts rather than get in each other's way? You have already pointed out a serious oversight on my part. Perhaps you could prevent me from making any further mistakes of that type, and I might be of assistance to you in some way."

"Oh? How do you figure that? I don't work with partners if I can avoid it."

"You admitted I am stronger and faster than you. You are good, but I am better. You may need help in that way, but I also have other talents that could be useful."

Steve was almost surprised to find herself seriously considering his offer that they work together. She had a lot more questions to ask him before she would trust him, but they were not accomplishing anything, standing here arguing. If he was truly an

Interpol agent, she could verify it with Dokes later. In the meantime, it might be better to keep this guy close enough to see what he was really up to, and working separately only guaranteed they would continue stepping on each other's toes. They could both end up losers that way.

"All right. We'll work together for now, but we've got to do something to make you less recognizable. What have you got in your bag?"

"I have another set of clothing identical to what I am wearing."

"Swell. Let's see what I've got in the van."

Wordlessly, he followed her, carrying his tote. She retrieved her gun and handcuffs, then climbed into the van. A moment later she reappeared, carrying her bag of tricks. Steve rifled through her belongings, searching for a simple yet effective disguise for Falcon.

"Take off your shirt and put this on." She held out a large white, vee-necked tee shirt. As he stripped off the black shirt and made the trade, Steve knew she was staring, but could not seem to ignore the visual treat he offered. His skin was a golden tan stretched smooth over squared shoulders and firmly muscled arms. The nipples on his bare chest hardened beneath her gaze, and she found herself making fists with her hands to keep them from grazing that smooth expanse. He looked like a Greek statue.

Steve wished he *was* a cold block of sculptured marble instead of the warm flesh and blood she had already encountered a bit too familiarly. She frowned slightly when she realized that her tee shirt, which hung loosely on her, showed off more of his masculine appeal than his own shirt had, but at least it provided him with a disguise.

Holding up a plain, white painter's hat, she appraised his thick hair. "We'll have to tuck it up and hope the cap holds it there. I don't have any hairpins." When Falcon cocked his head, she didn't bother to explain. "Here, hold this." Steve handed him the hat and reached to gather up his hair. *Oh. God, it's like petting an angora cat!* She took a deep breath to get on with her task and realized how close they were standing. Her breasts brushed against him as her chest rose and fell. She could smell the scent of soap and it made her think of him in the shower.

"I can't do it," she murmured, quickly backing away. "Your hair's too . . . Uh, there's just too much of it. Maybe you can do it."

Falcon bent over at his waist and efficiently twisted his hair into a knot that the cap secured well enough. Suddenly he pulled the neckline of the borrowed shirt up over his nose and inhaled deeply, before letting it fall back in place. "It smells like you. I would not think this piece of clothing would fit you very well."

He was not touching her, but his eyes held her. "I . . . I sleep in it." Her voice came out in a sultry whisper that implied much more than her words revealed.

Falcon continued to watch her for several seconds, but again Steve could not fathom what was on his mind. She wondered if he ever played poker. The odd thought seemed to break the spell.

"Is there anything more to this disguise? If there

is not, I think we should be on our way."

"Oh, yeah, one more thing." Steve handed him her large sunglasses. She pulled a San Francisco Giants' baseball cap out of her bag and put it on. "That's it! Let's rock 'n' roll."

He looked at her inquisitively, shrugged his shoulders, and walked around to the passenger's side of the van.

As they came to a stop in front of the shack, Steve laid down the rules. "I'll do the talking. You'll be a trainee, so you won't have to look like you know what you're doing. I understand it's like a maze down there, so the only hope we have of getting to Underwood's office is if we're taken right to it. His private line has been put out of commission, and his security people are expecting a telephone company repairman. If the data I've been given is accurate, they already have the van on their monitors and someone will appear to escort us in."

Steve had also been told they would only pat her down or ask for ID if she had come uninvited. She decided to trust that information and remain armed. From what she had seen and felt, if Falcon was carrying, she didn't know where, and she wanted one of them to be holding something more substantial than self-confidence if they were walking into a trap.

Steve got out of the van, and buckled on the utility belt that completed her cover. Just as they opened the door to the shack, a section of flooring slid open and a stainless steel monolith rose up through the gap. The front of the tall rectangular box swung toward them, and a uniformed security guard greeted them from within.

The guard looked from her to Falcon and said, "We were told only one repairman, a woman I mean, would be coming. He'll have to stay here until you're finished."

"Him?" Steve waved at Falcon. "He doesn't count. He's a trainee, assigned to follow me everywhere I go. You know, like he's attached at my hip. But, hey, if it's a problem go ahead and clear it first. You might get through to somebody for an okay before the end of the day. You know how the phone company is. Meanwhile, I've got one more job back in Vegas that has to be done before five this afternoon and no way am I gonna take the blame if it's not done. You know, it's one of those big-shot casino guys, and they have ways of getting back at you when they don't get what they want!"

"Okay, okay, forget it. I guess it's all right. Mr. Underwood would probably be angrier if his phone's not fixed than if I let in some trainee. Come on in then." When they entered the steel closet, he closed the door and pushed a button on the wall panel. Instantly, they made their descent below ground.

Steve had expected the unusual elevator, but assumed a telephone repairman might not react nonchalantly. "Wow! That's really cool! I heard this place was like something out of a science-fiction movie. I'm kinda sorry I promised not to say anything to anybody about what I see here. But they told me I'd lose my job if I opened my mouth, so I guess I'll just have to keep it to myself, or I should say *our*selves, right, Bob?" Steve nudged Falcon in his side a little harder than necessary, and he agreed with a grunt.

The guard nodded approvingly and held the elevator door open for them as they exited into a lobby. "You'll have to sign in first."

Steve quickly signed for the both of them. The guard led them through a set of double doors and directed them to take a seat in a waiting golf cart.

When they were all settled, he asked, "Will you need to go to the central communications room or to the telephone they're having trouble with?"

Steve continued to look around as if dumbstruck. "Oh, uh, take me to Mr. Underwood's office first. Maybe it's some little thing I can fix on his phone. I'll let you know if I need to get to the main board." Steve was pleased that Falcon was going along so obligingly. Perhaps it was a good thing they came to an agreement before they got in here. Now, if they could only catch up to Underwood!

They rode for several minutes through a series of corridors. Eventually, they stopped at an ornately carved wooden door. As they entered, the guard held his arm out toward a secretary with carrot-orange hair. "Miss Preston, these are the people from the phone company. I'll wait outside for them."

Miss Preston Three got up from her chair and walked to a door on the far side of her large office. Steve was a little surprised that it was not a duplicate of Underwood's other two offices, but then this whole setup was different from the norm—except for the redheaded secretary.

"I hope we won't be putting your boss to too much trouble," Steve said quickly.

"No problem," Miss Preston answered. "He was here yesterday, but there was an emergency in San

Francisco and he had to go back last night. It was just as well. He would not have been very patient about the phone being out of order this morning."

Damn! They had missed him again. Steve followed the secretary into Underwood's office knowing it was futile, but she had to finish the charade before they could get out of there. The woman remained in the office with Steve while she turned the phone over and removed a screwdriver from her belt. As Steve pretended to make an adjustment, she kept an eye on Falcon, who was wandering around the richly appointed office, touching various objects. He was good. His meandering made the secretary watch him instead of Steve. Even in his impromptu disguise, he was a man at whom a woman stopped whatever she was doing to get a better look. Hiding his hair and eyes had not made any difference. Steve had not disguised his hard, lean body, nor had she thought of suggesting that he alter his walk that made her think of a prowling jungle cat.

She was about to put the phone back together and ignore him *and* his walk when he closed in on the redhead.

"You have a smudge," he said in his low vibrating voice. It clearly had the same affect on the secretary as it had on Steve. "Let me get it for you." He lifted his hand, the first two fingers extended, and gently touched the side of her face by her temple. Steve stopped what she was doing.

The position of his fingers was the same as she had seen him do to her. The moment he contacted the woman's temple, her eyelids drooped, and for an instant her features completely relaxed, as if she had gone to sleep. Falcon removed his hand and the woman's lashes fluttered open again.

"Thank you," the secretary said as he stepped away from her.

Steve thought she had seen the woman go limp for a moment when Falcon touched her, but it had happened so fast, and the woman made no comment about what he had done, that Steve convinced herself she must have been seeing things. After all, hadn't she practically melted when he kissed her? His nearness *was* pretty devastating. Maybe this woman was so susceptible to his charm it only took a touch.

What a monumental ego he must have if every woman he touches conveniently falls apart for him. Steve pondered what it would be like to have men react to her in such a way. Now *that* was a really ridiculous idea. She had not even been able to hold on to the man who had married her!

"Okay, all set." Steve jammed the screwdriver back in her belt and headed for the outer office. "The main office will have the telephone back in working order by five today. It was just a short. Let's move it, Bob!"

She got into the golf cart without waiting to see if Falcon followed, and the guard had them back on the surface a few minutes later.

Once in the van, Falcon looked concerned, or at least that was what Steve supposed the slight change in his expression indicated.

"You are angry again? You are disappointed that Underwood was not there. I, too, am somewhat disappointed."

Steve could not answer right away. She was not

sure her mood swing was entirely connected with missing Underwood, but that was all she intended to discuss with a man who was a virtual stranger. "Yeah. I'm disappointed. If I could have gotten here yesterday, I might have had him!"

"No, you would not."

"No? Why do you say that? You heard the secretary."

"She prevaricated. We are being led along a false trail. That was only what she was told to tell anyone who asked. Underwood has not been in that office for several weeks."

"Now hold on a minute. I'm not saying you're wrong. I have a feeling you hit it right on the head, but you sound like you know it for a fact."

"It is the same for me as you, Steve. I have . . . a *feeling*. Perhaps I have more faith in my intuition than you do."

"Okay, I'll buy that . . . for now. For a second there I had the crazy idea you were going to tell me you were reading her mind when you wiped the imaginary smudge off her face."

"Yes, that is a crazy idea. Do you have any others?"

"Crazy ideas?"

"Maybe. I was actually wondering if you had a *feeling* about where we might try next. I sincerely doubt if Underwood is in San Francisco since that appears to be where he wants us to go."

Steve caught his use of the word "we" and let it go for the moment. Until she found out who he was for sure, she was not going to accept or reject him as a partner on this case. They were back at the spot where they had met earlier, and Steve stopped the van.

"First, I've got to get this van back to Vegas and check in with my office. Going back to San Francisco is probably a waste of time as far as finding Underwood is concerned, but that's where I live and work, so I don't have much choice. My expense account doesn't stretch far enough for me to go traipsing around the world to every one of Underwood's offices in hopes that I accidentally bump into him. I'm going to have to wait until he surfaces somewhere or somebody comes up with another lead."

"Steve, I have another feeling. The secretary in the San Francisco office is important to Underwood. I believe she is the one who would know where he is."

"That's more than just a feeling. It's in his file. There were several notations that conjectured that she's his number-one Girl Friday, in spite of his lack of imagination when it comes to his secretaries' hair color and names."

"Then it would be reasonable to return to her."

"Why? Do you think you could melt the old biddy into a pool of desire and get her to confess everything she knows? Don't kid yourself, Falcon. Even *you* aren't that good. She's made of stone and one hundred percent loyal to her master."

"You are right, Steve."

"Yeah? About what?"

"You do have very crazy ideas. Why did you call me Bob before?" Subject changed.

"Because Bob is a very common name, and Falcon is not. I didn't want your identity known. Your name would be remembered, believe me. Now answer a question for me. How did you get out here, and how did you intend to return to the city? And just what was it you were doing wandering around like that when I first saw you?"

"I believe that was three questions, and one comment that deserves a response. You are right about my name. I do understand now if you must call me by another name in the future. I was brought here by a taxi. He did not wait, as you can see, but it does not matter now. You will take me to wherever we are going."

His explanation left her thinking he was either a good liar or a total rube! "How lucky for you that I came along then. Although I don't usually pick up hitchhikers, I guess you can come back to Vegas with me. Now, question number three?"

"I was looking for a way in."

"Didn't Interpol give you any background at all?" Steve caught her breath in a small gasp, and her voice revealed her worry. "Oh, God, don't tell me you're a rogue! I manage to get into enough trouble all by myself without getting mixed up with something like that." She saw his brows draw together, and assumed he did not understand the term. "A rogue—an agent who goes off on his own, without orders. Someone who rejects the rules of the game and makes his own." Steve did not consider herself a rogue; she simply failed to go by the book when the rules became too constricting. Lou had extracted her promise to behave on this case, and she did not want anyone else getting her into a jam when she was trying so hard not to.

"No, Steve, I am not a rogue. I am here alone, but with Interpol's knowledge. Since I seem to have been seriously uninformed, however, I hope you will agree to assist me, as we discussed earlier."

Steve felt her stomach tighten a little. She had already decided to have him checked out, and maybe they could help each other find Underwood. It was the man, Falcon, not the agent, who made her question the sensibility of such a plan. He made her feel and think things she had consciously chosen to shut out since her divorce. "You mean for the duration?"

"It is reasonable."

Several times on the way to Las Vegas, Steve contemplated starting a conversation and changed her mind. For one thing, Falcon did not show any interest in talking. For another, she was not at all sure she wanted to promote communication with a man who made her remember that she was a woman. Lastly, if he was not really an agent, she did not care about anything else he had to say because it would probably be a lie, too.

They delivered the van to the phone company's service building in Las Vegas and, after telling Falcon to wait for her outside, Steve found a pay phone inside the building to call Dokes. It did not take long to bring him up to date.

"I can't say I'm surprised," Dokes replied when Steve finished speaking. "I warned you Underwood seems to have a sixth sense about these things. When I made all my calls last night, I asked everyone to let me know if they hear anything about a time or place where he's expected to show up. Plus, I put out a few feelers in the civilian corner today. Considering all the businesses he owns, there must be something he attends to personally. Where can I call you if we come up with anything solid?"

"Before I answer that, I need you to check on something for me. The guy I described to you last night turned up in the desert today. His ID says he's Interpol. Name, A. Falcon. I tend to believe it, but I'd like confirmation. He's after Underwood, too. Either I work with him or run the risk of his getting in my way, unless he's not on the level."

She agreed to wait by the phone while Dokes contacted Interpol. It took about a half-hour for Dokes to call back, but Falcon never came inside to question the wait, a small favor for which Steve was grateful.

Dokes confirmed Falcon's identity and description. "The person I talked to didn't know him personally or very much about his assignment. Apparently, it's highly confidential. In fact, it sounds like you know more about what he's doing than they do. I'd hate to see them get the drop on us on this one. Work with him, Steve. It's the only recommendation I can make under the circumstances. Since he suggested it to begin with, there should be no problem, but keep a close eye on him anyway. Look at it this way, if anything goes wrong, we can always blame Interpol!" Dokes laughed and Steve joined him, knowing there was more than a grain of truth to his joke.

As long as Falcon agreed with what she had already decided to do, she concocted a way to keep her bird of prey under her wing. He might be legitimate, and her little voice might tell her she was safe with him, but that did not mean she could trust him not to double cross her. Steve did not want to risk his taking off ahead of her, leaving her holding nothing but excuses. If she returned home to San Francisco, he would be free to go his own way.

"Listen, Lou, I have an idea or two on how to handle this Falcon character, and I can accomplish it easier if we stay here for tonight. I'll give you a call later to let you know what hotel we're in. Hopefully, you'll come up with a new lead by morning."

"Fine. Be good, Steve," he said with an unprofessional send-off.

Steve made one more call to her mother to let her know she would not be home, and spoke at length with her children. She had not spent a night away from them in over six months, but guilt pressed heavily on her anyway. They could always call Uncle Lou if they needed anything before she called again.

After weighing several ideas of where they could spend the night, she picked a hotel that might even be some fun. Falcon complacently agreed with her plan when Steve explained that Lou expected to have something better for them to do than revisit the first Miss Preston, and it would be more efficient to stay put in the meantime.

A few minutes later they were in a cab on the way to the famous Las Vegas Strip.

"Falcon, are you wearing contacts?"

"Contacts?" he returned cautiously.

"Contact lenses. In your *eyes*! What is it, do you have another name for them in Wales?"

"Oh, my lenses. Yes. I did not realize they were noticeable."

Marilyn Campbell

"They're not, really, but I've seen how you keep rubbing your eyelids like one of my friends does when his lenses start irritating him, and your eyes are a little bloodshot, too. Don't you have some drops you can use?" Steve had no doubt that she had managed to fluster the unflappable agent. He must be more vain than she guessed if it embarrassed him to have someone know he wore contacts.

"No, I . . . forgot to bring . . . drops."

The cab dropped them off in front of the Mirage Hotel. On the way into the lobby Steve suggested, "Look, why don't you go by the gift shop and buy some eyedrops. They will soothe your eyes until you can take the lenses out later. By the time you get back, I'll have us both checked in."

A loud roar stopped Steve in her tracks, but Falcon continued on directly to the source. There in the lobby were two magnificent white tigers in a glass cage. The closer Falcon got to them, the louder they roared.

Catching up to him, Steve commented, "They're beautiful, aren't they? But so noisy! It's almost like they're trying to tell you something."

Falcon turned to her and almost smiled. "I will look for the eyedrops now."

As he walked away, Steve congratulated herself. Except for his one show of defiance in the desert, Falcon was proving to be quite malleable. A second surprise awaited her at the registration counter. Behind the employees was a glass wall through which Steve could see a man-eating shark swimming back and forth. Only in Las Vegas! she thought wryly.

When Falcon returned carrying a small paper bag,

she held up a key and gave him an apologetic look. "They only had one room available. There's a couple of big conventions in town and not a decent room left. We were lucky to get this one. They assured me it has two beds, and I figured if I didn't mind, you shouldn't. Okay?" She was worried that her nervousness about the sleeping arrangements would make her lie about the available rooms sound false.

Steve intended to keep him within sight, even if it meant sacrificing her privacy. *Hah! Who are you kidding, Steve?* By sternly reminding herself to keep her mind on the case, she managed to banish the images she conjured up at the thought of spending the night in the same room with Falcon.

He looked directly into her eyes for several long seconds. Although she could not tell what he was thinking, she had the uneasy sensation that he knew she was lying, but once again he nodded his agreement without uttering a word.

Steve wanted to dispel the uncomfortable feeling quickly. "As soon as we've dropped our bags in the room, I'll let Lou know where we are, then we can have some fun. I think it's my duty as an American to show a visiting official a good time. You've never been to Vegas have you?"

"No, I have not."

"Good! You're in for a real treat then!"

Chapter Six

Rich men rule the law.—Oliver Goldsmith

Gordon Underwood took another glance at the fuzzy videotapes of the man and woman who had appeared in his two California offices. Miss Preston was correct in that the woman was almost unrecognizable in her disguises, obviously a professional. Only the audacity of her two performances gave any clue that something was in the wind. The man had made no attempt to change his appearance, and his excuses for being in the two offices were extremely flimsy. He was either an amateur or over confident of his abilities. It did not really matter. Between the two of them, Underwood knew now that someone was looking for him.

It had taken the last three hours, considerable use of his computers and a handful of phone calls, but he had learned who they were and what one of them was up to. Private Investigator Stephanie Barbanell was indeed working on the Nesterman case. Apparently, Nesterman had managed to leave a clue behind that pointed to Underwood in some way. But it could not be a very revealing one, since it took six weeks to uncover it, then turn it over to a private agency instead of the police.

The man was A. Falcon, an Interpol agent, on special assignment in the United States. Unfortunately, none of Underwood's contacts could come up with more than that, although they promised to keep trying. Interpol! What could *they* want? He was involved in too many deals in too many countries to narrow the possibilities down without more information.

Usually, Miss Preston's instincts were exceptional when it came to protecting him. The fact that the two agents did not appear to know each other did not rule out the possibility that they were working on the same case. Underwood decided it was time to have another chat with Nesterman, and find out what projects the scientist had been working on before he was brought to Alaska. If he was involved in a government project, that might help piece the puzzle together.

In the meantime Underwood needed more time with Nesterman. Each day brought him closer to convincing the computer whiz that he had been justified in his actions. Delphina's appearance had almost won Nesterman over. Underwood was certain that if another of her people could be lured in, one with superior knowledge or powers, Nesterman would realize the importance of what they were doing and become an ally rather than an enemy. He firmly believed another alien would be arriving any day now.

Marilyn Campbell

With two different detectives trying to locate him, though, Underwood knew he could only stay hidden for so long, and he did not want to risk moving Delphina from Alaska. He assumed it would be easier for her people to find her if he kept her where she had appeared. Underwood needed to keep his pursuers running around in circles for a while longer. This could be accomplished by throwing out a few deceptive crumbs for them to follow, combined with a little sleight of hand to keep them interested.

He made a call to Miss Preston to give her his instructions for the misdirection of Barbanell and Falcon. For the magic he summoned King.

Chapter Seven

A lion among ladies is a most dreadful thing.
—William Shakespeare

"I can't believe you've never been to Monte Carlo!" Steve teased. "Here I thought all of you international agents hung around glittery casinos wearing tuxedos and looking debonair like James Bond."

"James Bond?" Falcon looked at her curiously.

"You know, Double-O-Seven! Geez, don't they give you time off to go to the movies over there?"

"Oh, yes, the movies."

Steve had the distinct impression he still had no idea what she was talking about. But this guy never seemed to understand what she was saying. His speech, what little there was of it, was extremely stilted. Perhaps she should try to use a little less slang, for his sake. Then again, what did it matter if they did not speak exactly the same language? They would only be together until they got the job done.

"Well, here we are," Steve said with a wave of her

hand toward the brightly lit casino. "Las Vegas is known for its extravagance and neon lights. Some of the places get downright tacky, but this place is one of the nicer ones. The tables will be honest, too. What would you like to try?"

"I will leave it to you, Steve. I am not familiar with these games."

"I'm not much of a gambler myself, but I know enough to show you around. The one-arm bandits are my favorite. Worst odds in the house, but even a complete amateur can try them. Watch some of the people playing for a minute while I break a twenty for some silver dollars."

Steve left Falcon staring intently at the whirring machines. In the next row someone had gotten lucky, as evidenced by the loud ringing bell, flashing lights, and clinking of coins into the metal tray.

When Steve returned, it took her only a few seconds to spot Falcon. He was listening to a buxom cocktail waitress in a skimpy costume, who seemed to be offering him much more than a drink. Steve had changed into the purple sweater dress, as it was the only appropriate thing she had with her. Even so, the waitress's blatant charms left her feeling somewhat insignificant. Falcon, on the other hand, was so attractive and dangerously male in his all black attire, every woman in the area paused to sneak a peak at him or openly ogle. One elderly woman next to Steve asked her if she knew his name, certain he was a famous movie star. Just then Falcon turned and walked to where she was standing, as if he had known she was there all along. Steve could not resist a gloating smile toward the waitress and a wink at the older woman. They did not need to know there was nothing between them.

Falcon looked slightly confused when he reached her. "I understand how the machine works now. You were right about the odds. Why would you put your money into such a unit?"

Steve laughed. "For the fun of it, I guess. And the chance that it's my turn to hit the jackpot."

"Would that make you happy, Steve? To hit the jackpot?"

"Are you kidding? I'd be happy to win enough to buy groceries next week. You can't imagine how much it costs to keep my family fed." Suddenly she realized how presumptive that sounded. "I'm sorry, Falcon. For some reason I assumed you don't have a family of your own to feed."

"I do not."

Steve knew she should let it lie, but she could not resist the urge to be certain. "You're not married, or anything?" Falcon was looking at her strangely again, and she felt her cheeks flush.

"I am not married . . . or anything, Steve."

How did he make a simple name like Steve sound so sexy? She *had* to stop reacting to everything this man did. Steve turned away from him, put a dollar in the machine in front of her, and yanked on the arm harder than necessary. The colored fruits spun madly inside the glass window, finally stopping on an orange, a banana, and a black bar. Steve shrugged and began to insert another coin into the same machine when Falcon stopped her.

"Not that one. You will lose again. Come." He touched her elbow and led her slowly down one row and up another. "This one."

Steve smiled. "Another *feeling*, Falcon? Oh, well, your choice is probably better than mine—beginner's luck and all that. Would you like to pull the arm since you picked the machine?"

He shook his head no, but placed one hand on the side of the machine and concentrated on the blurred pictures.

One bar. Double bars. Triple bars. Bells clanged! Lights flashed!

Steve let out a squeal and threw herself against Falcon, giving him a strangling hug.

"I won! I won! I can't believe it! Thank you!" Steve realized she was choking him and quickly released her hold around his neck. It made her instantly aware of the secure hold he had on *her* in return, and the strength radiating from the length of his body pressed close to hers. Steve's heart was pounding from the excitement of the win, yet she recognized the moment her reaction switched from her luck to his nearness.

Falcon smoothly slid his arms back to his sides and stepped back from her. "Is that a lot of money?" he asked, not looking at her.

"I . . . I think so." Steve busied herself counting her loot as she dropped the silver dollars into a plastic bag. By the time she had it all gathered up her breathing was under control, even if her thoughts were not. "I just won $257 thanks to you. Let me know if you get any more of your feelings!"

Steve tried several more machines without any luck. Falcon seemed distracted, or perhaps the one-arm bandits simply were not challenging enough for him. "Falcon, would you like to try one of the tables? I can explain roulette and blackjack, but I'm afraid craps and baccarat are over my head."

"What are they doing there?" He pointed to the section of the casino where the semicircular black-jack tables were located.

Steve explained the rules of twenty-one and the betting involved while they watched a few of the players in action. After a few hands Falcon suggested they try the game.

"Okay, but let's go over to that table where no one is playing. It's a five-dollar minimum, but if you're the only player the dealer won't mind if you're a little slow or stop to ask questions. Anyway, we'll be playing with the house's money."

They sat down in front of the table, and Steve placed a stack of silver dollars in front of Falcon. "You play this time. I've never been very lucky at blackjack."

At first Falcon won a few hands and lost a few. After about five minutes his luck began to improve. One hour later Steve found herself sorting tall stacks of various colored chips, trying not to think of the enormous amount of money they represented. They were no longer alone at the table. Every seat was occupied, and spectators stood three-deep behind them. Suddenly Falcon stood up and handed the dealer a black chip. *Damn! Steve realized. A five-hundred-dollar tip!* He moved away from the table, leaving Steve to pick up his winnings. Her hands were shaking so badly the dealer had to help her gather the chips.

Steve hurried to catch up with Falcon, who was

making his way to the roulette tables. "What happened? Why did you walk away? How did you pick up on card counting so fast? That is what you were doing, wasn't it?"

Falcon flashed Steve a mischievous grin that stunned her. It was the first real smile from him she had witnessed.

"I became bored once I figured it out. It was not fair for me to continue. There were two men watching us who did not seem at all pleased with my luck."

"Fair?" Steve's voice raised in disbelief. "There's no such thing as fair in gambling. Those two men in tuxedos wouldn't know what fair means. Okay, forget it. Do you have any idea how much money you just won? It's a small fortune!"

"It is not my money. It is yours."

"That's ridiculous! It may have been my stake, but *you* played the game. It's yours!"

"I have no need for it, Steve. If you do not want it, we can return it to the casino," Falcon said seriously.

"Are you some kind of crazy man? What do you mean you don't need it? Don't tell me, on top of everything else you're loaded, too! Geez! Never mind. We'll share. I'm not about to look a gift horse in the mouth. Since we have money to burn now, let's play roulette. Okay?"

"Whatever you wish."

Again she explained the rudimentaries of the game, and they found seats at a quiet table. Over and over again, the little ball dropped into a slot on the wheel which bore one of the numbers Steve had bet on. In no time the stacks of chips in front of them multiplied several times again, and another crowd collected around their table.

Abruptly, their luck changed. Nothing Steve bet on came up. Caught up in a gambling frenzy, she put more and more chips out on the felt board, only to watch the croupier drag them away with his stick. Inadvertently, Falcon brought her back to her senses when she caught sight of him rotating his fingertips over his closed eyelids. The smoke must have been bothering him terribly and Steve had not given him the slightest notice for some time.

She stopped playing and gathered up their remaining chips, marveling at how easily she halved the fortune amassed during the game. Winning and losing colored chips kept you from thinking in terms of dollars.

"I'm so sorry, Falcon. I guess I got carried away there. I can see your eyes are bothering you again. It's still your money if you want to keep playing, but I don't like losing very much, and our luck definitely seems to have gone sour."

"I do not care to continue playing."

"What do you say to dinner and a show? We can certainly afford to treat ourselves."

Falcon nodded. It took a little time at the cashier's cage to exchange the chips for $2,000 in cash and a cashier's check for $24,750, which Falcon insisted be made out to Stephanie Barbanell. While she completed the information for the IRS, Falcon excused himself to put more drops in his irritated eyes.

Steve asked the cashier about the dinner show in the hotel. By the time Falcon returned, a casino pit boss appeared to escort them to the showroom. The man seated them in the center booth of the first raised tier from the stage, unquestionably the best table in the room. Steve handed him a generous tip. He wished them a pleasant evening, compliments of the house, and hoped to see them back in the casino later.

Steve felt like she was floating on a golden cloud as she ordered the most expensive dinner on the menu to be accompanied by an equally expensive bottle of wine. Normally she never drank while on duty, but she was technically not working and this was all too good not to celebrate. Falcon seemed to enjoy his simple fare of broiled snapper and refused the wine. Before the show started, Steve ordered a second bottle for herself.

She had seen a variation of this show some years ago, when it was at the Frontier Hotel. It remained her favorite of all the glitzy extravaganzas. Aside from the usual music, dancing, and elaborate costumes that failed to cover the dancers' physical attributes, this show had Siegfried and Roy, two of the most beautiful blond men to have ever set foot in America. Automatically, Steve amended that evaluation when she glanced at Falcon.

The show combined magic with a company of well-trained jungle cats. There was no barrier between the stage and the audience. Only Siegfried and Roy's talents as expert animal trainers kept the ferocious lions and tigers from joining the diners. At the climax of the show there were twelve large cats poised around the stage, several of which were elegantly sprawled on overhead balconies with their tails swishing above the stage. It was absolutely breathtaking. Suddenly the cats began to roar, one after the other, until they drowned out the orchestra. They became increasingly agitated, and Siegfried and Roy moved swiftly from one to another, cracking their whips and ordering their silence in German. The animals quieted after a moment, but then the lions on the higher perches leapt down to join the other cats as they all stalked toward the center runway. It was so perfectly choreographed it appeared to be part of the act, until Steve caught a look of concern pass between the two trainers. Their animals appeared to be enacting a quiet rebellion, and the men were unable to stop whatever the big cats had in mind.

Falcon reached over and clasped Steve's hand. "Do not be afraid," he murmured. He stared straight ahead at the huge lion that led the pack. "They only want to say hello."

Steve looked at him as if he had lost his mind. He was completely at ease, except for the powerful grip he had on her hand. Steve's gaze darted around the room. There were a few curious expressions on the faces of some of the patrons, but no one in the audience seemed aware that anything unusual was happening.

The lead lion jumped off the stage, followed by the other eleven. In close order drill the mighty king paraded his court through the crowded aisle toward Steve and Falcon's table.

Falcon gave Steve's hand a final squeeze and slid out of the booth. "Stay seated. There is nothing to fear." As he moved in front of the table, the twelve sleek cats surrounded him, then bowed their heads.

Falcon stroked each one on the nose or between the eyes until he had all of them purring contentedly.

Steve imagined her eyes were bulging out so far she would never get her eyelids closed over them again. The cats' purring was almost identical to the sound she had heard from Falcon when they were in the desert.

This had to be some sort of hallucination. Steve heard Falcon say a few words, but they were foreign to her. He was speaking to the cats! In unison the animals rose and returned to their assigned places around the stage. Falcon gave a small salute to the two men who were still standing at the end of the runway, doing their best to look calm. Quickly improvising, Siegfried held out an arm toward Falcon and encouraged the audience's applause. Roy and Siegfried responded like the true professionals they were. Everyone thought Falcon was part of the act.

Except Steve. Her hands trembled and she stared at Falcon with a mixture of awe and fear, until he did something she had seen him do before. For the merest second he brushed her temple with his fingertips, as if he were pushing a strand of hair off her face. Immediately, she relaxed. Each time he touched her, he made her aware of how vulnerable he made her feel. There did not seem to be any way to prevent her response to him, nor did she honestly care if he realized it.

By the time they returned to their room Steve was able to find the whole evening terribly funny. A bottle and a half of wine helped to promote a case of the giggles.

"God, Falcon, that had to be the wildest thing I have ever seen! I think those cats thought you were one of them. Must be that mane of hair," she slurred unintentionally, reaching up to touch his silky strands as she spoke. But he smoothly moved away before she made contact.

"Perhaps we should get some sleep now, Steve. You may have the shower first." He opened up a brochure he found on the nightstand and leafed through it.

Steve was too wound up to think of sleep. She had won a half-year's salary in one night, seen a miracle, and had had a generally terrific time with a man who kept her pulse at its peak workout level just by being in the same room.

"I don't *want* to go to sleep yet." Steve thought her voice sounded sulky and tried to improve it. "You know what I *do* want to do?" She waited for Falcon to look up at her. "I want you to show me how you got out of that hold I had you in today. I'd like to be able to do that if somebody ever got me in that position—not that anyone ever has, mind you, but you never know."

"I think it would be better if you went to sleep. I believe you have overindulged in alcohol. I would not want to hurt you by accident."

Steve marched up to him and poked her finger at his chest. "I have *not* had too much to drink to handle *you*! I think you're scared, Mister. You probably couldn't do it again!"

"You do not know what you are saying, Steve. Go to sleep."

She refused to be put off. In a move only slightly

123

impaired by her inebriated state, she had him face-down on the carpet between the two beds, with his arm bent behind his back. "Now. Show me what you did or I won't let you up." Steve could no longer remember why she was insisting on this, but she had an inkling it had something to do with wanting to be handled by him again.

While she contemplated that, she missed whatever it was he did, and she was once more pinned beneath him. "You did it too fast," she complained, sounding like a whiny child. As the seconds ticked by, however, all thoughts of fighting and tricky moves slipped away.

This was why she had pushed him into action. *This* was what she had wanted to feel again—his warm breath against her face, his weight heavy upon her, being completely enveloped by him. She felt his heartbeat racing with hers, his body growing hard on top of her.

Steve watched his mouth come closer. As his lips touched hers, she lowered her lashes, and sighed her willingness to take *this* a step further. Instinctively, her hips tilted to accommodate the change in his body.

Suddenly she felt the room's air-conditioning replace his heat. Her eyes opened in time to see him grab the room key off the table and open the door.

"Go to sleep, Steve."

He was gone.

Steve sat in the middle of the floor, feeling incredibly foolish, and tried to clear the fuzz from her brain. All of Vinnie's insults combined had not made her feel so unfeminine. No matter how often her ex-husband had accused her of wanting to be a man because she was not much of a woman, all she had ever had to do to prove him wrong was to spread her legs and he climbed aboard. He had never rejected her sexually; he had rejected everything else about her instead.

What mistake had she made? For the first time in three years she had met someone whom she found desirable, the time and place were perfect, and he had been as aroused as she. Yet he had walked away.

Sobriety returned with a throbbing headache. She took a quick shower and crawled into bed. If Vinnie's harsh words had not convinced her she was worthless, she was certainly not going to let some stranger's rejection do it.

The more she thought about it the more firmly she believed Falcon had not walked out because of lack of interest. She eliminated the possibility that he was homosexual. He could not hide the fact that his body had been aroused when it pressed against hers.

Perhaps his Welsh background gave him a higher moral standard about what was proper professional behavior, especially when the lady in question was three sheets to the wind. So much for the promiscuous super-spy myth! Yes, that had to be it. Hadn't she always refused to date any of her coworkers or other law enforcement officers she knew because she believed a man and woman who worked together in the field should not have a more personal relationship that might distract them?

It had to be the wine and the excitement. Otherwise, she would never have acted like a horny twit. Tomorrow she would show him she was just as professional as he was!

Damn! This nightshirt smells like him now.

Falcon strode down the Strip with the determination of a man very late for an important appointment. Thousands of neon lights lit the way, but he paid little attention to the complex designs and colors of the brilliant hotel signs. He intended to walk until he was too exhausted to do anything but sleep when he returned to the room.

He needed time and space to sort out today's events, as well as to unwind the tight control he had sustained all day.

The moment he saw Steve in the desert Falcon knew he was in trouble. Against his better judgment he had coerced her into working with him. He told himself it was because he needed some guidance and, in a sense, she was a tracker like himself.

She had surprised him with her strength and ability, and he believed it would be more efficient if they worked together. Undoubtedly they could assist each other, for there were so many things about her world with which he was not familiar. But kissing her had had nothing to do with efficiency or learning about her world.

Keeping her from knowing just how unfamiliar he was with his surroundings turned out to be a serious problem. Steve was trained to look for clues, anything out of the ordinary. If he spoke, she evaluated what he said. If he was silent, she took that as his agreement to whatever she said. For the most part he had little objection to letting her give orders, at the moment. If she could get him close to Underwood, then he would take over.

He reasoned it was better to say as little as possible rather than to make up lies to explain about himself or his abilities. How could he explain that he had touched the secretary's mind to learn the truth, or that he could *see* events and *hear* conversations that had occurred during the previous twenty-four hours by touching objects in the room where those events had unfolded?

Added to the obvious problem of concealing his true identity was that his eyes were killing him, though the drops Steve had suggested had helped somewhat. But he could not risk removing the lenses in front of her. He would have to wait until he was alone in the bathroom taking his shower. Then he would clean them and reinsert them before he went to sleep. That would have to do for now.

It would have been easier for him if she was not such an emotional creature. On the two occasions when he had touched her mind to calm her, he had resisted the strong urge to learn her exact thoughts; it was bad enough knowing her feelings every minute. In the desert he had felt her aggression, her readiness for battle, her elation when she thought she had overpowered him, her fear when she had lost the fight. He knew she had lied about the room, but not why. In the casino he had absorbed her excitement, and during the show he had known her panic when the cats had approached them. Through it all, he had felt her desire for him, strong, powerful, and more compelling than anything he had ever known.

He wondered briefly, as he had before, if it was her desire that had prompted him to kiss her, not once but thrice. And, as before, he knew he could not use that as his excuse.

Falcon thought he had been fighting the temptation to give in to desire for months. He had not known what a real fight it was until today. Like fuel laying stagnant in a puddle until a lit match was thrown on it, Steve seemed to be a catalyst to his emotional explosion. He was not simply aware of what she was feeling, he was *feeling* it as well. By the end of the day he had not been able to differentiate between her happiness and his, her desire and his. He needed more practice, but that was not an available option at this time.

It was one thing to be aware of the emotions of others, and to help ease their pain, but Falcon had always considered emotionalism a terrible burden that others had to bear. Yet tonight he had gotten a glimpse of how wonderful it could be. Happiness was quite nice actually, like being underwater in a whirlpool and feeling all the tiny bubbles skipping over your bare flesh on their way to the surface.

For now he would have to work harder to control all the strange sensations his newly developed emotions were causing. He needed all his abilities intact as he searched for Underwood, and he still had no way of knowing what would happen to those abilities if he allowed emotions to become a permanent part of his life.

That brought Falcon to consider the other surprises he had experienced tonight. He had been able to control the machine Steve called the one-arm bandit, and, until his eyes began to blur from the strain, he had directed the ball in the roulette wheel. At the blackjack table he had first thought he was seeing through the backs of the cards, in spite of his obstructive lenses. Then he had realized he was receiving pictures of the cards in his mind, as long as he kept his hands on the table, close to the shoe the dealer used. Were these powers he had always had but never tested, or were they new, like the emotions?

Calling the cats had been an accident. They were so beautifully primitive he had longed to touch them, and they had come. He had communicated with them as easily as he did with humans. Had he always been able to do that? He did not know; he certainly had never thought of trying to talk to animals before.

Was that also happening with Steve? Was his desire for her so strong he called to her without realizing it, rendering her powerless to his desire? Or was she so sensual he could not resist her? That would explain why in all the previous months his sexual need never focused on a particular female . . . until now. There were too many questions, and Falcon did not dare seek the answers.

It had been terribly cruel to walk out on Steve, knowing what she was feeling, especially if what was happening between them was all his doing. He could not have stayed in that room with her and not have taken what she had offered, nor could he have explained his rejection of her.

There was no help for it; he would just have to

keep from touching her and control his thoughts while he was with her, until they found Underwood. Then he would separate himself from her as soon as possible.

Chapter Eight

When we think we lead we most are led.
—*George Gordon, Lord Byron*

Ring! Steve's hand lashed out for the receiver before the telephone had another chance to sound its alarm.

"G'mornin'," she mumbled through what felt like a mouth full of alcohol-dried cotton.

"Don't tell me you're just waking up! In case you've forgotten, today is *Thursday*, not Saturday or Sunday." Dokes was teasing, of course. He knew very well that with her two young children she was always up with the sun.

Steve forced one eye open to look at her watch. Eight o'clock already. "Oh, gawd! Let me call you right back, Lou. Ten minutes, okay?"

She hung up, glancing briefly at the other bed where Falcon began to stir. Quickly, she headed for the bathroom, deciding to put off facing him for a few more minutes. As she splashed cold water on her face, she assessed her physical condition. Her head pounded ferociously, but some aspirin would take care of that. Stomach queasy, but not rebellious. Juice, coffee, and Danish should help. She had not had so much to drink since the night her divorce was final, and now she remembered why not. Hopefully, Falcon was the understanding sort; he had told her at dinner he never drank alcoholic beverages. So now he had proven he was faster, stronger, more professional, *and* smarter.

Slowly, she opened the door, preparing her apology as she did so, but the words never left her mouth. Falcon stood by the bed with his back to her—his very naked back.

Steve knew the polite thing would be for her to turn away or to clear her throat so he would be aware of her presence in the room, but that would be like one of her children giving back a lollipop after taking the first lick.

Seeing him completely naked for the first time, she was struck at how magnificent his body was: from his wide, solid shoulders, down his muscled back, to his sculpted thighs and calves. Narrow-molded buttocks flexed as he bent over to slide one long leg into his slacks. No wonder when he had touched her she had felt every intimate inch of him so clearly; he wore no underwear.

The back of Falcon's body was flawlessly smooth, like his chest and arms, and if he had any body hair, it was so blond and fine it was unnoticeable. Steve understood American Indians had little or no body hair, but Falcon said he was from Wales. She could not help wonder if he turned around . . . .

He did—just as his fingers closed the waistband on his perfectly fitted pants. Steve warmed under his hungry gaze that swept over her from her head to her bare toes. An image of the lead lion from last night's show flashed in her mind. Her heart picked up its pace as she realized that the little her cotton nightshirt covered was clearly outlined for his view. She tried to stop the instant tightening in her breasts, and failed. Steve had the distinct impression he had been aware of her appreciative scrutiny, and was returning the compliment. Unlike her, however, he was not the least bit embarrassed.

"Good morning, Steve," he said in his penetrating voice that stroked her like velvet. "That shirt looks familiar. I believe I like the way you fill it out better." He gave her a crooked grin and turned around again as he donned his black shirt.

Steve could not be positive, but it sounded like he was actually making a joke. Damn! His lack of a sense of humor was the one thing she thought she could find fault with. As she rooted through her bag for clean clothes and a toothbrush, she decided to get the worst of her discomfort out of the way.

"Uh, Falcon, I want to apologize for last night. I know getting drunk was stupid, and it's hardly an excuse for behaving like a child. I mean, it was very unprofessional of me, and I can assure you nothing like that will happen again. I was just really excited about the money and . . ."

"It is quite all right. Please do not upset yourself further about it. Who was it who called?"

"It was Lou. I told him I'll call him back," Steve answered automatically as she headed for the bathroom, then stopped. "Wait a minute. Why should I be ashamed of what I did last night? After all I'm not the one who started it. *You* did! In the desert. You kissed me twice without my invitation." Hell, she had enough to feel guilty about without feeling bad about something that was not her fault.

"You started the fight, Steve, not me."

"There's a hell of a lot of difference between fighting and kissing!"

"Yes. And I have decided I like kissing much better."

"I don't give a damn *what* you like! You owe me an apology."

"No."

"And why not?"

"I am not sorry. As I said before, you taste very interesting. I do believe, however, that we should refrain from such activity during our search as it does tend to be distracting."

"*We* should refrain? Of all the . . ." Steve was across the room in four big strides. With a frustrated grunt, she shoved him onto his bed. "*You* just keep *your* hands and *your* mouth to yourself and we'll do fine, because I have no intention of touching you again, even for a much-deserved punch in the nose." In a huff she disappeared into the bathroom, slamming the door behind her.

Falcon sat staring at the closed door and suddenly laughed. Steve might have been upset with him, but she still felt attracted to him. What a beautiful contradiction she was! In spite of the fact that he had spent most of the night reminding himself why he had to keep his distance from her, he had to admit being around Stephanie Barbanell was too much fun for him to stay away from her. He had never considered that this journey would be as entertaining as it was educational.

Steve brushed her teeth with more vigor than usual. How dare he! She had never met a man who could make her want to kiss him one minute then knock him down the next. Lou had warned her to keep her temper in check, and she was trying, Lord knows, but this man was so-o-o . . . aggravating!

Once dressed in her jeans and pullover shirt, she paid attention to Falcon only long enough to ask if he wanted anything from room service, then turned her back on him while she called for breakfast. When Falcon went into the bathroom, Steve returned Lou's call.

"I'm almost human now. What's up?"

"What's wrong, Steve? You still sound strange."

"You are not going to believe what happened last night, and I'm not going to give you all the details now, either. Suffice it to say Falcon and I won a bundle in the casino, we were almost devoured by wild animals, and I got stinking drunk. So, what have you got on Underwood?"

Dokes shelved the obvious questions and got right to business. "We hit the jackpot on Underwood, too. He's got a big merger in the works between one of his oil companies and a competitor's. Since it's supposed to be a friendly move, all the directors and their spouses from both companies have been politely commanded to spend this weekend at the Fontainebleau Hotel in Miami Beach. The arrangements were made rather suddenly yesterday, but everyone is expected to show up.

135

"I was told that Underwood will be personally involved in the negotiations. He'll be staying on his yacht, which is docked across the street from the hotel. I couldn't find out exactly when he's expected to arrive, but I got you a front row seat. The houseboat docked next to his yacht has been reserved for you for four nights starting tonight. The key can be picked up at the hotel's front desk. Give them my name; it's already paid for.

"I can't give you any specific schedule of events, either. Even the guests won't be given it until they check in. You'll have to poke around until you find out which meetings Underwood will be attending."

"Dear Uncle Lou, you never cease to amaze me with what you can accomplish with a telephone and what I will guess was another sleepless night. Okay, we're heading for Miami. Anything else?"

Dokes passed on the few other tidbits he had picked up and gave her the details of the travel arrangements he had made for her and Falcon. "I assumed our foreign friend would want to accompany you. How's the baby-sitting going anyway?"

At that moment Falcon came out of the bathroom, and room service knocked on the door. Steve motioned for him to take care of it. "The *baby* is too big for his britches I think, but I'm handling it. I *said* I would, didn't I?" Steve bit her tongue to make it stop flapping.

"Temper, temper, young lady. Yesterday you talked like you had him heeling nicely. Maybe you'd better take a minute to tell me more of what happened last night after all."

"Never mind. I'm just tired and hung over. I'll call you in the morning. I better call Mom now. Bye." Steve hung up before he had a chance to interrogate her further.

The call to her mother went as expected. Mom nagged about how Steve should have taken a desk job like her brother, but assured her she and the kids would be fine for a few days. Mary Ann and Vince each got five minutes to tell their sides of a story that made no sense from either angle. Steve successfully distracted all three of them by telling them about the money she had won and promising a surprise for them when she got back. Maybe a real vacation. She had only been gone one night and already she missed her children terribly.

After loud kisses and good-byes to all, Steve stiffly joined Falcon at the small table where he had already laid out their breakfast. It was a nice gesture, and she thanked him for it before remembering that she was still slightly miffed with him. They were both content to eat in silence.

Over a second cup of coffee, Falcon asked, "How old are your children, Steve?"

"Mary Ann's seven and Vince is five. It's hard to believe they'll both be in school in another six weeks. I still think of Vince as my baby."

"Yes, I heard you refer to a baby when you spoke with your friend, Lou."

Steve flushed when she realized he had heard her nasty comment and hoped he really did think she was referring to one of her children. "Anyway, I hate to leave them like this, but it goes with the territory, and it doesn't happen all that often, thank goodness.

I'm lucky to have my mother with me."

"She lives in your home, also?"

"Actually, we live in her house."

"And where are your mates?"

"Mates? Oh, you mean husbands. My father was killed in a car accident five years ago. As to my mate, he found somebody more compatible than I was."

Pain! The sensation speared Falcon's mind so suddenly he closed his eyes against it. It was horrible! How could she casually speak of something that hurt her so much?

"Falcon!" Steve jumped up quickly, knocking her chair over backward. Dropping to her knees in front of him, she grasped his clenched fists in her hands. "My God, what's the matter? Are you ill? What can I do?" Her voice was strained as she searched his face for some indication of the source of his pain.

Falcon regained control and slowly relaxed his hands, turning them over until he was holding hers instead. "I am so sorry, Steve. Let me help you." He released her hands and lifted his fingertips to the sides of her face.

When she saw what he was about to do, she pushed herself away from him. "I don't know what that is you keep doing, but I told you I don't want you touching me anymore. I thought you were in some kind of pain."

"I would not hurt you, Steve. It is not my pain, but yours. I feel I can ease it for you. I must help you because your pain is hurting me." His voice was barely a whisper of sound as he held his hand out to her. "Let me touch you. *Please.*"

It was the desperate way he said "please" that did her in. Mechanically, she moved toward him and knelt again at his feet. His hands lifted to her face. When his fingertips gently touched her temples, she felt her eyelids close against her will.

Steve had not been aware that she carried a heavy burden, but she suddenly had a vivid picture in her mind of a huge boulder strapped to her back, weighing her down as she struggled to walk. Falcon came to her side and undid the ties. Effortlessly, he lifted the boulder from her back and tossed it aside. The weight had been there for so long she had thought it was part of her, and now it was gone. She was free! Her body felt lighter. Steve opened her eyes when Falcon removed his hands from her face.

"What are you?" she murmured. "A healer? Like an evangelist or something?" She became more skeptical as the vision of the huge boulder faded from her consciousness. "I don't believe in that kind of thing. What did you just do?"

"I think a healer is an adequate term. I am able to help people feel better, emotionally. You *do* feel better now, and therefore, so do I."

"It's hypnosis, isn't it? You better not have left any post-hypnotic suggestions or anything like that in my mind." Now she was afraid that her guess was right. If he was a hypnotist, that would certainly explain how she was so easily drawn under his spell.

"You are much too suspicious, Steve. I would not force you to do something against your will. I have already explained myself to you as much as I am able. Now I would like you to advise me of your

139

conversation with Lou. I gather we will be going somewhere today."

Steve decided there was nothing he could say that would make her believe he had the power to heal, even if she did feel less depressed and pounds lighter than she had in years. It was obviously a trick of some kind. Again Steve assured herself she would not let him touch her in the future.

She repeated Dokes's end of the conversation for Falcon, filling him on the upcoming meeting in Miami. "The real kicker is that Underwood actually did come out of hiding just a few days ago. He was seen by a half-dozen different people in his New York office. The oddest thing was that he bought an entire wardrobe of women's clothing designed in the style of the Napoleonic era. I'll bet the trashy newspapers will have a field day with that information."

Falcon leaned forward in his chair. "Why do you say that?"

"Underwood isn't supposed to like women, at least no one has ever discovered a romantic relationship serious enough to warrant his buying clothes for a woman. It wasn't like he was picking out costumes for a party, either. All the clothes were to be made for one woman's measurements. The lady in question wasn't there. It's almost as if he's found himself a lover and he's dressing her up in private for some crazy fantasy of his. I wouldn't put anything eccentric past him, but it really doesn't fit in with everything else I know about him."

Steve noticed Falcon's forehead wrinkle in deep thought. She congratulated herself that perhaps he was beginning to let his guard down.

"Falcon?"

He stood up and paced for a moment before answering her. "Steve, you told me you were looking for a man, and that Underwood might have something to do with his disappearance. I, too, am looking for someone who has disappeared, but it is a young woman. Her name is Delphina, and we have reason to believe she is with Underwood." Falcon refrained from telling Steve about Delphina's talent for bringing other people's fantasies to life. She would never understand. It was her comment about Underwood having a crazy fantasy that convinced him Delphina was definitely with the man. "I must go now. Give me the address of the hotel in Miami you spoke of."

"I beg your pardon?" Steve asked sarcastically. "I must not have heard you right. It sounded like you're thinking of going without me, and I know you couldn't have meant *that*!"

"Steve, I am sorry, but I can travel much faster without you. You cannot know how vital my mission is to my people."

"*Your* people? What about *my* people? I *knew* I couldn't trust you! You bastard! What have you got, a private plane stashed somewhere? Is that how you got out to the middle of the desert? Well, let me tell you something. We're doing this together, and if you have transportation that's faster than mine, you better believe you're taking me along with you."

"I have no plane."

"Oh? No, wait. You sprout wings and fly through the air, right? Or better yet, I'll bet you have a Superman cape hidden in that bag of yours. Well, I don't care. If the man in the blue tights can take Lois Lane for a flight, I'm sure you could do the same!"

Falcon cringed inside. He could not reveal the truth, nor did he feel comfortable with the idea of abandoning her. He rationalized that he still might need her help. It would have to be her way for now.

"I have made you angry again. This time, however, I believe you are justified. Of course we will go together. When do we leave?"

Steve was only slightly mollified. He was hiding something, she was certain, and knowing that would help keep her guard up against him. "We are already booked on a flight this afternoon. With the three-hour time difference and two stopovers on the way, I'd say we won't get into Miami until at least midnight, but that should still get us there before Underwood boards his yacht. If we take turns watching and sleeping, we should be able to get to him the moment he arrives.

"In the meantime I don't have enough clothes for either an extended stay or for a variety of occasions. I need to hit a store before we catch the plane. Maybe I'll pick up a bathing suit, too. We can stop on the way to the airport."

Not knowing precisely what "hitting a store" entailed, Falcon merely nodded his head.

"Good. I'm sure we'll have time for you if you need anything. And don't worry about the money. We're rich!"

Steve's estimate of the travel time to Miami turned out to be wishful thinking. It was three o'clock in the morning by the time they were settling in on the houseboat. Falcon took the first watch, insisting he was wide awake.

She shook her head as she considered why he was in that condition. The man was a white-knuckle flyer.

Falcon listened to the water gently lapping against the sides of the houseboat. The subtle rocking motion began to calm him in spite of his inner turmoil. Never in his wildest imagination could he have thought it was possible to survive what he had just experienced.

He knew the plane itself was rather primitive and that the risks of traveling on it were much too high for his peace of mind. What he had not expected was the blind fear emanating from several of the passengers, one of whom had bordered on hysteria. To make matters worse Falcon had absorbed the worry of one of the flight attendants. When he had touched her, he had learned that one of the cockpit crew was intoxicated and belligerent.

By the time they had landed, Falcon had experienced firsthand the heart-pounding, stomach-wrenching results of pure terror—an emotion he would not care to feel again in a thousand years. It had completely wiped out the bewilderment he had felt as he had accompanied Steve in the shopping mall. Romulus had certainly been right about that aspect of Outerworld life.

The sun was well above the horizon when Steve appeared on deck. "Good morning, Falcon. You shouldn't have let me sleep so long. You must be exhausted. Any sign of our man?"

"Good morning. No, it has remained dark on his yacht. I believe I will be able to sleep a little now." He rose, gave her a cheerless nod as he passed, and slipped inside.

Steve made herself comfortable on a chaise longue in the sun. She had put on a pair of shorts and a sleeveless tee shirt thinking she might catch a few rays while she took her watch. Opening the paperback romance she had picked up at the mall, she thought she looked like any other tourist along the Intracoastal waterway.

The parking valets and bellhops in front of the Fontainebleau Hotel were hustling madly. Steve guessed that at least a few of the couples arriving in limousines were associated with the Underwood gathering.

The Underwood yacht sat in the water directly in front of her, about a hundred feet away. A crew of men were topside. They must have all been asleep below when she and Falcon had arrived, but they were moving with a sense of purpose now. A shiver of anticipation followed Steve's awareness that Underwood was clearly on his way.

This time she did not think deception would help. Her plan was to approach Underwood head on, present him with what she knew, threaten to turn him in, then offer to make a deal. All she needed to do was get his attention.

Two black limousines pulled up to the curb. The sight of a small army of black-suited men exiting the limos made her drop her book. There was not enough time to wake Falcon. Quickly, she left the houseboat and headed for the far end of the yacht where a gangway had been extended to the sidewalk. Then she saw him—a bald head surrounded by dark-haired ones, surging toward the gangway.

"Mr. Underwood!" she shouted, breaking into a run. The men did not even slow down. Steve tried to wedge her way into the moving mass of bodies protecting her prey. "Please! I need to speak to Gordon Underwood! It's very important!" She yanked on one man's arm. He turned to look down at her through his dark sunglasses, but never missed a step. While several men continued to surround Underwood as he made his way onto the yacht, four huge men blocked Steve from following any further.

"It's about Nesterman!" she screamed at his back in a last-ditch effort to gain his notice. One movement gave him away. It was barely perceptible, but he had cocked his head automatically at the sound of the name. Then he was out of sight.

"I'm sorry, miss," one of the bruisers stated. "Mr. Underwood has had a tiring trip and will need to rest before seeing anyone. If you would like to leave your name—"

"Never mind my name. He knows what I want to see him about. I'm staying on that houseboat next door. Tell your boss to make it easy on both of us. He can come see me, or I'll catch up to him eventually. At the moment, I only want to talk."

Steve turned her back on them and crossed Collins Avenue to the hotel, as if she really did not care if they passed on her message.

Counting on the assumption that Underwood would not be leaving the yacht any time soon,

Steve decided to abandon her post on the houseboat and do some snooping. A stop in the Conventions Office and a little white lie got her a copy of the schedule and locations of the Underwood group's meetings and banquets. Nothing was scheduled for that day, Saturday was crammed full, with separate groups meeting at the same time in different rooms. The final event was a brunch on the yacht Sunday morning.

Steve wandered out to the pool area, where a sizable tip to the cabana boy obtained her a chaise longue next to several wives of the directors involved in the merger. As she sat down, Steve dropped the schedule of events on an older woman's rounded stomach.

"Oh, excuse me," Steve said as she retrieved the paper.

The woman opened her eyes, then smiled when she recognized the schedule. "I'm Irene Wilson, Tom's wife. I don't think we've ever met." She extended her plump hand bearing no less than ten carats of diamonds on her fingers.

Steve returned the limp shake. "Hi. Sue Smith. My husband's one of the attorneys for this deal." She assumed there were dozens of lawyers involved, and she just hoped that one of them would have a common name like Smith.

Irene introduced her to the other women in her group, and Steve quickly involved herself in their conversation. A wave at the cabana boy brought a pitcher of *mai-tais* and iced glasses. Two hours later, Steve felt the heat of the sun on her bare legs and arms and a flush in her cheeks caused by the two drinks she had slowly nursed. It was a small sacrifice. She now knew which meetings were preliminary rounds and which one Underwood would definitely attend.

Before he was completely awake, Falcon knew he was alone. The female's physical presence was gone, leaving only a weakening trail of brain waves. A weight against his chest prevented him from taking a normal breath. *Where is she? Is she all right?* Unbidden, an image of Steve sitting on deck appeared in his mind. Accustomed to allowing his powers to work for him, he closed his eyes again and relaxed. He saw her drop her book and dash off the houseboat. There was no sound, but he had no trouble comprehending the meaning of the scene that followed. Of all the rotten luck. If he had had the watch, he would have had no trouble breaking through the wall of muscle protecting Underwood. All he would have needed to do was touch him for a moment and the game would have been over.

Touch? Falcon realized he had not touched anything just now and yet he had seen the events involving Steve as if they were occurring at this very moment. Even when he picked up images from touching inanimate objects, the picture was usually blurry, not clear like this. What had prompted this vision? His questions? Quickly, he tested that theory by asking himself several more, about other people and places, including some about his mission, but nothing more came to him.

Was it only questions about very recent, local events then that triggered such lucid images, or was

147

it because the questions involved Steve? He recalled the uncomfortable feeling that had accompanied his thoughts about her and knew that had to be part of the answer.

But still he was puzzled. He thought of Romulus and Aster who were his friends. He cared for them, and yet he had never felt such concern for their safety, only absorbed their worries about each other.

Falcon wanted to work this out logically. There was no doubt he had acquired another new power, but a new emotion had been uncovered as well. He could not help but wonder. . . .

Footsteps alerted him to Steve's return. He would analyze the changes later. Right now he had to deal with her.

Steve smiled. Falcon had apparently slept through her absence. To be certain, she tiptoed up the narrow stairs to the bedroom.

An obstacle burst into her path, almost causing her to fall back down the short flight. Two strong hands gripped her shoulders and shook the breath from her. The sight of topaz eyes glittering with anger temporarily immobilized her.

"What do you think you were doing?" Falcon growled in a voice too loud for the close space.

Steve recovered from her shock enough to determine she was not in serious danger. "I—I was only coming up to see . . . Is something wrong, Falcon?"

"Yes, *something* is wrong. You were not here when I awakened. It was irresponsible of you to go off on your own. We are *supposed* to be working together." His voice quieted, but he did not loosen his tenacious grip which held her balanced one step below him.

Steve's temper caught fire. "Irresponsible? Who the hell do you think you are? I *told* you I don't work with partners, and I never agreed to take orders from you. What *would* have been irresponsible is if I had wasted the time to wake you up first. As it is, I came back here with more information than we had to begin with, and I would never have gotten it if you'd been with me." In spite of her irritation with him, she related what she had learned.

As she talked, the pressure of his fingers eased from her shoulders and began a creeping ascent up her neck and into her hair. His thumbs found the pulses beating below her ears and rested there. Nowhere else was he touching her, yet she was aware of him in every cell of her body. The reason for her annoyance was forgotten.

"So, uh, we now know he, uh . . ." Steve kept her gaze on his eyes, where his anger melted into desire. She slowly moved her head to rub her cheek into his palm, wanting greater contact. " . . . will be at the four o'clock meeting tomorrow."

Want . . . more . . . she thought.

Falcon pulled his hands away from her so abruptly she had to grab the railing to keep from falling. He was at the bottom of the stairs when he spoke without turning back to her. "I am taking a walk. Do not wait dinner for me."

Once again Steve was left staring at empty space.

Falcon ran blindly, oblivious to the people he passed on the sidewalk. He crossed the street between two hotels and ran toward the ocean. Tearing off his shoes and socks, he ran in the wet, sucking sand.

He ran until he thought his heart would explode through his chest. But he could not escape what was happening to him.

He had laid his hands on her in anger. How could he have done such a despicable thing? He still felt her satiny skin against his fingertips and carried her sweet scent in his nostrils. He had no idea what she had said to him; he was lost in her eyes, and would have pulled her closer and kissed her again, had he not heard the two words "want . . . more." He had not touched her mind, nor had she spoken. Yet the words had come to him all the same. They jolted him because he had never before heard an untrained person's thoughts that way. They frightened him because they were an echo of his own thoughts. Was it truly her wish, or had he unintentionally planted the desire in her mind?

His powers were increasing. He knew that and was prepared to adapt, but the struggle between his two selves was escalating in spite of every attempt he made to suppress his awakening humanity. The emotions bubbling inside of him, unexpectedly taking over at the oddest times, had to be some sort of challenge to his worthiness to handle greater powers. It was as if his human half was demanding he acknowledge his weaknesses.

Then what did that make Steve—the ultimate test? Resist her and acquire the gifts of the most powerful felan. Give in to her, accept his humanity, and lose, not only the chance to reach a higher mental level, but perhaps the powers he had had since birth.

Not long ago the wiser choice would have been obvious.

Chapter Nine

*There is no great genius without a mixture of
madness.—Aristotle*

Gordon Underwood grunted as he ended his telephone conversation with King. So, the two detectives
had pounced on the bait, and Barbanell revealed
that she had made a connection between him and
Nesterman. Regardless of what she had to say, he
was not ready to hand over the scientist to her, even
though his efforts to turn Nesterman into an ally
had not yet succeeded. His frustration led him to
giving King a free hand in Miami Beach, so long
as none of his actions could be tied to Underwood.
Barbanell and Falcon were like two annoying flies,
and he wanted them swatted away.

Work held little appeal for him this morning. With
a resigned sigh, he headed for the parlor, where
he knew Delphina would be right where he had
left her.

"You look very tense, Gordon," she noted with
concern. "May I be of some assistance?"

Sitting down next to her, he took her slender hand in his. "You help just by being here, my dear."

"I am able to do much more. I am aware that Outerworld morality is less open in some ways than I am accustomed to in Innerworld. It occurs to me that you might not understand what my job as an entertainer at the mining camp would have entailed." When Gordon raised an eyebrow at her, she continued, "I am a fantasizer. For a short time I can make you believe you are whoever you wish to be. Although you would never leave this room, mentally you can be any place, any time.

"A sexual release can relieve tension, but combined with a fantasy, it is considerably more effective. You have never requested my services in this manner. I do not know if you were hesitant to ask or if you have not found me desirable."

"Not desirable?" Gordon took a long slow breath to steady his erratic heartbeat. "You are the first woman I have desired in years. From the moment I saw you I wanted you." He pulled his hand from hers and looked away. He was embarrassed as if he were an adolescent on a first date. "But it doesn't matter."

"If you have wanted a sexual release with me and not satisfied the need, that would explain your frustration. It is not healthy to deny a natural physical urge such as sexual gratification. I am here for you, Gordon." She placed her hand on his cheek and turned his face back to her.

He met her gaze, watched her tongue wet her lips in anticipation of his kiss. Hesitantly, he bent his head until his mouth touched hers. A small spark caught, and a long-forgotten stirring began in his groin. He deepened the kiss, pulling her into his arms, seeking her tongue with his own. Her hand moved slowly from his cheek, kneading the muscles of his shoulder, discovering his sensitive nipple through his shirt, down over his belt buckle to the semi-hardness between his thighs.

He tried, desperately wanting it to be different with her. The past would not allow it. It intruded with images that reminded him of what he needed to satisfy the wretched creature in his trousers. With a groan bordering on a sob, he pulled away from Delphina and strode to the window.

"Gordon?" She glided to him and placed her hand on his arm. "Have I done something to offend you?"

He looked at her in disbelief, opened his mouth, but failed to find a satisfactory explanation.

"You do not need to tell me, you know. I could touch your mind and see whatever it is that is so difficult for you. Perhaps in the sharing you would find comfort as well."

Gordon felt an overwhelming need for the comfort she offered. He had never confided in anyone, about anything, least of all his secret. "Delphina, whether I told you or you learned it in your way, you would be too repulsed to allow me near you again. I don't think I could stand that. You see, I can't ... I'm sorry I kissed you. Let's forget it, all right?"

"I do not believe that would be the best thing for you, Gordon. I am very knowledgeable about sex, and I could never be repulsed by anything about you. Please tell me why you cannot come to me for your pleasure."

Could she be right? Was there any way she could know about him and not hate him? Would this beautiful woman from another world grant him the satisfaction he had so long denied himself? "I would not know where to begin," he finally said with a shake of his head.

Delphina took his hand and led him back to the sofa. She made sure he was comfortably seated, walked around behind him, and placed her fingertips on his temples. "Relax now, Gordon. Close your eyes and remember. Let me see what I need to do to please you."

As soon as Gordon closed his eyes, a scene crystallized before him. At first he knew Delphina was planting the image into his mind. A moment later, all awareness of present time and place was gone, and he was reliving a memory, physically and emotionally, not merely watching it.

He was thirteen again, sitting at Miss Preston's kitchen table. His knuckles smarted from the whack she had just delivered with her wooden ruler. Not for the first time, she reminded him that she was hired to tutor a genius, not to teach manners to an adolescent.

But he couldn't seem to help himself. Ever since his friend, Frankie, had told him about what men and women did in private, he hadn't been able to get it out of his head. Maybe if he didn't love Miss Preston quite so much, or if her red hair, green eyes, and small body were not quite so beautiful, maybe then he could keep his eyes from wandering over her, and stop wondering what she'd look like without her clothes.

That day she changed her tactics. Accepting the fact that his highly active curiosity about every academic subject had naturally extended to sex, she took on the responsibility of satisfying that curiosity in order to get his mind back to his studies.

Gordon could not believe his dreams had come true when she undressed for him, and when his hesitant first touch made her moan, he was certain she loved him, too. She showed him how to please her with his hands and mouth, but a moment after she seemed satisfied with his performance, she turned on him.

He had to be punished for his wicked behavior, she scolded him. She had to help him learn not to be ruled by the mindless devil in his pants. By threatening to tell his father that Gordon had raped her, she forced him to accept the punishment she believed would teach him the self-discipline he needed.

Gordon's father preferred to use his fists or his leather belt to enforce strict discipline in his house. Miss Preston's weapon was her wooden ruler, but she was equally proficient at inflicting punishment with her hands, fingernails, and teeth. But that day through it all his erection never relaxed, as if that part of him truly did have a wicked mind of its own. That was enough to convince him that she was right about having to learn to discipline himself before the stupid appendage between his legs destroyed his intelligence, the only thing his father could not take away from him.

When she felt he had been sufficiently chastised, she allowed him to climax with a few impersonal jerks of her hand. Then they both got dressed and returned to the calculus lesson as if none of it had happened.

Each lesson after that began in a similar way, with Miss Preston continually finding new, inventive ways to punish Gordon for his evil male thoughts. When she did take him into her body, she tainted that joy as well, with tricks such as viciously biting his nipple or sticking him with a hatpin at the moment he climaxed.

For two very formative years he anticipated and dreaded their time together. As in all subjects, Gordon was an excellent student. By the time they parted company, pain, pleasure, and guilt had permanently meshed together inside him. From several futile attempts with other girls and women, he also knew he could not maintain an erection without the pain. Eventually, he gave up trying. He had an empire to build instead.

The years flew by in a sexless void with the exception of two notable incidents.

Gordon's father stopped beating him for his many offenses when, at age sixteen Gordon topped his father's six-foot, two-hundred-pound frame, but his mother's torture worsened. He considered his mother a weak, spineless creature, a victim if there ever was one, but that was no excuse for what his father put her through. He hated his father. And he hated himself for being the same gender.

For years Gordon stood by helplessly as the old man took out his anger on her verbally, but when he had used his meaty fists, breaking her jaw and blackening her eye, Gordon had had enough. In a fit of accumulated rage, he had used his own fists, just like his father always had, but he had not stop with injury. He had not stopped until the older man lay in a bloody, lifeless heap.

His mother had observed him wordlessly as he removed all his father's identification and folded the body into a large garbage bag. Gordon had weighted the bag and dumped it in the river. It never occurred to him that he could be caught. It simply was not in his destiny. He had returned home to find his mother had cleaned the bloodstains and was calmly waiting for him to take her to the hospital for her jaw. As far as anyone ever knew, her husband had left home one night and never returned. The matter was never discussed at all between her and her beloved son, but ever since that day she believed she owed him her life and her freedom, and he could do no wrong.

That night, with adrenaline still racing through his system, Gordon Underwood had masturbated, each purposeful stroke matching a remembered punch to his father's face.

The second incident occurred exactly fifteen years after he and Miss Preston had played out their fare-well performance. One night she had appeared on his doorstep looking much older than her fifty years. She had allowed her own hatred and anger to take its toll, but her greed had not dwindled at all. She had read an article about her one-time star pupil, she had informed him, saying that life was treating him well and that he was wealthy and gaining prominence daily.

Underwood had been tempted to turn her away, then thought better of it. He had listened to her reminders of their relationship, which she said could be renewed openly now that he was of age. After all, she had helped to make him what he had become. By showing him his weakness he had overcome it, hadn't he? Shyly, she had spoken of financial assistance. Blackmail was such an ugly word, she had whined, and he had coolly agreed.

They had been alone in the house; no one knew she had paid him a visit. He had shut out the vision of the scrawny hag she had become, and remembered the beauty he had worshipped; she who had taken his innocent, pure love and had turned it into a grotesque perversion. It had been so long he told himself, then had told her aloud, with a hard, punishing kiss on her tight mouth. Her teeth had clamped down on his lower lip, breaking the skin. The taste of his own blood pushed him over the edge. It had been too long for both of them. They had undressed hurriedly. He had allowed her inflictions of pain and verbal abuse, and he had grown stiff and anxious, as he had known he would. But he was no longer a boy who could be cowed by threats and promises of dark pleasures. He was a full-grown man with a glowing future and enemies who would use his weakness against him if they knew of it.

Unexpectedly, Underwood had pushed her down on her back and mounted her. He had savored the look of surprise and fear that touched her cold, green eyes when she saw the size his weapon had grown to, and it grew when she screamed from the pain of his thrust into her skinny, unprepared body.

"I loved you, Miss Preston . . . once upon a time." His hands had closed around her throat as his hips slammed into hers. Miss Preston had absorbed his final climax with the last beat of her twisted heart . . . .

Delphina's fingertips moved from his temples and stroked the skin of his head for a moment before releasing him completely. Reliving every sickening incident left him too spent to raise his eyelids. Nor did he want to see the change in Delphina now that she knew of the ugliness inside him. And yet, for some reason, he did not feel so ugly anymore.

She took his icy hands, and warmed them with her breath. Only when she settled herself on his lap with her arms around his neck and her head on his shoulder did he dare look at her. Delphina smiled. He was so elated by her reaction, he found himself running his hands over her, kissing her, and murmuring nonsense against her neck.

"Gordon. My Gordon. You have very dark memories, but that is all they are—memories. I cannot change them and neither can you. You must not let them affect the present. It is against our laws to do violence to each other, even if it is for the purpose of pleasure. But I still want to try to please you. Remember, you cannot disappoint me. Whatever happens, I will be here for you."

Delphina unbuttoned his shirt and toyed with the sparse hairs on his chest. "I like the man you are, Gordon. In Innerworld, a man with such a beautiful body would be in demand by many women. You should never feel shame about your natural physical needs." She kept talking, telling him what a good thing it was that he was a man, how much she needed him, exactly as he was, and how much she wanted to be needed by him.

Marilyn Campbell

Minutes passed. Or was it hours? Gordon could not be sure. He was entranced by her voice and the butterfly movements of her fingers over his naked body. A thought floated by that this was one of the fantasies she had spoken of, but he wanted it to be real, and so it was.

Her skin warmed to his touch. She melted for him. And he was all man for her.

"I love you, Delphina. You are mine, now and forever."

She moved against him in answer and he wanted her . . . again . . . and again.

Chapter Ten

It is not good to wake a sleeping lion.
—*Sir Philip Sidney*

It was one o'clock in the morning before they could attempt the next step in Steve's plan. She appraised her bikini-clad figure in the mirror. Falcon would probably think her donning the skimpy suit was another one of her flimsy attempts to attract him. She grabbed a tee shirt and pulled it on. Two seconds later she took it off again. The hell with what he thinks, she thought angrily. Swimming was easier without excess clothing, she reasoned, and he probably would not notice anyway.

Out on deck Falcon waited with even less covering than she wore, but she vowed not to notice. "Don't you think you ought to take that off?"

Falcon paused. He had understood nudity was not generally accepted in public, and although her attire left nothing to the imagination, the female parts of her anatomy were covered . . . more or less. *Don't think about it!* "I do not understand. You picked

161

out this swimsuit. Is it not appropriate?"

Steve's mouth opened and closed as she realized what he thought she meant. "Oh geez, no, I, uh, I was referring to your ring. Opals aren't supposed to get wet, are they?" As far as she was concerned, nothing could make the showy thing less attractive than it already was, but he did seem attached to it. "Is it your birthstone?"

Falcon turned his ring hand away from her line of vision, and said the first thing that came to mind. "It is not a genuine opal. The water will not hurt it. Yes, it is my birthstone."

"Not genuine? No kidding?" Steve reached for his hand to get a closer look at the fake, but he put his hand behind his back.

With his other hand, he pointed at the two-foot long, black, cylindrical tube she was holding by its grip. "What is that?"

Now why wouldn't he want her to see his stupid ring? The thought of trying to force the issue held some temptation, but she decided not to give him another reason to think she was a twit. "I've never used it in the field myself, but it's the latest technology in mountain climbing. When I press this button, the top opens and twenty feet of rope shoots out wherever I point. A four-pronged grappling hook on the end opens like an umbrella, with rubber tips. As long as there's something for it to grab onto, it will support up to six hundred pounds.

"It sure would have been nice if Underwood had taken my bait and invited us on board by the front door, but I guess that would have been too simple. I just hope there's no alligators in that water."

Falcon raised one eyebrow at her. It had not occurred to him that there might be living creatures in such dirty water. Fortunately, they would only have to swim a short distance. "And I hope the moon stays behind those clouds. Steve, I know you work alone, but will you please stay close once we are on board? It would be inefficient, and possibly dangerous, to separate."

Steve felt like refusing just to be ornery, but it was exactly what she was going to suggest, so she agreed. "Fine. Ready?" She prepared to slip over the side into the waterway when he stopped her.

"Steve?"

She turned back to him, wondering at his frown.

"I wish to apologize for my outburst earlier. I had no right to touch you in anger."

Steve laughed in spite of his serious expression. "Hey. No problem. It did my heart good to see you act completely human for once."

Falcon winced. "Why would you say that? Do I not seem human to you?"

"To tell you the truth, Falcon, there are times I'm not sure what you are. Now let's go." Again she started over the edge, when another voice stopped her.

"Sue! Sue Smith!"

Coming up the houseboat's gangway were the ladies Steve had met at the pool and three men, who could only be the husbands. She groaned and hurriedly whispered in Falcon's ear, "Your name is Smith and you're an attorney for Underwood." She smiled broadly at the small party cramming themselves on the deck. "We were just about to cool

163

off with a dip. Care to join us?"

Irene Wilson scanned Steve and Falcon's bathing suits, then looked down at her elegant cocktail dress with a grin. "I think we're a mite overdressed. We were invited on board for drinks with Gordon, but he never came out of his suite. When I saw you two out here, I thought we would have more fun sharing some of the bubbly with you. Tom, pop that cork. Break out the glasses, Sue. And *you* must be her *darling* husband!" She stroked Falcon's cheek with one stubby index finger as her gaze slid down his body. "You didn't tell us he was gorgeous, Sue, dear. I would have made a point of visiting earlier!"

Falcon gave her a look that thanked her for the compliment and told her he was not available without insulting her. Steve was amazed at how smoothly he extricated himself. There was no help for it, though. They would have to be sociable for a short while at least.

Irene may have been fascinated with Falcon, but her husband was on the verge of erupting. Falcon felt his simmering frustration as soon as the man came on board. The other two men could not take their eyes off Steve's barely covered curves. He did not need to sense their feelings to recognize the same lustful thoughts that had taken up residence in his head.

Steve nearly jumped out of her skin when Falcon moved behind her and put his arms around her waist. Accustomed to flowing in and out of whatever character suited the moment, she automatically became the loving wife, smiling up at him and covering his forearms with her own. What on earth was this all about? She tried to laugh at the jokes and join in the conversation around her, but his proprietary hold kept her from composing any rational sentences. His heartbeat drummed against her shoulder blades; the heat of his near-naked body burned her skin.

Falcon pulled her back with him as he leaned against the railing. Steve's breath stopped short when he tucked her between his open thighs and she discovered the hard reason he was keeping her in front of him. If she thought for one moment that she was the cause, she would have squirmed around a bit, just to tease him, but she was not at all sure that this was not a reaction to Irene's advances. When it came to Falcon, she could not be sure of anything.

"Oh, damn!" complained one of the other wives. "We left the party too soon."

Everyone turned to see why she was pointing at the yacht. It was pulling out! Falcon and Steve shared a grimace of exasperation. Their visitors had delayed their plans long enough for the Underwood yacht to leave the dock. Like a clock striking twelve, the sight of the ship moving past them abruptly ended the gaiety. In a matter of minutes the three couples finished their drinks, said good night, and departed.

"Do you think that was planned?" Steve asked.

"It is certainly a possibility. Do not be upset. From what you learned, he must return before the four o'clock meeting tomorrow. We will catch up to him then."

A short time later Steve lay in her bed, unable to sleep in spite of the hour. Naturally, Falcon had made no mention of the minutes spent cuddled together on deck. After all, it was only an act, wasn't it? Then why did her chest tremble when she remembered how he had looked down at her so possessively? Everything about Falcon made her think of a fictional hero in a spy novel. He was a devilishly handsome international agent, and could be charming when he chose, but his aloofness and secrecy turned him into a walking mystery. Actually, she could have made him up from her own fantasies.

She only wished she had enough experience to take advantage of his appearance in her life.

The yacht had returned at dawn, and at a quarter to four that afternoon Underwood was ushered into the limo, driven across the street, then hustled into the hotel. Already aware of the man's destination, Falcon and Steve were able to follow at an unhurried pace. They were temporarily detoured by the sight of his bodyguards checking identification outside the conference room. But Steve had already planned her entree into the room. She was dressed in a borrowed waitress's uniform and wore her own curly red wig. All it had taken for her to replace the waitress assigned to set up the coffee service was a small bribe. The woman had been more than happy to take a break.

Now Steve left Falcon at the end of the hallway with a promise to return to the same spot within a half-hour. Hopefully, by that time, she would have a commitment from Underwood to confer with them both privately. Her intention was to confront him in front of his business associates, when it would be to his advantage to talk to her.

Standing in the shadows, Falcon closed his eyes and called on his newest gift. Making his mind go blank, he thought: *Steve*. As before, a picture of her came to him clearly. He saw her pushing the service cart past the guards and into the meeting room. The board members were in the midst of a heated discussion, several people appeared to be talking at once. Steve set up the service on a table in the back of the room and took her time looking around. Every chair around the big oval table was occupied, but Underwood was not one of those present.

Steve left that room and went into the next one down the hall. Another meeting, much more subdued, was in progress. The three men who had boarded their houseboat the night before were there, but again, there was no sign of Underwood and no empty chair to signify someone's absence. There was only one more room on this floor where meetings had been scheduled, and Steve checked it out next, with the same disappointing results. They had definitely seen Underwood enter the hotel minutes before they did, but he was not where he was supposed to be.

There was no time to waste. Falcon walked down the corridor and approached the two guards in front of the conference room doors. Before they had a chance to stop him, he raised his arms and touched each man's temple, freezing them in place.

Steve pulled the cart out of the third room in a state of confusion. Nothing was making sense. She looked up in time to see Falcon standing in front of the two guards. He was *touching* them like he had done to her! As she walked by, Falcon backed away from them and entered the elevator with her.

"What were you doing? You could have blown the whole thing! Why did those guys let you touch them like that?"

"There was something I had to do."

"And?"

"It was not successful." The two guards were little more than morons. They only knew they had escorted Gordon Underwood to that floor and were to prevent anyone matching Steve's or his description from entering any of the rooms. Thanks to Steve's propensity for costumes, the two men had failed in that respect.

Steve sighed. She would feel better if she had some idea of what he was up to, but it was obvious he was not going to say any more. One of these times she was going to stand her ground and make him give her a straight answer for a change. "Well, don't feel too bad. I just served coffee to a bunch of businessmen and didn't even get a tip. It was another wild goose chase."

Falcon frowned. A wild goose? Why had he not seen the creature? He realized his mistake when Steve shook her head with an air of endless patience, then went on to relate her movements. Falcon gave her his attention, nodding occasionally, as if he had not seen exactly what had happened.

The hours were slipping by, and they were no closer to Underwood than they had been a week ago. They would have to try to get on board again tonight.

Just as they started to cross the street, fortune smiled on them. Underwood was entering his black limousine without his usual entourage.

"Come on!" Steve shouted, and took off for her car parked on the opposite side of the street. Falcon barely closed the door on the passenger side when the car lunged out of the space and headed south after the limo. She despaired that she had lost it when she suddenly caught a glimpse of it moving west over the Arthur Godfrey Causeway.

With a little experienced maneuvering, she closed the distance, but remained concealed in the moderate traffic. At one point she noticed Falcon clutching the dashboard, but she did not want to take the time to assure him of her abilities. It was taking all her concentration to watch the limo and follow the expressway signs. A series of lane changes took them into the city of Miami. The fact that Underwood was making this trip without bodyguards, at a time when everyone thought he was in a meeting, led Steve to believe she would be well rewarded if she could stay on his tail.

Once they exited the expressway, it became extremely difficult to follow the limo without sticking close, but every time Steve thought she had made a wrong turn, the black limo would come into view. The quality of the city deteriorated a block at a time, until they were in the midst of an area that sported the special street lamps used predominantly in high-crime neighborhoods.

Underwood's chauffeur pulled the car to a stop in front of a four-story building that should have been condemned, but the evidence of a few drapes and a sheet hanging out a glassless window indicated that people lived there. Steve stopped close enough to survey the immediate area around the limo. There was not a building on the block that was habitable. Broken garbage bags and trash littered the sidewalks and fenced-in dirt yards. Several small groups of young blacks lounged in front of doorways, drinking from containers in brown paper bags, and sharing their smokes. Apparently, black leather jackets were out this year; black sweatsuits were the uniform of the day, in spite of the heat. Several ghetto-blasters competed for the greatest volume, and both the limo and her car were noted with considerable interest by more than one of the music lovers.

Even though it was not yet dark, Steve knew this was not a place she should have come to unarmed. She also knew Underwood had some shady dealings from time to time, but whatever he was doing here went far beyond shady.

Underwood stepped out of the car and headed toward one of the apartments.

Steve pressed on the gas pedal and spun out with a squeal. She slammed on the brakes right behind the limo.

Falcon grasped her arm as she pushed her door open. "No! Stop!" he shouted, but she was already out and moving toward where she had seen Underwood enter a dilapidated building. Falcon jumped out of the car after her. He was frantic. Hostility and anger surrounded them. It was all pervasive. They were in serious danger. He had to get her out of here.

He caught up to her, grabbing her arm and pulling her around, but it was too late. They were suddenly surrounded by jeering black faces. At least ten young men and boys were within arm's length and behind them were twenty more.

Steve gave herself the time it took to take one breath for self-recrimination, then prepared to get herself and Falcon out of the situation she had caused. She gave Falcon her back, knowing instinctively he would protect it, and tried for diplomacy.

"Hey, guys. What's happenin'? We have some business with the dude that just went inside, so, if you'll give us a little space, we'll do our thing and be out of here."

"Don't think so, Mama," one of the older teens taunted. "This here's a private club. You paid your dues yet?" The horde inched closer, and Steve pressed herself against Falcon's back.

"We could pay your dues. Let us go back to my car. I left my purse."

The gang leader leered at her and fingered the sleeve of her shirt. "No need. We'll take our dues in white sugar."

A young man, shorter than Falcon but three times his girth, pushed his way forward. "You can all have her. I want me this here pretty thing." He grabbed Falcon's hair in his meaty fist and jerked him away from Steve.

Steve did not get a chance to check Falcon's response. The leader grabbed her upper arms, and her body sprung into action. The side of her hand slashed across his throat a second before her foot connected with the groin of the boy next to him. By the time the gang's stunned comrades came to their senses and attacked *en masse*, she was poised and ready. Her speed and agility more than countered

171

their numbers and individual sizes. In a chorus of cries and grunts, her opponents fell victim to her ax-like chops and perfectly aimed kicks. She received a fair share of punishment in return, but as she had been trained, she shut out the pain and forced her muscles to perform on demand.

One brave soul pulled a knife on her after several others had run off. He could not know how the sight of it infuriated her. Up to this point, her efforts were confined to defending herself while delivering temporary discomfort.

Her attacker lunged, his knife aimed at her gut. In one fluid motion, Steve sideswept and grabbed his wrist, locking his elbow, and the knife flew out of his hand. The side of her free hand slammed into his forearm to the accompaniment of the sickening crunch of splintered bone. The boy screamed in pain as he scurried after his friends into their hiding places.

Spinning around quickly, Steve eyed the results of Falcon's defense. On the ground around him, eight boys appeared to be sleeping peacefully, curled in the fetal position, two of them sucking their thumbs. Falcon was being circled by the last two assailants. When Steve moved to join his fight, they backed off.

"Screw this, man! We ain't paid to get ourselves killed!" one angry teen yelled before they both fled.

Steve's adrenaline-rushed system had her looking for another victim when her wild-eyed gaze landed on Falcon. Other than getting his hair mussed, no one would have guessed what he had been doing. He wasn't even breathing hard, while she was sweating profusely and huffing her little lungs out.

He gave her a bored look. "*Now* can we leave?"

"I'm afraid not," a deep voice said behind them.

As one, Steve and Falcon whirled to face a towering, dark-haired man with Oriental features. Knees and elbows bent, hands angled and circling in front of his body, his fighting stance warned of experience in the martial arts.

"You did very well against the untrained children. Now you will deal with me."

The momentary respite had allowed fatigue to set into Steve's overworked muscles. When her brain sent out the message to defend herself, they took a split second too long to respond. The man's hand slammed into her diaphragm, knocking her to the ground as if she were weightless. She struggled to take a breath into her paralyzed body, trying not to panic. The numbness would only last a few minutes, but that was long enough to keep her from helping Falcon.

Pain! echoed in Falcon's head. Steve's paralysis threatened to immobilize him as well. As soon as he controlled it, he became aware of a powerful, dark emotion rising inside him. *Let it come*, he told himself.

The Oriental moved cautiously around Falcon, not yet striking a blow. Suddenly one word came clearly from the attacker's mind: *Kill!*

No! This animal had no right. *How dare he hurt her!* Falcon's anger coursed through him like a drug. He leapt into the air, landing a kick to the man's chin that hurled him back several feet before he fell. But he rolled and jumped up immediately, delivering a

173

steady stream of blows an instant later.

Falcon blocked, spun, struck, and kicked again. Repeatedly, he came within an inch of touching his assailant's temple. Repeatedly, he received blows so staggering he could not block them out. Falcon was now feeling the man's pain as well as his own, and knew he had to end the confrontation quickly.

Steve drew a ragged breath. She could not imagine how either man could withstand the punishment they were each meting out. The Oriental's nose and mouth were bloody and swollen. Falcon had blood all over him, but she could not tell the source. If she could just stand up. . . .

Falcon grasped the taller man's right arm in both his hands, and yanked him off his feet. Using strength he had not known he possessed, he whirled in circles, lifting the man's huge body off the ground as he spun round and round. As if he were throwing a discus, Falcon relinquished his hold. The Oriental flew into the side of the building and collapsed in a heap. Falcon limped toward the body, reaching out with his two fingers.

"Hold it right there," a gruff voice shouted from behind him, but he did not freeze until he heard Steve cry his name. He turned to see the chauffeur pointing a weapon at him.

"Come to me, nice and easy like." The uniformed man waited as Falcon neared him. He motioned for Falcon to stand beside the immobilized Steve who was sitting on the pavement. Then the man walked to where the Oriental lay and leaned over to touch the pulse in the man's neck without taking his eyes or the gun off Falcon and Steve.

"You gonna be okay, Mr. King? C'mon, ya gotta help yourself into the car and I'll get you outta here."

King groaned and blinked several times. Slowly, he rose and dragged himself to the limo, his driver close behind. In a stench of burning rubber, they sped away.

Falcon helped Steve struggle to her feet and to walk to the car. "Will you be able to drive? I . . .I don't have a license."

"Why doesn't that surprise me?" she mumbled to herself as she opened the car door. "I'm okay. But you look like hell. Is anything broken?"

"No. I am also 'okay.' A shower will help immensely."

With Falcon's occasional reminders as to which direction they had come from, they managed to get back to Miami Beach. Steve could feel the results of her exertions setting in rapidly and silently wished the houseboat came equipped with a hot tub. To get her mind off her pain, she drew Falcon into an analysis of the case, even though he seemed content to sit and brood.

"Listen, I know that was all my fault back there, and I'm sorry. I thought for sure we had him this time, but it looks like I walked, or rather, I raced us right into a trap. You heard that one kid say they were being paid." Falcon continued to stare straight ahead. "Hello? Falcon? Are you sure you're all right? You look kinda green around the gills."

Falcon turned to her. Gills? He hid his confusion this time. "Excuse me. I was preoccupied. You need not apologize. There is no question we have been misled several times this week. I also believed I saw

Underwood enter the limo."

"Of course! It was a disguise. I should have thought of that myself. Got any ideas for our next move?"

"I need to get on his yacht. Perhaps tonight we will not be interrupted if we try again."

"Fine with me." When Falcon began to lapse back into his own thoughts, Steve demanded, "There's something else, isn't there? I can tell you're bugged. What is it? You do blame me, don't you? I said I'm sorry. What do you want from me?"

"Nothing, Steve. I am 'bugged' with myself. I will work it out."

The only time she had seen that tense expression on his face was in their room in Las Vegas, right before he touched her temples and fed her a story about being a healer. "I don't understand, Falcon, and I want to. I've never seen anyone fight like you did back there, but you couldn't expect to win against a gun. You *had* to back off. I've had to do the same thing myself in other situations."

"I cannot explain it, Steve. Please let it be." How could he tell her that he had just broken one of the basic laws of Innerworld? He had allowed his anger to rule him, and committed a vengeful act of violence. Along with the anger had come incredible physical strength. He had barely tapped into it to finish off his opponent. Falcon knew, in that moment, he had been capable of taking another life. The shockingly sweet taste of power had instantly turned to bile.

With that realization came another. His human emotions were continuing to surface with increasing resistance to his control, yet his felan powers were not diminishing, as he had anticipated they would.

In fact, he was discovering new talents each day. Falcon decided it was too soon to draw a definite conclusion. Only time would give him the answers he sought. Clearly, he was no longer in control.

Steve let him sulk and found herself doing the same. She should not be annoyed that he did not care to confide in her. The only thing she was to him was a temporary partner on a case. A partner who almost got him killed because she could not resist being a hot dog P.I. Wouldn't Lou Dokes like to hear her admit that!

Neither one moved very quickly as they boarded the houseboat. Falcon accepted Steve's offer to take the first shower, and Steve gave in to the need to collapse on her bed.

She had not meant to doze off, but knew she had when his voice came to her from a different plane, telling her she could use the shower.

Steve's eyelids fluttered open, then squinted shut again. She was fairly certain there was not an inch of her body that was not in serious pain. Slowly, she tested her toes and fingers, but when she tried to rise, she fell back with an audible groan.

"You are in much pain, Steve. Let me touch you. It will help."

He stood expectantly beside the bed as he casually tucked a towel around his waist. Steve wanted to assure him that she did not need his help, but the sight of him turned her tongue into a useless appendage. Smooth, hard-muscled thighs were braced inches from her face. Forcing her gaze past the towel, above his still-damp chest, she could not stop her slight intake of breath. His incredibly beautiful features were more pronounced with his wet hair brushed back, curling behind his ears and onto his bare shoulders. She was simply struck dumb, and he took it as her assent.

Steve braced herself to feel his fingertips against her face, but when he sat down next to her, he picked up her hands instead. She watched him carefully, determined to figure out what he did when he touched people.

Falcon held her hands in his and closed his eyes. Like every other part of her body, her fingers and palms radiated discomfort and tension. He concentrated on passing his strength to her, and lessening the physical pain in the same way as he would an emotional one. A gentle, shimmering warmth centered in his hands at the same time he visualized various parts that made up hers. The bones, muscles, nerves, and blood vessels took on a bright reddish hue where the damage was worst. He moved his fingers to those spots and pressed, massaged, and pressed again. The color cooled. He kept his eyes closed, using the anatomical image in his mind to guide his hands up her aching arms, bringing relief as he progressed.

Her shoulders, neck, and arms received the same, efficient treatment. Falcon felt a certain exhilaration in the knowledge that she was not only improving by the moment, but allowing his touch without her usual wariness. Before he could work on her feet and legs he had to remove her shoes, socks, and jeans, and did so in a quick, impersonal manner, leaving her in her tee shirt and underwear.

Steve told herself to think of him like a doctor. Hell, her gynecologist saw more of her than this, and usually caused more discomfort than relief. If Falcon could pull off her jeans and not notice that she was a woman, she would not feel insulted this time. He was making her feel too good to complain, and not only because he was doing a great job of massaging her aches and pains. His hands heated her skin and left it tingling wherever he made contact. By the time he reached her thighs, she was vibrating with a different kind of ache, one she did not want to go away. At least not too swiftly.

Falcon had made a serious mistake. He had opened his eyes for the brief minute it took to remove her jeans. A glimpse of white satin kept intruding on the more physiological image of muscle and bone he was trying to hold on to. Steve herself was making his task of healing impossibly difficult, not only with her tempting, female body, but her thoughts that sporadically made themselves known to him.

Stop. Don't stop. Touch me. Please. Higher.

He could touch her there, as she needed, and not take pleasure himself. That was a lie! He was already receiving more pleasure than he dreamed possible just by handling her arms and legs.

He lifted his hands from her thighs and carefully slipped them under her shirt, wrapping his fingers around her rib cage. One bone had suffered a small crack. Falcon discovered he could take away the pain, but not repair the bone. The injury would have to heal in the usual manner. In spite of that limitation, he acknowledged the magnitude of this gift. The talent to draw pain from the physical body

179

was rare among felans. He also admitted that he had never felt more desire for Steve than he was experiencing at this moment. The power and the emotions were not separate, competing entities, but partners, growing together. He had been wrong all along. His felan gifts would *not* desert him if he accepted his human emotions. So there was no reason to deny himself any longer.

When he felt the last remnants of Steve's pain recede, Falcon raised his gaze to hers. She wanted him to do precisely what he wished. As carefully as he had touched the rest of her body, his fingers crept up until they encountered her satin-covered breasts. When she continued to welcome him with her eyes and thoughts, he molded her into his hands, and brushed his thumbs over her taut nipples. The urge to see what he was touching became overwhelming.

Steve's world altered into one of slow motion, one where sensation replaced the thought process. His massage had left her languid and wanting at the same time. When Falcon stretched out beside her and hesitantly returned one hand to her breast, she gave in to her desire to touch him in return. The velvety texture of his skin against her fingertips seemed somehow new and wondrous. Steve stroked his cheek, the outline of his ear, and trailed downward to discover his nipples were as hard as her own. She had not known a man's skin could feel so soft, like down on a baby bird.

Falcon inhaled sharply at her exploration. Steve's touch excited him beyond belief, and her scent filled him with a craving he was certain could never be satisfied. He lowered his mouth to hers, intending to caress her with infinite tenderness. Gentleness was discarded when he tasted her, and a ravaging hunger guided his actions. The beast demanded to be unleashed.

She had forgotten how strange his tongue felt until he used it to outline her lips and stroke the roof of her mouth. At once it tickled, teased, and consumed her like nothing she had ever experienced.

One of Falcon's legs slid between hers. The towel around his waist slipped aside, and Steve felt his rigid manhood throbbing insistently against her thigh. He pressed his hips forward, wordlessly requesting her touch. But she was not ready to look at that part of him, let alone lower her hand, not even to investigate whether his skin felt so smooth all over.

It shocked her to realize she was actually shy. Of course, she had good reason to be. The only lover she had ever had was Vinnie Barbanell, and the last time she had lain with him was almost four years ago. As if Falcon was aware that her mind had wandered, his tongue grazed a burning path to her ear and down her neck while his hand snaked down her abdomen, silently forcing the return of her attention.

Falcon's mouth stifled Steve's moan as his fingers glided over her panties to the sensitive flesh of her inner thighs. Lightly, he stroked her skin, coming close but never quite touching the center of her desire. She thought perhaps he understood her need to go slowly, to savor each plateau as she came to it. Was his touch really more sensual than Vinnie's had been or had it just been so long since she'd felt a man's touch that it seemed that way? She could not remember anything quite so delicious.

Despite his drugging kisses, her stubborn common sense intruded again. What was she doing? Why was she letting a virtual stranger handle her so intimately when she had refused men she knew much better? Men who were clearly more deserving of her gift?

"Falcon?" she managed to say in an exhale of held breath.

He stilled his hand and raised his head to look at her. His topaz eyes glowed with a golden fire that reflected what little light was in the room. It was enough to convince her she was right to want to know more about him before going on.

"How do you do the things you do?" Falcon withdrew his hand, but Steve felt him withdraw much more than that. "I don't know if you can understand this, but please try. I've never been with any man but my ex-husband. I thought I could do this—enjoy an hour of passion, no strings attached, but old habits die hard. I want you to make love to me, but it isn't that simple for me. You have too many secrets for me to be comfortable with you. I want you to share one with me.

"You decide. Pick one incident and explain how you did it: how you got from San Francisco to Los Angeles ahead of me, how we had so much luck in the casino, what happened with the jungle cats, what you do when you touch someone's temple?" Steve took a deep breath. "How you make me melt just by coming near me?" She closed her eyes, shyness now giving way to embarrassment. She had seen all these things, yet refused to question them, because underlying all of it was her own primal urge to be possessed by him no matter what he did. But in the end, it mattered.

"Is it not enough to let me pleasure you? You cannot know how long I have waited for this same hour of passion."

"No. I need to know."

"And it is something you must not know. I cannot answer any of your questions. Will you not accept anything else?"

"No. And thank you for reminding me of my priorities." She rolled away from him and off the bed. "You do great massage, Falcon. I feel like a new woman. I believe it was my turn for the shower."

Falcon's body ached with unfulfilled passion, but he hurt from something far worse than his aborted sexual release. He had never understood how a human could have a broken heart until he watched Steve, her back straight, leave the room, and felt her unshed tears. Surely, his own heart would never be whole again. Raising his hand to his face, he closed his eyes and inhaled deeply. But the memory of her would be with him always.

Chapter Eleven

I can believe anything, provided it is incredible.—Oscar Wilde

Steve descended the staircase in her bikini, her chin lifted defiantly, her eyes warning Falcon to keep his distance. The sight of her brought back the chest-clenching, stomach-churning sickness he had experienced earlier that night. He had classified it as guilt—another human emotion he would have rather done without.

She walked by him, picked up the grappling device, and exited. Falcon was certain there must be a dialogue appropriate for these circumstances, but his life experience did not prepare him to deal with the melee of emotions emanating from Steve: anger, disappointment, sexual frustration, and embarrassment, all directed at him.

A splash alerted him to Steve's departure from the houseboat. Falcon hurried to jump in the warm water and swim after her.

Staying close to the side of Underwood's yacht,

they were able to remain in the shadows caused by the bright moon and streetlights over the ship. A few lights shone on board, but there was no sign of anyone.

Steve tried to tread water and aim the hook, but could not hold it steady with one hand. Falcon immediately assisted by placing his hands on her waist. She twisted from his touch.

"You need both your hands, Steve. Allow me to help."

She glared at him for a moment, then braced herself for the contact. Why did such an inconsequential action have to make her pulse race? Why did a stranger have to be the one to have such power over her? It did not seem at all fair.

Less than a minute later, they were on board, retrieving the rope they had used to shimmy up the side. Falcon touched her shoulder and pointed in the direction he thought they should take. Steve stayed close to him as they crept along the superstructure and down a stairway to the cabin area. He ran his fingertips along the walls and railing, occasionally coming to a stop and closing his eyes. Without comprehending, she knew he was doing more than simply feeling his way along the passageway. It gave her the creeps, but she continued to follow his lead.

At one door Falcon paused, placed his palm flat against the wood, then opened it. Steve quickly stepped in behind him and closed the door again. A bit of moonlight entering a porthole made it possible for Steve to discern that they were in a fair-sized stateroom cramped by an executive desk and a full complement of office equipment.

Steve waited, wondering why Falcon had chosen to come in this room, yet sensing that she should not interrupt him. His hand roamed in small circles over the desk and chair, then halted on the telephone. His eyes closed tightly, his head slightly angled as if straining to hear, he remained frozen for what seemed like an eternity. What was he doing now?

When he opened his eyes, he said, "Gordon Underwood has never been here, Steve. His employee, King, has been enacting a masquerade for our benefit. His orders were to waylay us in any way he could, including bodily harm if necessary, as long as it looked accidental."

Suddenly he turned his head from left to right. He seemed to see something Steve could not. His fingers toyed with his ring in a strangely purposeful manner as he stepped around the desk.

"Someone is coming," he whispered as he drew close to her. There was no time for explanations. In a move that brooked no argument, Falcon pulled her against his chest and wrapped his arms tightly around her.

Steve was incensed and confused one moment and terrified out of her wits the next. The floor dropped out from under her; the room then the world disappeared. She fell into a void where she no longer had a body. The resulting sensation was similar to a roller-coaster ride in total blackness, followed by no feeling at all. Was she dead? Had they been discovered and killed? She had always assumed that the brain ceased functioning when one died. Maybe she was in a coma. That might explain it.

Before she adjusted to that idea, reality returned. Her feet stood on a solid surface, Falcon's arms held her in a death grip, and she smelled a trace of the soap he had used in the shower. Instinct told her to proceed cautiously. Had seconds passed or some greater amount of time while she was comatose? Her sense of balance restored, she raised her head to look at Falcon and pushed away from his grasp.

"There was no other way," he said quickly. "Please stay here. Do not move from this location until I return." Falcon moved his fingers over his ring.

As Steve opened her mouth to protest, her eyesight faltered. Falcon's features blurred, then there was nothing. Well, not exactly nothing. She was outdoors, in a city, in front of a building. *Underwood's building*! Spinning around abruptly, she saw the Transamerica Pyramid. Okay, she was in San Francisco. Alone in the dark. Was she suffering from amnesia or insanity? Weren't she and Falcon in Miami Beach? Did he really command her to stay there then disappear?

She could not simply stand around indefinitely. A chilly gust of wind blew over her causing her to hug her body and look for shelter. It was freezing out here. Realization careened through her head. She was still in her bikini, still wet from her *recent* swim in the Intracoastal Waterway. A cold drop of water slid off her hair, intensifying the shiver that ran down her spine.

In a reverse of his disappearing act, a blurred vision of Falcon appeared before her, clarifying into the real thing as she gaped. He was fully dressed and had both their traveling bags.

As he pulled her shivering body into the recessed entranceway of Underwood's building, he said, "I believe I retrieved all your possessions. You had better get dressed before we go further." He handed her her bag and turned his back, offering himself as a shield against the eyes of anyone who might pass by.

What kind of an explanation was that? Steve tried to question him, but her chattering teeth refused to cooperate. Later. Unzipping her bag, she knew the only way she would get warm was if she got out of her wet bathing suit. Shivering uncontrollably, she managed to change into warmer clothes using a variety of contortions and as much speed as she could muster. As soon as she was dressed, Falcon turned around and pulled her into his arms again.

"Sh-h-h-sh," he hissed, as his hands ran up and down her back.

Delicious warmth swept through her. It felt too good to let her pride get in the way. But with the return of comfort came the desperate need for explanations, and her body tensed in preparation. "What the hell is going on?" That one question summed it up as far as she was concerned.

Falcon swallowed hard. He would have told her another falsehood, if one had occurred to him, but absolutely nothing came to mind that she would rationally accept. "I am unable to explain. We are back in San Francisco, and I need to get into Underwood's office." He released her and tested the door. "This entrance is locked and appears to have an alarm attached to it. Would you know how to gain access?"

Steve blinked and shook her head in disbelief. "That's it? Business as usual? Listen, pal, I just aged twenty years because of that last little trick." As her temper rose, she started pacing back and forth in the protected entranceway. "How silly of me to think you had secrets before. I hadn't seen anything yet, had I? I don't even *want* to know anymore. I don't understand any of it, and I'm scared to death that knowing would be even worse." She came to a decision and turned to confront him. "Okay. I'm going home. Have a wonderful life. I hope I never run into you again."

Grabbing her bag, she strode down the sidewalk with hopes of finding a cab. What the hell time was it anyway? They had climbed onto the yacht around two, so it must be about eleven o'clock now.

"Steve."

Falcon's raspy voice brought her to a stop more effectively than his hand on her elbow. It vibrated through her like a kitten purring against her breast. He should *not* be allowed to do that!

"Please, do not go. I need your help." *And you*, he added to himself.

Steve fought to reinforce her resolve. Apparently, he thought he could dissolve her into a mindless pool of gelatin with his sexy, pleading voice and the pained expression on his handsome face, and the way his thumb caressed her elbow, and . . . Oh, damn! He was doing it to her again.

She took a deep breath, stepped back, and crossed her arms in front of her. "Explain." To make sure she did not give in without getting an answer from him, Steve stared at a building in the distance instead of his eyes.

His words came out haltingly, and he hoped she could not tell he was making it up as he went along. "I have a few psychic abilities. I was afraid it would frighten you if you knew."

"So, I'm frightened and not terribly surprised by that news flash. How did we get here from the yacht? And how did you zap back and forth like that?"

"My ring is . . . an experimental transportation device. Very few people are aware of its existence."

"Let me get this straight. You expect me to believe that some brainy scientist figured out how to dematerialize and transport people across thousands of miles in a matter of seconds, using a fake opal ring. Then he decided to test it with an Interpol agent." Falcon's eyebrows raised a notch. "Don't look so shocked. I've seen every episode of 'Star Trek.' I know all about things like dematerialization. I also know no one in this time period has invented it. Of course, you could have come here from a future time. My, God! That's it, isn't it?"

Falcon's face relaxed into a smile. He wondered, if she could accept his being a time traveler, could she accept his being from another world? His intuition responded negatively. He would allow her to believe whatever she was most comfortable with. "No one must know where I am from, Steve. Will you keep my secret?" At least he had not actually lied to her.

Steve's excitement had her pacing again. "I can't believe it, but I do. How can I not after everything you've done? Will you tell me about the future, Falcon? Where, I mean, *when* are you from? Is it fantastic? Do we find a cure for cancer? Does the . . ."

Falcon stopped her by placing his hands firmly on her shoulders. "Please do not make this more difficult for me. I can tell you no more than you already know. I am here on a mission for my people. Will you continue to help me find Gordon Underwood and not speak to anyone about my being here?"

Steve's smile vanished as she removed his hands and stepped away from him. "On one condition." Keeping both her eyes and voice lowered, she stated her terms. "Stop seducing me. You don't need to do that to get my cooperation."

Falcon was momentarily confused by her demand and her reasoning. He sensed that her desire for him had not lessened, and she seemed fairly satisfied with his explanations. He reached out empathically for understanding and felt the answer—her pride was bruised. When he tried to take her hands, she retreated another step. "Steve, with the exception of what happened earlier this evening, I have worked very hard at trying *not* to seduce you. I would not use such a method to obtain your cooperation, even if it resulted in something I wanted very much. But if that is your condition for keeping my secret, I promise to do my best not to entice you. If you will be honest, though, I should make the same demand of you."

If she had to be honest, they were equally guilty when it came to seduction and rejection. But when he referred to something he wanted very much, why did she still wish that she, not Underwood, was that something? Regardless of his meaning, his secret had just put the seal on her resistance to his charms. Any hour he would be gone, not only from her life, but from her time.

She needed to get back on track. "I appreciate your promise, and return the same to you. Now, why do we need to get into this building?"

"When we were in the office on the yacht, I overheard a telephone conversation between Underwood and King."

"What? You never picked up the phone."

"It is one of my abilities, Steve. When I touch objects, I can sometimes see and hear things that have occurred a short time before. You are doubtful, I see. If you do not want to hear the answers, I would rather you not ask the questions."

"Sorry. Go ahead."

"I told you what I learned. I neither heard nor saw anything that revealed where Underwood was during that conversation. I have deduced that the secretary here knows where he is. She was too suspicious to let me near her before, and now I am sure she would be more so. We do not know how many people Underwood has instructed to stop us. If we could gain access to his offices when no one is around, I am sure I would discover a clue to his whereabouts."

"Why can't you just zap yourself in there with your trusty ring?"

Falcon smiled in spite of her sarcastic tone. "I do not have an exact floor plan or a signal to home in on. I would not care to transport myself into a wall or piece of furniture. I had the exact coordinates of this location since it is where I originally arrived, and, although I had calculated the houseboat's position, this was the one I thought of first when it became necessary to leave the yacht immediately. You see, I recognized King's aura as he approached the office."

Steve pushed down her next dozen questions with a groan. "Okay, but there's no easy way to get into that building once it's closed, and it won't be open until Monday morning, at least thirty hours from now. In the meantime, you're welcome to stay at my house. I can only offer the couch tonight, since Mom and the kids are asleep by now. Tomorrow I'll rearrange them a little to give you a bed."

She did not wait for his acceptance before going on, "My car's still at the airport. We'll take a cab out there, then head to the house. I may as well warn you. My son is an early riser, so I'd suggest you get what sleep you can as soon as we get there. He has no sympathy for adults who sleep in late."

After picking up her car at the airport, the trip to Kensington was quiet, but not uncomfortable. Steve was too tired to try to get Falcon to satisfy more of her curiosity about him, and he had closed his eyes minutes after they got in her car. Whether he was sleeping or deep in thought, she decided to leave him alone.

After tiptoeing into the house, she found him a pillow and blanket and retired to her room. She was positive she would never sleep after everything that had happened, but her head met the pillow and exhaustion drove her straight to dreamland.

Falcon tried every possible position, but it was impossible. The couch was too short, he could not sleep fully dressed, the lenses had been in his eyes so long the drops no longer helped, and he had too much on his mind. Since he sensed Steve was asleep, he went into the bathroom, removed the lenses, and

193

cleaned them. He desperately needed to leave them out of his eyes for a few hours. Deciding the blanket was cover enough, he shed his clothing. Both the lenses and his clothes could be replaced in time if he made a point of programming himself to arise as soon as the first person, probably the boy, began to stir—if he ever fell asleep at all.

By propping the pillow under his neck and resting his head on the cushioned arm of the sofa, he was able to extend his legs fully. If only he could cleanse his mind as easily as the lenses, the last obstacle between him and Morpheus would be removed.

His thoughts were not exactly *un*clean. They were just tormented with images of a small scrap of white satin—a fabric that took second place to the delicate softness of Steve's skin. And he had touched so much of it. With no effort he recalled the tangy fragrance that was Steve's alone, and the salty-sweet taste of her tongue. How close he had come to discovering the ultimate human pleasure when they had been on the houseboat after the fight. He had meant to protect rather than hurt her by refusing to answer her questions. At that time he had had no way of fore-telling that she would discover some of his secrets anyway.

Falcon tried not to dwell on how differently things might have been between them had he known that she would accept a story as unusual as his being a time traveler. But even if he had thought of that lie instead of her, he would not have expected her to believe it.

And now that his secrets were no longer a barrier, he had promised not to seduce her.

Would once have been enough? Or, after his first release within her body's grasp, would he have needed to repeat the experience over and over again, until he had made up for countless years of abstinence?

If he had been uncomfortable before, his present state was bordering torture. The harder he tried not to think about her, the harder he became. He could not stop himself from imagining what it would be like to be completely enveloped by Steve.

Steve's dream mechanism shifted into high gear. Falcon had appeared fleetingly in another dream, on another night, but its content had been forgotten upon awakening. Tonight's dream was so much better. They were back on the houseboat, lying together, kissing, touching. This time she did not stop him or get up and leave. This time she wore nothing at all.

He moved over her, positioning himself between her spread thighs. With one long, slow drive, he entered her body. The low simmer of sensation flared into frenzied need. She could feel him throbbing, holding back. Didn't he understand? She didn't want him to hold back. Her body was ready, waiting breathlessly to be carried over the edge of the rainbow. She opened her eyes to convey her urgent need. Two flames of golden fire leapt from his eyes to hers, blinding and burning her in a climactic burst of passion.

Steve bolted upright, her chest pounding furiously. There was no man in her room. It had been a dream. Her nightgown was bunched up around her waist, her inner thighs were damp and sticky, and her body trembled. She had never experienced a dream so intense, so erotic . . . so *real*.

She got up from bed and walked down the hall. She had to assure herself that Falcon was asleep on the couch. In the darkness she could make out his form. His breathing was strained, erratic, as if he was struggling for air.

Not certain if he was ill or having a nightmare, Steve stepped cautiously toward the couch. "Falcon?" Then her own breath became a strangled gasp that exited in a frightened whimper. It was Falcon. And it wasn't. It was a being with inhuman eyes—glittering, golden eyes with black, marquis-diamond pupils that reflected her face like twin mirrors.

Falcon jumped up and grasped her upper arms. Steve's eyes had adjusted well enough to see that he was naked and aroused, and her fear escalated to terror when he touched her.

"*Please*. My children. My mother."

He gave her a rough shake. "Stop it! Stop the fear, Steve. There is nothing to be afraid of." He tried to pull her into his embrace to comfort her, but it only frightened her more, and when she began struggling in earnest, he gentled his hold without releasing her. Holy stars! Her fear was directed at him! "Tell me. What has frightened you?"

Steve was confused. He sounded the same, he felt the same . . .

"Your eyes. My God, Falcon. What are you?"

What am I? He could not think past her paralyzing fear. He raised one hand to her temple.

Steve pulled her head away. "No! Don't touch me!" Her voice was a frantic whisper, torn between a desire to scream and a prayer that her family would not awaken and leave the safety of their rooms.

Falcon would not relinquish his hold. He was desperate to reach beyond her fear. "Steve. It is me. Falcon. I have never hurt you, have I? Think! Let go of the fear and think. I have kept my eyes masked only because they are different. I could not afford to call attention to myself. I am still the same person you have been with all week." He closed his eyes. "Look at me now, Steve. What do you see?"

Calling upon her long-established courage, she lifted her head. As long as she could not see his catlike eyes, she could tell herself he was Falcon. Her terror subsided, leaving her shaking in its wake. Steve raised one trembling hand to his cheek. Her fingertips confirmed his identity. "I don't understand," she murmured quietly.

Falcon took a slow, deep breath. Perhaps the Noronian code of honesty *was* the best policy. He found he could not bear any more lies. "I will tell you the truth, if you are sure you want to know it. Would you prefer that I replace my lenses before we talk? They irritate my eyes. I removed them, thinking you were asleep."

"I . . . I'll be okay now. Leave them. I just wasn't expecting it . . . on top of the dream." She prepared herself for a second look as he raised his eyelids. When she looked at his eyes this time she was not frightened. In fact, she had to admit, his eyes were even somewhat fascinating.

Falcon let her take as long as she needed to get accustomed to his real appearance. He had never had anyone react to him that way. Aster was a Terran, but when she met him, she had already accepted the incredible fact that she had been transplanted to a strange world in the center of her planet. All things considered, his eyes probably seemed rather insignificant to her.

He knew Steve was no longer afraid of him, but she was still wary. "You said you had a dream. Was it a nightmare? Is that what brought you to me?"

Steve slipped from his arms and turned away from him. "No, not a nightmare. It was so real. I thought you were . . . Never mind. It's not important."

Falcon suddenly realized what had awakened her. If she had not been so terrified, he would have smelled it immediately. The musky aroma of sex surrounded her like a cloud. Somehow his fantasy about her must have invaded her sleep and become her dream.

He stared at her stiffly held back. The modest nightgown could not prevent him from seeing her as nature had formed her. Perfect. Beautiful. Instantly, he regretted using his talent for seeing through objects, as his body responded against his wishes. "It was not real, but my thoughts were very explicit. I had no idea they would affect you in your sleep."

Steve jerked her head toward him as she absorbed his words. He *gave* her that dream? Glancing at his condition, she immediately turned around again. "Please cover yourself. Then I want to hear the truth."

Sitting on the couch, he drew the blanket over his lower half. "Please sit with me."

After making sure he had done as she asked, she sat gingerly on the opposite end of the sofa. She was getting used to his strange eyes, but she had lingering doubts about the rest of him.

"Steve. Come closer."

"No. I can hear you from here."

"Halfway then. Close enough to hold my hand." She did not move. "I will talk when I have your hand." It was a way of keeping her there until she had heard everything and accepted it. He longed for the contact. When she scooted only the minimal distance required to place her hand within his reach, he knew he was right for insisting.

"You're not a time traveler, are you?" Steve stated to get him started.

"No. I am a tracker, not so different from you. I come from Innerworld, where a thousand people died and a female vanished due to Gordon Underwood's criminal behavior. He stole a ring like the one I wear, and my assignment is to retrieve it before he causes more damage."

Steve listened intently, without interruption, as he told her of the world in the inner core of the Earth, of the doorways, and accidental transplants of Outerworlders. He spoke warmly of Aster, a female Terran, like herself, who recently joined with his friend, Romulus, who was the governor of Innerworld; how Aster had been his guide on two brief visits to Outerworld, and why they had needed to come out.

It was as if he had been storing up conversation all week, and it all came out at once. He finished by detailing the events that led up to his present mission. At least now she understood why Underwood needed Nesterman's assistance.

"I don't know what to say," Steve said with a shrug of her shoulders. "I shouldn't believe anything so outlandish, but I do. Are you doing something to my mind to make me believe you?" she asked suspiciously.

He squeezed her hand once. "No. Only if I touch your temple, can I plant information in your mind. I have told you the truth."

"Can you read my mind?" Steve frowned at the idea.

"By the same method, yes. Except with you, when your emotions are exceptionally strong, I discovered I can pick up an occasional word, without touching you.

"What do you mean, 'except with me'? When did you discover this?"

Falcon saw no reason to keep the rest of it from her and explained his empathic powers and the gifts he'd always had. He revealed how his talents had expanded slightly in the last few months in Innerworld, but that powerful new abilities had abruptly come to him in the short time they had been together.

Steve was so pleased that he was finally talking openly to her, she did not allow herself to judge the content of his statements too harshly. "In other words, you're going through a kind of mental change-of-life."

The analogy made Falcon grimace. He needed to tell her all of it. "It is physical, also. My strength has increased, and there has been another change which I will tell you about, so that you can understand some of what has happened between us. As an empath, I never experienced emotions of my own. Shortly before we met, my emotional side began developing unexpectedly. Contact with you stimulated the growth that much faster."

"Contact with me? What did I do?"

This time he gave her a broad smile. "What did you do? For me, it seems, your very existence threw me into a state of frustrated confusion." He turned her hand over and traced the outline of her thumb and fingers, drew a circle on her palm, then repeated the pattern.

Steve felt the goose bumps rise on her arm in response to his absent-minded caress, but rather than pull her hand away, her fingers flexed to give him better access to the sensitive skin between.

"The first time I saw you, I desired you. I do not expect you to comprehend my reasoning completely, but I believed giving in to desire would result in the loss of some or all of my gifts. I thought I was being forced to make a choice between my mental abilities and emotions. Yesterday I finally realized my powers have increased in a vein parallel to my emotions."

She felt her cheeks grow hot and had to look away from him. "So that was why—."

"I quit fighting my attraction to you," he finished. "You are nervous now. There is no reason to be. I will not break my promise." But he did not stop his sensuous stroking of her palm.

"I still don't get it. Why would making love to me be different from any other woman you've been with? They do have sex in Innerworld, don't they?"

Falcon laughed. "Yes, Steve, they have sex. In fact, they are much more casual about that physical activity than your people seem to be. But, as an empath, I had no personal knowledge of desire, until recently. What makes you different is that you are the first woman I desired."

"But surely . . . You're shaking your head. You can't mean I would have been the first?" He nodded. How ridiculous! This had to be the greatest come-on line she had ever heard. A man that looked like him should have had hundreds of conquests by his age. The whole concept of a grown man being a virgin was completely alien to her.

She tensed with comprehension. Falcon stilled his hand. "There's one question you haven't answered yet. What are you, Falcon?" When he did not answer, she prodded, "Are you human, or something else? Your eyes are so different." Her fear returned. "Oh, God. You even asked if you seemed human to me." She tried to pull her hand back, but he held it tighter. "Let me go."

"Please let me explain. I said I will tell you the truth, and you have not given me an opportunity to respond. I am half human. My father was a human, from the planet Norona. My mother is felan, from the planet Emiron. I inherited my gifts from her; my appearance, with the exception of my eyes, from him. Therefore, I am human *and* something else." He did not want to know what she was feeling, but he could not stop it from coming to him. Her hand had become cold and clammy, and she swallowed several times, as if attempting to control a rebellious stomach. He only wanted her to know about him so she would not be frightened. Instead, she was repulsed by him. There was no comfort he could offer her when he was suddenly in urgent need of it himself. He opened his hand and let her pull away.

None of this is real, Steve told herself. *It's more of the dream, and I'll wake up in a minute, and everything will be normal. And I will never have hungered for love from an alien life form.*

For the second time in twelve hours, Falcon watched Steve walk away from him, without knowing how to make things right. His chest felt as if a battle-ax was lodged in it. Having feelings might have some positive aspects, but the negatives were truly unbearable. Falcon had never been disturbed by his mixed heritage, nor had he ever been a target of prejudice or disapproval because of it. Suddenly, through Steve's eyes, he saw himself as a freak of nature. "What are you?" she had said. He recalled the explanations he had been given in his youth, and never thought to question them.

For a thousand years the felan population on Emiron consistently declined. They devoted their lives to developing and improving their mental powers, particularly empathy. In doing so, they gradually relinquished their physical strengths, and replaced their own personal emotions with those they absorbed from others.

At first, only sexual desire faded, then the ability to reproduce ceased altogether. Although a felan might live for two hundred years or more, the old ones began dying off, without newborns to replace them. Experiments to create life outside the body failed. Before the race became extinct, they came up with a plan to integrate stronger species with their own. The result would be a mixed breed, but the offspring would still carry felan genes. The hope was they would be strong enough to interbreed themselves and perpetuate the race in that way.

Athletes, dancers, and other performers from across the universe were invited to Emiron to participate in a great fair. In this way, they were assured of drawing strong, healthy members of many species. Of those who attended there were several whose physical bodies were structurally similar to the Emironians; the humans of Norona were one such group.

Sperm samples were removed from the male visitors without their knowledge and used to fertilize felan eggs. Using a hypnotic power, the Emironians held the female guests after the males left, and their bodies were used for the gestation period. After the births, the females returned to their home planets with an artificial memory of the lost time supplied to them by the Emironians.

Their actions would not be considered honorable by many cultures, but the plan was moderately successful. A generation of mixed breeds were produced who, although only half felan, might be able to reproduce, thus preventing total extinction of their people. Now that Falcon knew he was capable of the act required for reproduction, while still maintaining his felan inheritance, he believed the experiment had been worth it. Most of the children remained on Emiron, as had been the hope. A few, like himself, chose to relocate elsewhere in the universe. Intentionally, the only records kept regarding the biological parents pertained to the father's race and native planet.

Falcon matured in a loosely knit circle of unemotional adults, all of whom accepted responsibility for his welfare and education. During his stay on Norona, he acquired a great appreciation for the human method of raising children in a small, loving, family unit. He should have realized then just how human he really was.

Chapter Twelve

Every human heart is human.
—Henry Wadsworth Longfellow

The familiar sounds of a wide-awake household drifted into Steve's bedroom, bringing her to consciousness. Surprisingly, she had managed to catch a few hours sleep.

Falcon was out there. The memory propelled her from her bed. What if he did not like children? What if he liked to eat them for breakfast? Good grief! How could she think such a stupid thing? Too many movies. A triumphant "Pow! I gotcha!" assured her that, not only had Vince, Jr. not been devoured, the presence of a stranger in their living room had not deterred him from his favorite activity. She should have been up in time for introductions, especially for her mother. Steve figured she would never hear the end of this one.

How was she supposed to behave after what he told her last night? Hopefully, better than she had at the time. As she dressed, she tried to put it into perspective.

Falcon said he picked up on people's feelings, but not their exact thoughts. The slump of his shoulders and the crestfallen look on his face when she left him told her he had read her reaction to his confession quite accurately. An alien had touched her intimately, driven her crazy with longing. The realization had turned her stomach, and he knew it. She would swear she had hurt his feelings. Had he really never experienced human emotions until recently? Had he really never . . .She didn't even want to *think* about that confession.

The only thing to do was get out there and face the music. The scene she encountered in the living room made her smile, in spite of her reservations about the central character. Vince had hauled out every truck, tank, jet, and miniature Army man in his vast collection and engaged Falcon in a major battle. Sitting cross-legged on the floor, opposite her son, Falcon had obviously been coerced into being the bad guys against Vince's much larger battalion of good guys.

But Falcon had a couple of recruits on his side of the floor. Mr. Spock lay sprawled with his head resting on Falcon's thigh, obviously enjoying a thorough petting. Fickle animal. On his other side, Mary Ann sat chewing on the end of her long, dark ponytail, pretending to be interested in the maneuvers, while taking frequent peaks at their visitor. Fascination shined in her big, brown eyes.

Steve walked the rest of the way into the room and knelt down beside her son before she was noticed.

"Mommy!" Vince squealed as he threw himself at

her, knocking her onto her back.

The next instant Mary Ann pushed him aside to get her hugs, and the both of them started wrestling on top of Steve.

"Get off!"

"I was here first!"

"But I missed her more!"

Steve separated them, sat up, and put an arm around each one. When they were both certain they had received an equal number of hugs and kisses, they dove headfirst into an account of the adventures and problems they had had in her absence.

Mary Ann was the first to remember their new acquaintance. "Falcon said you were really tired and to let you sleep. He said we could call him Falcon, okay?"

"Yeah. He's real cool, Mom," Vince added.

Steve made herself look at him directly. She was not sure what she expected to see this morning, but it was just Falcon, looking like he always did. "Yes, Vince, he's real cool." She tried to force a smile, but her mother appeared before she succeeded.

"Well! Sleepyhead finally got out here. We all introduced ourselves long ago, as you can see." Ann walked over and gave Steve a kiss on the forehead. "Welcome home, honey. Breakfast is on the table everybody." She hustled into the dining room, expecting them to follow her lead.

Mary Ann stood up and reached for Falcon's hand. "I'll show you where you can sit."

Not to be outdone, Vince jumped up and grabbed his other hand. "Yeah! Next to me." Mr. Spock barked once in agreement and followed on Falcon's heels.

Before he was pulled into the dining room, Falcon twisted his head back to Steve, who was getting up off the floor. The smile he had worn with the children faded uncertainly.

"Welcome to the nuthouse," she said with a shrug, then followed them in to breakfast.

The table was set elaborately with her mother's best china and silver. An array of fancy platters overflowed with more food than ten people could finish at one sitting.

"What's all this about?" she asked in shock.

Her mother's glare and reddening cheeks informed her she was supposed to act like they ate in this style all the time.

Enunciating each word with a clenched jaw, Ann explained, "I thought it would be nice for a change, Steve. After all, you've been away and we *do* have a guest."

Steve smirked and raised one eyebrow at her. Who did she think she was fooling? So, her mother had fallen under Falcon's spell as easily as the rest of the family.

"Your table is beautiful, Ann, and I am extremely hungry." Falcon held the back of her chair as she sat down, then moved to do the same for Steve. Too stunned to do anything else, Steve sat. Falcon caught Vince's eye, looked to Mary Ann, then back. Vince's mouth dropped open in dismay as he figured out the subtle order, but he held Mary Ann's chair for her anyway.

Steve could not have gotten Vince to do that with anything less than a death threat. When Falcon looked back at her, he winked. Steve was certain she would never have pancakes again without remembering this extraordinary meal.

As soon as the children ate their fill, they asked to go play, but Ann stopped them. "Don't you want to hear about the money your mother won while she was away?"

Steve was left with little choice but to relate the tale of their good fortune and listen to their ideas on how to spend it.

Ann interrupted the children's excited chatter. "I've already decided how we're going to spend part of it." Everyone stopped talking and looked at her expectantly. Steve's mother was not usually the most decisive person. "I spoke to your brother this morning. It's all settled." She returned her attention to her coffee cup.

"Mother, you didn't finish what you were saying. You called John this morning? Or did he call you? Nothing's wrong, is there?"

"Oh, my, no. But he's been asking when we were going to come for a visit, so I called and told him to expect us tonight. You don't have to worry about a thing. I already called the airlines."

Vince and Mary Ann both squealed at once. "We're going to see Uncle John!"

"Are we really going on an airplane?" he asked.

"Will we get to meet the president of the United States?" she wanted to know.

Ann smiled happily. "Yes, we're going on a jet. And I don't know if the president will have time for us this week, but I'm sure your Uncle John will do his best. Your aunt and cousins are anxious to show you all the other wonderful things Washington has to offer, though. Now, go play. You can help me pack after I clean up the dishes."

When the children were out of earshot, Steve voiced her exasperation. "Mother! How could you do that? You know I'm in the middle of a case. I can't just take off. And to bring up something like that in front of them! You know how disappointed they'll be now if they don't get to go." Steve could not understand how her mother could be so lacking in common sense.

"I suppose I could take them myself," Ann offered, "especially if you're still on this case. Why, you might have to go out of town again, and if we're away having fun, the children would hardly notice."

Steve considered the suggestion. She had wanted to take them to Washington herself, but it probably would not make any difference who took them, and her mother and sister-in-law would be there.

Ann rose and started stacking dishes. At the kitchen door, she stopped and turned to Steve. "Actually, dear, it's just as well that you're still on the case. I only made plane reservations for the three of us." She slipped into the kitchen before Steve could find her tongue.

Steve closed her gaping mouth as she realized what her mother had done. No common sense, eh? Having discovered that her daughter had brought home an eligible man—and Steve had no doubt Ann requested his marital status before his name—she immediately put on her matchmaker hat. She purposely arranged a situation that would leave them alone in the house.

Gawd! Mom was miles off base with this one. She

should have asked Falcon's species. How could she explain why she didn't want to be alone with him? Of course, she could always refuse to let her mother take the children today and promise to take them herself right after this case was closed.

The clink of glasses broke into her thoughts. Falcon had helped clear the table while she sat there like a dummy. She was being foolish. Nothing was going to happen just because they were alone. It was only one or two more days at most. She stood up and carried her plate of uneaten toast to the kitchen.

Falcon was rinsing the dishes and loading the dishwasher as her mother was storing leftovers. Somehow, seeing them like that made her feel even more ridiculous. Mom and the children would have a ball, and she and Falcon would be perfectly fine without a proper chaperone.

For the next several hours, Ann bustled back and forth, doing laundry and packing for their impromptu vacation. Steve made a lengthy call to Lou, telling him they were back in San Francisco and bringing him up to date without adding anything he really would rather not know. Vince and Mary Ann vied for Falcon's attention any way they could. Mr. Spock did not care which of them got it as long as he remained within reach of Falcon's hand.

Steve kept a surreptitious eye on all of them. Falcon's patience seemed endless, as he played one game after another, ignored their petty squabbles, and never once tried to touch their temples to calm them his way. A quieter, group activity was finally agreed upon after Falcon asked how Mr. Spock got such a formal name.

"You know, *Mr. Spock*. From the movie!" Vince used a tone that implied Falcon must be kidding to ask such a silly question.

"I do not believe I have seen that one. Is it one of your favorites?" Falcon hoped that was a proper response.

Mary Ann snorted. "He's only watched it about a zillion times!"

"You wanna watch it with me, huh, Falcon, huh?"

"That would be enjoyable."

"I guess I'll watch it, too." Mary Ann pouted, but promptly stationed herself next to Falcon.

"Mom?" Vince's one-word question was his way of asking her to join them, combined with a request to put the movie video into the VCR.

A fan herself, Steve had several tapes that included dozens of episodes from the television series, as well as every one of the *Star Trek* movies, but Steve knew the fourth movie, *The Voyage Home*, was Vince's favorite, and set it up for him.

A few minutes into the film, Vince tapped Falcon's arm and shouted, "There. Him." He ran to the television and pointed. "That's Mr. Spock."

"He looks different from the others of the crew," Falcon observed as Vince sat back down next to him.

Vince laughed at this adult who did not know the simplest things. "Of course he does. He's a Vulcan. He can do a whole bunch of neat stuff even Captain Kirk can't do."

"A Vulcan? You mean he is not a human."

"Yeah, I guess that's what it means."

Mary Ann was quick to show off her superior

213

knowledge. "Spock's *mother* is human. His father is Vulcan. Sometimes it mixes him up."

"I can imagine it would," Falcon said quietly. "Tell me, Vince. Is Mr. Spock a good guy or a bad guy?"

"Oh, he's a good guy. They killed him off once, but he came back to life so they could make another movie."

"I see. In other words, it is not necessary for a man to be entirely human to be a good guy." Falcon did not hear Vince's response. He had been watching Steve as she followed the exchange. Her eyes were glassy with moisture. Her mouth shaped three syllables. There was no sound, but he heard her clearly. *I'm sorry*.

His nod told her he felt her sincere regret, and when he touched his fingers to his lips as if to blow her a kiss, she understood that he had forgiven her.

Throughout the rest of the movie, supposedly for Falcon's benefit, Vince kept up a running narrative, which required Mary Ann's constant corrections. The end result was that Falcon couldn't possibly have followed the movie itself, but he convinced the children it was the best movie he'd ever seen. Steve couldn't help but wonder if it was the *only* movie he'd ever seen.

The time soon came for Steve to drive her family to the airport. Before leaving, Steve answered Falcon's questions about using the telephone, as it was time for him to check in. With whom, she almost asked, but did not.

As soon as they left the house, Falcon picked up the receiver, and pressed the series of numbers he had been given in Innerworld to reach his Outerworld contact. When the emissary answered, Falcon used the push buttons to identify himself and the ensuing dialogue was conducted numerically. Even if a determined listener broke the code, they would need to know a particular Noronian dialect to translate the conversation accurately.

"Falcon, here."

"Recording report. Proceed."

"Mission incomplete. Delays unavoidable. Progress anticipated within twenty-four hours."

"Report cannot be passed on at this time. All communications jammed by unknown source. Tensions running high. Man disintegrated upon entering transmigrator unit.

"Do not—repeat—do not use ring as computer extension even for Outerworld relocation. Do not return to Innerworld until mission completed. Romulus and Aster send regards. Over."

"Thank you. Over." Falcon was numb with shock. Another senseless death added to Underwood's list of crimes. Yesterday, he had no way of knowing their cross-country trip carried more risks than merely raising Steve's suspicions. He had put her in grave danger. Being ordered not to return to Innerworld was too ludicrous to consider. He had to succeed. There was no place for him in this world of violent emotions and people with human eyes.

Steve returned from her airport run, bearing several small white-and-red cardboard boxes. "Chinese food for dinner okay? I hate to cook, and I leave the fancy table settings to Mom. We'll eat in the kitchen." Falcon followed her wordlessly. "I've never seen you eat red meat. I opted for vegetable chow mein and fantail shrimp. I hope that's okay." As she carried on a one-sided conversation, she set out two plates, utensils, and napkins, opened up the boxes in the center of the table, and sat down. "Dig in."

Falcon followed her example, spooning the food directly out of the boxes onto his plate. The flavors were not unfamiliar, but he had little appetite.

Finally, Steve gave up trying to pretend nothing was wrong. "I thought we got past the silent treatment last night. If you're waiting for a formal apology for my acting like a twit, you've got it. You threw me for a loop. Unlike you, I am a *very* emotional person."

Falcon managed a sad smile. "No, Steve. I need no formal apology. Your actions were entirely understandable under the circumstances. I received some very bad news while you were gone. I have not yet adjusted."

"Can you tell me?" Steve's voice was soft. He looked so worried, and she would have taken his hand if things were different.

Falcon related the information he had received about the latest fatal accident and the orders he had received. "It could cause another delay in catching up to Underwood if we must use only Outerworld transportation."

Steve noted he still used the word "we." "I'm sorry about the man who died and all the others before." Steve had the feeling that was not what was bothering him most. "Are you afraid you won't be able to get back?"

Falcon looked into her eyes and read compassion there. He sighed. "Yes." There was little else to be said. "I find I am quite fatigued tonight. Where would you like me to sleep?"

Steve put fresh linens on her mother's bed, since it was the largest, and a few minutes later Falcon bid her good night and retired behind the closed bedroom door. Now that she thought about it, she was amazed she was still upright herself. As soon as the kitchen was back in order, she headed for her shower and bed.

It had been a lovely day from start to finish. Certainly a contrast to last night. The children, her mother, even Mr. Spock, were absolutely crazy about Falcon. How could they not like such a sweet, gentle, patient, gorgeous man? Wasn't there a saying about children and animals being able to see past the surface to the truth?

She could not stop her thoughts from running the gamut of what they had been through together this past week. Nor could she prevent the memory of the erotic dream from returning. He believed he put it in her head by accident. She was not at all sure he did, at least not in the way he thought. The fantasy of making love with him had crept into her every spare thought since she first saw him *before* he had ever touched her mind.

It had to be an unbelievable coincidence that she and Falcon crossed paths at the same time his hormones decided to perk up. She happened to be the woman at hand, so he wanted her, wanted her to be his first sexual experience.

What a kick! How many women would pant for some sack time with a guy like Falcon, regardless of where he came from? How many more fantasized about introducing a virgin to sex? For that matter, how many women had actually made love to an honest-to-God man from outer space, not counting the movies?

And soon he would be gone. She was positive they would find Underwood, Falcon would get the ring back, and he would return to his world. She knew in that moment she would miss him terribly, because no matter what he was she cared.

So what if she just happened to meet him at a time when anything female would have suited his needs? She had an extremely rare opportunity here. Only a complete fool, or a coward, would ignore it. And she was neither. For the first time in years she was relieved her tubes had been tied after Vince's birth.

Steve got up from the bed, put on a robe, and went to her mother's door. She tapped lightly, and spoke in a low voice, "Falcon? Are you awake?"

"Yes."

"May I come in? I need to tell you something." He took so long answering she thought he might have been asleep after all.

"Yes."

Steve opened the door and took a few steps inside. It was dark, but she could tell he was sitting up in the bed. "Falcon, are your eyes closed?"

"I have already removed the lenses. I was not expecting you to see me until morning."

"Oh, God. I really am sorry about how I acted last night. It was stupid and horribly rude. Please open your eyes." He did. "They really are quite beautiful."

"You said you had something you wished to tell me."

Steve kept her gaze glued to his, knowing he could see her clearly in the dark. "I wanted you to know that I believe we'll find Underwood. I have a good feeling about our trip to his office tomorrow. I'm sure you'll get back home."

"Yes. Of course I will."

"Falcon?"

"Yes?"

"I was curious . . . about your eyes. Can you really see me perfectly in this dark room?"

"Yes."

"And you can see through things, too?"

"Some. If the covering is thin enough."

"Can you see through my robe?"

Steve saw his pupils expand from a spindle shape to a diamond and back again before he answered.

"No."

He was lying. "No? What if I take off my robe?" She untied the belt and let the garment fall to the floor.

"Steve, I promised not to seduce you, and I will honor my word. I will also control my thoughts so as not to influence your dreams. However, it is much easier to do both if you are not in the same room with me."

"Hmmm. Yes, you did promise not to . . . I believe the exact word you used was entice me. And I respect you for being an honorable man. But, you see, Falcon, I can't always keep the promises I make." A little at a time, Steve gathered up her nightgown until the hem reached her knees, her thighs, her hips. With an exaggerated stretch of her torso, she raised the gown over her head and dropped it on top of the robe.

Falcon sucked in his breath and held it. Why was she doing this to him? She did not want to share her body with a man of mixed blood.

She did! Her desire came to him as strongly as her scent. She had not moved closer, but her husky voice seemed to close the space between them.

"I want to give you a gift to take home with you, Falcon. Something to remember me by . . . if you still want me. Do you want to know all that being human has to offer?"

"Please, Steve. Don't . . ." He struggled to complete the sentence.

"The word is 'tease.' And I'm not." But her breathy voice continued to taunt him as she glided to the edge of the bed and drew back the sheet. "This isn't fair. I can't see you." She dropped the sheet and moved to the adjoining bathroom to switch on the light. Pulling the door partway closed, she smiled reassuringly. "That's better. Your body is too good to keep in the dark."

Falcon's mouth went dry. She did not simply look at him. She devoured him with her eyes, piece by trembling piece. He was afraid to move, to reach out to her as he longed to, afraid she was a dream that would evaporate if he tried to hold onto it.

Steve leaned forward and combed her fingers through his hair. "Beautiful. Just like silk." Her sweet breath fanned his face, and Falcon angled his head to bring her palms into contact with his scalp.

He would have closed his eyes to savor the pleasure her slight touch gave him, but his gaze was captured by the full swell of her breasts rising and lowering before him with each of her breaths. Their dark rose-colored peaks had drawn tight the moment she removed her robe.

Steve dragged her fingertips out of his thick mane and placed them on his temples. "Do I need to do this to know your thoughts?" He could not answer. Steve's gaze scanned downward to his erect masculinity. "No, I don't think it's necessary."

She traced the features of his face, and ran her index finger over his sensitive lips until they parted. "Your skin is softer than a baby's. I never thought someone could get addicted to the *feel* of something, but I think I could stroke you all night, and enjoy every minute of it." Her finger pressed down slightly on his lower lip, then slid between his teeth and over the tip of his tongue.

"But this isn't soft at all. It's like a cat's—rough and firm. You shocked me when you first put it in my mouth, but it was one of the most sensual things I ever experienced. It made me think of how it would feel . . . in other places."

Her fingers trailed down and up his arms and over his chest. His muscles clenched and relaxed beneath her feathery caresses. When her exploration took her lower, his stomach contracted, and a low sound, so much like a purr, escaped his throat. But she did not touch where he anticipated, moving instead to his thighs and down to his feet.

"Mmmm, yes. All over. Soft skin over hard muscles. Absolutely marvelous. Now I understand how

221

a sightless person can see with their fingertips."

Moving to the foot of the bed, she placed a hand on each ankle and separated his legs. She climbed onto the mattress, into the triangle she created, running her fingers up his inner thighs as she progressed.

Falcon was certain he would die with each pounding heartbeat. Surely man was not meant to *feel* so much at one time. Some part of his brain told him he was supposed to be doing something other than lying there mesmerized, but for the life of him he could not make his limbs respond. He had never been completely helpless, under another's total control. It was intoxicating and exhilarating all at once.

"I have been wondering about this, Falcon." Her fingers trickled through the sparse curls at the base of his manhood. "You do have some body hair, but it's fine and silky and tickles my fingers. Another memorable feeling."

Her one hand moved lower to cup and roll his swollen sacs. Falcon could no longer keep his eyes from squeezing shut under the onslaught of pleasurable sensations she was creating. Her other hand brushed over the tip of his member, then down and up the sides, so lightly he found himself ready to beg for mercy.

As if she heard his silent plea, her fingers closed around him; he forgot to breathe, then inhaled with a gasp as her tongue flicked over him. Her mood changed suddenly. He felt her control slip with her first taste of him. Her actions became feverish, nibbling, sucking hungrily, until he was certain he *had* died, and this was heaven.

Falcon opened his eyes again in time to see her straddling him. He wanted her to hurry; he *needed* her to go slowly. She guided him to her, and he tensed, poised on the brink of the unknown. Unexpectedly, she regained control, seeming to understand his need to experience this first time in milliseconds.

Gradually she took his hardened length into her hot, moist recess. Would screaming help? he wondered as she lowered herself completely, and his strangled growl blended with her soft cry of relief.

Her muscles grasped him tightly, pulsing around him. Had a sheath ever fit a sword so perfectly? Impossible. Nothing could compare to this.

Until she moved. Falcon tried to make it last, knew he should wait for her, but his body would not heed his wishes. With an upward thrust his world exploded into shattering prisms of light and color, twinkling down around him like falling stars as he returned slowly to Earth.

Steve lay on top of him, her head nestled against his neck. He gathered enough strength to put his arms around her, but not enough to speak. His hands moved over her, finding relaxed muscles. She had needed no more than he to be satisfied. Knowing that made him feel a little less selfish.

Never had Steve felt so drained, yet so contented. She stifled a giggle as she realized Falcon was so much of a man he had given her the most glorious, thrilling climax in her life, without moving a muscle. Well, maybe just one. Good God. How could she ever settle for a mere human after that?

Steve felt him throbbing deep inside her, powerful and hard. He filled her and stretched her beyond what she believed possible, and he was ready and wanting more.

That did not surprise her in the least, and with one strong muscle contraction, she told him she'd be happy to comply.

Chapter Thirteen

For knowledge, too, is itself a power.
—Francis Bacon

"What the hell do you mean they vanished? I have never known you to fail so miserably, King. First you tell me this man overpowered you in a fight. You! Probably the most proficient martial arts expert on this continent. Then, while you were licking your wounds, your hirelings lost track of two people on an enclosed houseboat?"

"I know I have not performed to your satisfaction, Mr. Underwood. The man's strength was unlike anything I've ever seen. As to the men I hired, they swear they witnessed the man and woman jump overboard and swim toward the yacht. They immediately returned from their post across the street and reported this to me. Within minutes I personally conducted a search of every room on board. I was prepared to eliminate the intruders and turn their bodies over to the local authorities. As burglars, their deaths would have been justified."

"The operative words there were 'would have'. What makes you think they weren't simply taking a swim?"

"With an ocean and a heated pool across the street, no reasonably intelligent person would choose to swim in such polluted water. Also, there was a fresh puddle of water on deck and a trail of water that led below. I'm certain they came aboard."

"But you're not certain where they went after that, except that they did not return to the houseboat." Underwood barely contained his fury with King. The younger man had never been inept before. There was a piece missing, and he never tolerated dealing with an unknown factor. "Get the videotapes you picked up from Miss Preston. I want to look at them again."

King immediately prepared the first film for viewing, and stood by patiently as his employer watched the brief clip he had already seen numerous times in the past few days.

Underwood studied the screen as Barbanell went through her first visit to his office. Falcon entered. No, she had never seen him before, that much was certain. On the second tape, she barely recovered after running into him again in Los Angeles. Their subsequent working together had to be completely impromptu.

"Put that first tape in again." This time Underwood watched it run in slow motion. Barbanell's appreciative perusal of Falcon scanned him from head to toe. What did she see when she frowned right there? Using his remote, Underwood backed up the film and froze the action. His heart leapt into his throat. Every time he had watched this scene, he had watched their faces, and missed seeing what had disturbed Barbanell. Up to this moment he thought she had been looking at Falcon's traveling bag. But it was his hand that caught her eye, the ring finger on that hand to be precise, and the gaudy opal ring. Furious with his belated awareness, Underwood hurled the remote control at the two figures frozen on the screen.

Damn! For the last week he had been misdirecting the one person he had been waiting for. How had he allowed something so vital to elude him? The realization made him feel stupid and ordinary. His stomach clenched and bile rose in his mouth. His oversight was unforgivable, an insult to the gift of intelligence he had been born with. Underwood pulled himself together with the greatest effort.

"King, I shall give you a chance to redeem yourself. I want the woman eliminated. Be careful what method you choose, but not so careful that you fail again. I cannot risk leaving her alive with the knowledge she has undoubtedly acquired about that man. He's the one we want. It's time to let him find me. They haven't disappeared. They've relocated. My guess is they'll be found in San Francisco. Have someone go to Barbanell's home and verify it, then be sure they are delayed until you can get there yourself. And, King, a second failure will not be tolerated."

King bowed his head as he backed out of the room. Gordon Underwood did not make idle threats.

A moment after King left, Delphina entered the office.

"Ah, Delphina. You always know when I need you."

She smiled sweetly as she came forward and made an elegant show of sitting on his lap. His arms encircled her, one hand bracing the back of her slender neck. Urgently, he pushed her head close, crushing her mouth against his.

"I need you, Delphina. I need what only you can give me. I've made a grave error, an unforgivable mistake. But you can make it better."

"Of course, Gordon." Her dainty fingers opened the top button of his shirt, but he stopped her.

"No, not that, not yet. I love you, Delphina, more than I believed I would ever be capable of loving another. But, I—I need more today." He took her fingers and placed them on his temple. "I need the other. It will cleanse me and clear my mind in preparation for what is coming."

As he wished, Delphina planted the vivid memory in his mind. A second later, Miss Preston's ruler cracked across his knuckles. He would gratefully accept the punishment he deserved, and afterward, everything would be all right again.

Chapter Fourteen

Let us do or die.—Robert Burns

Steve sighed contentedly. The warm body against her back, the heavy leg overlapping her own, the gentle fingers playing with her nipple, all confirmed it had not been another erotic dream, but the amazingly, wonderfully real thing.

She turned to face Falcon, and stroked his outer leg with her foot. No matter how they had spent the night, she craved more of the delicious feel of him against her skin. Her tongue snaked out to get a taste of his shoulder, then the skin under his chin. When she lifted her head and leaned over to do the same to his mouth, Falcon captured her tongue with his teeth and pulled it inside his mouth.

One kiss and the heavy male part of him throbbed against her stomach. She was a little sore—who wouldn't be after last night's marathon?—but not so sore that her body couldn't respond instantly to the awareness that he wanted her again. Moving further up his side, she placed her bent knee over his hip, positioning and stretching herself for him. He found his mark without her guidance, and they each moved half the distance necessary to be completely joined again.

"Falcon." Steve whispered his name as if it were a sacred word. "Every time feels better than the last. For someone who swears he never did this before, you've certainly gotten the hang of it."

He kissed her with the same excruciating restraint that he used to ease himself in and out of her. "I had an exceptional trainer," he purred in her ear during another slow, deep thrust.

Steve tilted her head back a notch. "Is that right? What kind of 'trainer' teaches such a . . .sensitive subject?" Another plunge deep inside her caused her to moan softly.

Falcon's fingers ruffled her short hair and stopped to play with the fine strands at her nape. He murmured his answer between brief, fiery kisses. "One who possesses beauty, courage, and kindness beyond words. One who allowed this humble, unskilled male to practice on her incredible body all night long." He flexed deep inside her, and her body instinctively tightened around him.

"O-o-oh. I don't think *allowed* works in that sentence. Try welcomed, invited . . . seduced." Another flex in response.

"Nevertheless, I do not believe a simple thank you is going to suffice in this instance." His hand slipped down her spine to grasp and massage her bottom, then lifted her to meet his next thrust.

Steve closed her eyes to hold onto the ripple of pleasure a moment longer. "You're right. I think you'll have to buy me flowers, too. Oh, God, do that again!" He did, and her body broke out in gooseflesh. "But I couldn't have taught you about nerves I didn't even know I had." His strokes took on a rhythmic, building momentum which caused her to arch and tense in anticipation.

"I had knowledge of the female body without actually knowing it at all. With you, I have only to open myself to your feelings to know what pleases you. It seems to be a most satisfactory method." He moved harder, faster.

His point was effectively proven when Steve cried out her extreme satisfaction. One more time he took her to a world where nothing mattered but sensation.

When she finally regained enough energy to separate herself from Falcon, Steve said, "And now I'd like to teach you about a matter of great concern here in California—conserving water." At his confused expression, she laughed and kissed his ear. Using her huskiest voice, she explained, "Come take a shower with me."

Falcon admired her nude back heading into the bathroom. He wanted to make the most of every minute they had left. Like her, his intuition told him their efforts that day would bring them closer to Underwood, which meant his mission, his reason for remaining here, would soon come to an end. *How will I bear to leave you, Steve?*

Over the sound of rushing water, Steve called, "What did you say?"

"Noth . . ." Falcon's brow furrowed thoughtfully. He walked into the bathroom, but stopped himself from entering the shower where he could see a blurry image of her behind the glass. "I did not speak."

Steve slid the door open a few inches and peeked out. "I thought . . . Never mind. Come on in. It's just right." She wondered why he would deny that he had spoken, and why he looked so puzzled. His voice had come to her clearly a moment ago, at least her name had. It was possible that wishful thinking had caused her to imagine it.

Falcon stepped in behind her and closed the door. If she had truly heard what he was thinking, one of two things was happening. Either she was developing a telepathy with him, or his power to send his thoughts had improved drastically since last night. He would have to be very careful until he had tested his theory properly. Steve's soapy palms rubbing over his chest regained his attention. There was nothing in her expression or actions to indicate that she was hearing his every thought.

When she nudged him around to do his back, he mentally directed a sentence to her. *I approve of California's method of conservation.*

"I thought you might." Her slippery fingers ran over his firm buttocks, then clamped onto his hips to turn him back to her. She soaped her hands a bit more and proceeded to give him a thorough, intimate cleansing.

He had his answer. Apparently, the sound of the rushing water kept her from realizing she was not actually hearing his voice. Her gentle massage terminated his interest in the experiment. Later. For now he was determined not to miss a single, enjoyable second of her attentions.

Steve closed her eyes as his hands performed a reciprocal service on her body. She was locking away every touch, every shimmering feeling. The night would come when she would need to take the memories out to ease her loneliness. Her certainty of that was so strong it must have made her hear him say what she herself was thinking. How would she bear it when he left?

His fingers slid between her thighs and covered her mound with his palm. Steve felt the warmth entering her flesh, like it had in her arms and legs when he relieved her pain after the fight in Miami. As then, she felt the immediate soothing affect his magical touch brought with it. "Mmmm. Much better. Thank you."

Falcon urged her against him and kissed her tenderly. "I apologize. I am afraid in my enthusiasm I did not consider your welfare as I should have."

"Don't you *dare* apologize for giving me the most fantastic night of my entire life." She sounded like she was scolding him, but her smile gave her away. After rinsing and turning off the water, Steve opened the door and reached for the two towels she had laid out. Falcon promptly took them out of her hand and dropped them on the floor.

"I have a much more interesting method of removing the moisture. One I am positive a conservation-minded Californian would approve."

Steve did not have to wait to discover what that method might be. Falcon's head dipped forward as if to kiss her again, but instead his unusual tongue flicked out to lick up a drop of water from the tip of her nose. She could not prevent the giggle that escaped. It tickled. He licked the water from her cheekbones, her eyelids, and the corners of her mouth. Steve sighed and willingly gave herself over to his ministrations.

"Your emotions are so delightfully obvious, Steve." With the slightest pressure under her chin, he tipped her head slightly back and lapped up the tiny pool of water in the hollow at the base of her throat. Falcon drew his rough tongue across her collarbone, stopping to drink the moisture pocketed in the indentations there. He absorbed her dampness, just as he absorbed the recurring shivers vibrating through her body.

"You like the feel of my tongue. I am aware that my tongue is more abrasive than a human's. I never considered it a matter of importance." He used it to trace her fingers and drew each one into his mouth and out. His hot breath exhaling softly on her palms and inner arms was like a desert breeze, as he blazed a trail back to her shoulders. The dampness on her skin evaporated on its own, but he continued the task he had set for himself.

His tongue snaked a path down and around her right breast, outlining her fullness in ever-decreasing circles. Finally, he captured the peak between his lips, sucking and tickling, until Steve thought every nerve in her body had been drawn into that one tight nucleus. Only then did he move to her left breast and repeat the heavenly torment. Each crest was treated to a parting kiss before he continued his observations.

"I was of the mistaken belief that the purpose was to give me a more acute sense of taste." Falcon placed a kiss between her breasts. Steve gasped and contracted her stomach when he proceeded to gently scrape his tongue in a jagged line to her navel. That sensitive small indentation received a seductive swirl and another kiss as he knelt before her.

"It has occurred to me that there is something else it may be good for. I can touch you, satisfy you, in a way no man in your world can." The warning did not prepare her for the shock of his unique appendage easing itself between her thighs, tasting, stroking, learning all the ways she was different from him. Overcome with pleasurable weakness, Steve's knees gave out. Falcon quickly moved his hands up the back of her thighs, bracing her for his next attack on her senses.

He dragged his tongue slowly to the center of her passion. Steve knew she was breathing too rapidly; her heart was pounding too heavily. She could not survive. But she could not stop this exquisite torture, either. Trembling from head to toe, she pressed her fists into his shoulders. Her fingers clenched and unclenched, tangling and tugging on his hair. This was like nothing she had ever experienced before. Higher and higher, she spiraled. Toward what? Silently, she begged for release from the all-consuming tension building inside her mind and body.

Falcon must have heard her plea. His movements became controlled, limited to imitating the stroking that had brought her such pleasure when he was inside her a short time ago. She heard herself moan—

a sound that was part pleasure, part pain. Teeth gritted, eyes squeezed shut, head thrown back in near delirium, complete ecstasy swept through her like a cyclone.

Falcon absorbed the violent quaking of her body, and held her tighter. Suddenly she collapsed in his arms. Panic overwhelmed him. Had he gone too far? After all, what did he really know about human females? Gingerly, he touched her temple. In his mind's eye he saw the same twinkling prisms he had seen with the loss of his virginity. He shared her return to consciousness. When Steve's lashes fluttered, he removed his fingers.

"What . . ."

Falcon kissed her nose and smiled. "Apparently your body decided it was time for a nap."

"My God! I fainted! I've never fainted in my life." Steve blushed as she realized what had caused the lapse, but did not lower her gaze. "*That* was incredible. I'm just not sure I would ever want to go through it again—at least not today." She laughed and kissed his nose right back.

After indulging in a lazy breakfast, it required very little urging on Falcon's part to convince Steve to take a real nap before they set out on their mission. The plan was to leave in mid-afternoon wearing simple disguises, enter the Underwood building separately, and remain hidden until after closing time. Their information on the building's layout and security systems was extremely sketchy, but a test run was not a viable option.

Between the two of them they recalled that, although there was a desk and monitor in the lobby, no one had been at the security station when either of them had entered. More than likely a guard was posted only at night. During the day each floor probably had its own receptionist, as the executive floor had, to screen its visitors. As they exited from an elevator onto any level, they ran the risk of being stopped and possibly recognized. Falcon had seen two closed doors in the lobby, aside from the elevator, and they pinned their hopes that at least one of them led to a temporary refuge.

When Steve awoke a short time later, it occurred to her that she felt more rested than she had any right to, but immediately channelled her revitalized energy into preparing for the job ahead. She chose a simply styled, shoulder-length, light brown wig and donned a navy-blue, tailored business suit, white blouse, and low-heeled shoes. With the addition of a pair of tortoiseshell glasses and a slightly scarred briefcase, she could pass for an unremarkable sales-person.

Due to her limited resources, Steve could not change Falcon's appearance as easily. She final-ly settled on a variation of the Nevada cover. A black baseball cap to entrap his hair, sunglasses, a tee shirt and her utility belt changed him enough to fool a casual onlooker, but, if someone was actually looking for him, they might see through the props. They would have to be extremely cau-tious. To Falcon's relief, he could forego the false lenses as long as he kept the shades on. He had a feeling all his gifts would be called on this night.

Just as Steve unlocked the door of her Mustang, Falcon stopped her. "Wait. A man was here, at your vehicle." He closed his eyes and placed his outstretched palms on the hood.

Steve froze, not understanding, but obeying implicitly. When Falcon moved away from the car, she waited for him to explain.

"The image is fading, which means what I am seeing occurred many hours ago, at least twelve. The man's aura is dark but not truly evil. He opened this front segment and loosened two fittings on the driver's side. Then he left. Does this make sense to you?"

Steve frowned and bent down to inspect the asphalt under the car. Beneath the master cylinder was a small stain. Touching the spot, she discovered it was fresh. One sniff of the translucent, oily substance confirmed it was brake fluid.

She straightened, keeping her dirty finger away from her suit, and opened her briefcase with her other hand. While she located a tissue, she said, "At the very least, someone's tampered with the brake line, but I'd have to get in there to know for sure.

"This reminds me of the gang attack in Miami. If we had driven away from here without checking, we would almost certainly have had an accident on one of the hills. It would have slowed us down, might even have caused some injury, but the odds are we would have survived. I believe that was the intention with the fight. We were supposed to be sidetracked and injured, perhaps severely enough to be hospitalized, but that chauffeur didn't kill us when he had a clear shot. The only thing I can figure is Underwood hopes to discourage us without having to do anything as messy as murder."

"I am not so sure, Steve. I picked up a conflicting message from the Oriental. He would have been satisfied to cause my death."

"Well, either way they can't know we have some very unusual talent on our side." Steve winked at him. "At any rate, the only way I'd drive this car is after I bled the brake lines and replaced the fluid, and there isn't time for all that. We'd better call a cab."

Falcon followed her back into the house. "You would be able to effect those repairs yourself?"

"Oh, sure. Daddy made sure I could do anything he could do, including auto mechanics. Actually that's one reason I've never traded in this old classic. I know where every single part is located and how it works. It's easier to stick with things I'm familiar with."

Now it was Falcon's turn to frown. She had clearly made an exception to that rule in his case. He turned her to him, and his fingers traced the line of her jaw. "Regrets, Steve?"

His question could have pertained to a thousand different things, but she knew what he was asking. She took his fingers in her hand and brought them to her lips for a soft kiss, then placed them over her heart. Raising her hands, she removed his glasses and wrapped her arms around his neck. She could see herself reflected in his devastating eyes.

"Not one, Falcon." She stood on tiptoe to deliver a soul-wrenching kiss. His hands slid down her back and applied enough pressure to bring her flush against him. Using more will power than she thought she possessed, she broke the kiss. "And if you start that again, it will be too late to get into Underwood's building, and you know it."

Falcon had trouble surfacing from the sensual haze that had enveloped him the moment she looked into his eyes. "This emotion, desire, is most interesting. I would not have believed it possible, but now that I have . . . given in to it, it comes more easily, and more potently. A moment ago I was ready to forget my entire mission for one more hour in your arms. I suppose, in time, I will improve my control over it."

Steve laughed at his analytical manner. "Well, let's hope you don't start improving until you go home." The words hung in the air between them. It was Steve's turn to grow serious. Falcon opened his mouth to speak, but she stopped him with her fingertips. Steve forced the smile back on her face. "No. It's okay. I really don't want to talk about it."

By the time the cab arrived and took them into San Francisco, the marginal hour they had allowed themselves had been burned up. They got out a block away from the building and Falcon went first, as planned. The less time he spent out in the open, the better. Ten minutes later, Steve followed.

As Steve entered the building, two people exited the elevator. She walked to the directory and studied it intently during the seconds it took them to depart the building. From that location she scanned the lobby. The monitor and keyboard at the desk reminded her to keep an eye out for cameras. Where were the two doors Falcon had seen? At the far end of the lobby was a hallway.

Steve took a moment to be sure no one was about to exit the elevator. The motor was silent. Quickly, she investigated the hallway, which turned out to be no more than an alcove with two doors. Above one was the familiar red-lettered "Exit" sign. She opened the door to verify that she had found the stairs. Her hand touched the next doorknob. Instantly it opened, and she was yanked inside. The one glimpse she had before the door closed again told her Falcon, minus his disguise, had pulled her into the janitor's closet.

The only illumination came from a minuscule strip at the bottom of the door. It was enough to make her realize any light they turned on inside might be detected outside as well. Falcon's eyes glowed down at her. Of course, he could see fine. She could tell he was smiling, and whispered, "You think you're pretty smart, huh?" He did not bother to respond. "It's awfully cramped in here. Did you notice if the floor was clean enough to sit on?"

"Clean enough."

Steve did her best to get into a comfortable position in spite of her costume. Removing her jacket, shoes, and glasses helped. Falcon eased himself down, sitting Indian fashion in front of her. She glanced at the luminous digits on her watch. "We cut that awfully close. It's almost five now." She did not realize her whisper had gotten louder until Falcon placed his palm over her mouth.

I believe we should refrain from conversing, she heard him state in his normal, resonant voice.

241

"Shh-sh," Steve hissed back. "Your voice carries a lot further than my whisper!"

But I was not speaking.

Again his voice echoed through her, and she responded to his soundless order by placing her palm over his mouth.

Only you can hear me, Steve.

She kept her hand on his face. His lips had not moved. There had been no vibration against her palm as she heard his words.

Please, relax. Remember, I feel everything you do. Your fear is quite uncomfortable for both of us, and you know it is unnecessary. I discovered another talent this morning. I have always been able to feed my thoughts directly to a trained mind, such as most adult Noronians possess, but I do not believe you have that training. Since you are the first untrained person I have been able to do this with, I have no way of knowing if it will be so with any individual or if our sexual sharing has made a difference. That was a very nice emotion you just had. I assume my making reference to our intimacy caused that. Yes, I feel that, too.

Steve did not need to be hushed as she removed her hand from over his mouth. She was totally speechless. The fact that he had picked up on her emotional state so easily had been confusing at first, but how did he get in her head? Could he read her mind now? She was afraid to hear the answer, so she refrained from asking aloud.

Steve, I would appreciate your assistance with an experiment. I wish to know if you have any telepathic powers that would explain how you can hear my thoughts so clearly. She nodded, knowing he could see the movement. *Thank you. I told you there were a few times I picked up a word or two of your thoughts when you were excessively emotional. For the moment, try to think of something passive, perhaps a mathematical table. Now, in your mind, say it as if you were talking to me aloud.*

She did. "Well?" she whispered close to his ear.

Nothing. It would have been quite nice if we could have conversed in that manner.

Again she leaned close. "You mean you can't read my thoughts unless I'm all worked up?"

Basically, that seems to be the case. Unless I touch your mind, as you already know. I suggest, for the remaining hours we are in here, if you need to speak, place my fingers on your temple and think your words directly to me. I assure you I would not invade your privacy by probing further. He placed his hand in hers.

Steve tried to adjust to the idea of communicating without voices. She was relieved that he could not read her every thought, and, when she was emotional, he usually knew what she was thinking anyway. He would abide by his promise to allow her her privacy. She pressed his fingers to her temple. It could be an interesting way to pass the time.

Like this?

Yes. I hear you. There is a lot going on in your mind, however. If you work at concentrating on a specific word at a time, it would be easier for me to disregard all others.

She removed his hand so she could plan what she wanted to say, then tried again. *We lucked out on the surveillance system they're using.*

That is somewhat better.

There's only one monitor with keyboard control. The guard doesn't have to make rounds of the floors. Instead, whenever he's due to patrol, he just runs through his list of cameras. The odds are with us, but when we move, we'll have to do it fast and be sure to keep your head down. I didn't see any evidence of cameras when we were here before, but they're around. Also, no elevator. He would be aware of it instantly. Since the stairs are only two feet away, and out of the guard's line of vision, we should manage fine, if the door doesn't creak. Hey, this is fun!

That is because you are not the one trying to sort out all the words you are thinking at lightning speed. Perhaps you would oblige me by limiting yourself to one sentence at a time.

Steve started to reply and realized he had withdrawn his hand. The sliver of light was not sufficient to see where it was. But she could see his eyes, and from them, she found his shoulder with her hand and followed his arm downward. She felt the muscle in his upper arm tense as she made her way to his elbow. That joint was bent at his hip, and her nails glided along his strong forearm.

He was not very good at hide-and-seek. She knew exactly where to find his hand and refused to play his game that easily. A tug on his wrist made no difference. If she wanted his hand, she had to get it his way. She felt her way along the back of his hand and gingerly tried to grasp one of his fingers without brushing against the part of his anatomy it was resting over.

Falcon smiled, knowing she could not see him. He had never completely understood the playful teasing his human friends enjoyed so much. In the last twenty-four hours, he had not only learned how delightful being teased felt, he discovered a whole new meaning for the word "play."

When he resisted again, she decided to change tactics. Pressing her hand against his, she molded his fingers over his rigid flesh. Once she ascertained his condition, she scraped her fingernails down the swollen muscle, knowing only the thin material of his slacks protected him. He flinched, and she quickly grabbed his fingers and pulled them to her face.

Behave yourself!

Why?

I said if someone caught us in a closet, we could let them think we were having a rendezvous. I did not say we had to be doing anything to be convincing. I have no intention of being caught with my pants down, literally, just because you haven't yet learned to control your new horns.

I am not familiar with that expression, but I think I comprehend your meaning. May I continue my experiment? It will not involve touching you physically.

Steve knew he would not say that if he did not mean it. *Okay.*

Remember, no talking, only thinking. He pushed himself a few inches further back.

She sat a little impatiently, waiting to learn about this next experiment. He kissed her softly on the nose. Her hand automatically went to the spot, while her gaze darted to his eyes. He had not moved. His mouth brushed hers, and still his eyes were several feet away from her. How was he doing that? His lips touched hers again and stayed.

The feeling was real and familiar, and yet her reasoning denied the reality. When his tongue dipped into her mouth and softly scraped the roof of her mouth, Steve had to stifle a squeal. She now understood his "experiment" involved toying with her senses on a mental level of some kind, and decided to keep her eyes locked on his to remind herself he was not truly making any physical contact.

Then why could she feel his hands cupping her breasts beneath her blouse? Repeatedly, he rolled the pebbled tips until they were sensitized beyond belief.

Stop it! Please. You're driving me nuts.

Falcon heard her clearly. He was right. When her emotions, particularly her passions, were aroused, he could read her without touching her. He could stop the experiment now, but he wanted to confirm another suspicion while she was cooperating . . . more or less. Had he actually invaded her dream the other night? Could he please her just because it was what he desired to do?

Close your eyes, Steve. And let go. Trust me.

His fingers were between her thighs, stroking and kneading her. Trust? With her body or her mind? She gave up the brief struggle and closed her eyes.

Falcon, beautiful Falcon. Standing proudly before her in all his naked splendor. Briefly, she wondered how her own clothes had mysteriously vanished and how she had come to be lying on silken sheets. She lifted her hand to caress the loving shaft he offered and continued to stroke him as he positioned himself over her.

Steve gasped when he plunged completely into her with one powerful drive. He was too excited to go slowly. But suddenly so was she. It was not enough to simply arch into his every thrust, she felt compelled to ram herself mercilessly against him. Her explosive climax hit without warning. She felt as if her entire body had been inserted in an electrical socket and jerked back out again.

Falcon kissed her lips and she raised her lashes. This was real. He was holding her tightly, with two fingers pressed to her temple, and . . . chuckling! Steve felt the rumble in his chest and gave him a punch on his shoulder. *That was not funny!* She could feel him working at suppressing his laughter.

The experiment was a success, in case you are interested. I can indeed read your thoughts when you are in a highly emotional state. Unfortunately, you tend to become incoherent beyond a certain point. Have I ever told you how much I like the way you smell? He inhaled deeply.

She punched his shoulder again. *You are developing a strange sense of humor. Let's see how funny you think this is.* She wriggled out of his arms and ran a hand over the closure of his pants. A small tug at his waist and the zipperless opening gave way.

When her fingers encircled his aching manhood, Falcon discovered just how hard it could be to form a coherent thought. *You said . . . what if someone . . . found . . .* Her mouth came down on him and the thought was lost. *Drek!* What was she doing with her teeth? He found her temple and pressed.

What I am doing, and what I am going to do, is just a little experiment of my own. I want to see if I

*can drive you out of that gifted mind of yours. And, by
the way, I said I had no intention of being caught with
my pants down. Yours are a different matter entirely.
Relax, Falcon. Close your eyes. Trust me.*

He complied with her second and third com-
mands. The first was utterly impossible for the
duration of the extraordinary, purely physical experiment she proceeded to conduct. When he could think
clearly again, he decided teasing and playing were
two more of the positive aspects of being human.

The next five hours passed quickly, with Falcon
doing most of the think-talking. Once Steve started
asking questions about Innerworld, Norona, and his
home planet, her curiosity got the best of her. The
more he told her, the more she wanted to know. After
all, she would never see these places for herself.

In her briefcase, she had packed sandwiches and
sodas, which came in handy, and a deck of cards,
which did not. Steve was beginning to wish she had
packed a porta-potty as well. After they got upstairs
there would be lavatories they could use, but she
warned Falcon not to flush. The plumbing system
would also be hooked up to the guard's computer.

During their wait, they had propped a stepstool
against the doorknob to prevent any surprise visits,
but so far, no one had shown any interest in the
storage room. Assuming there was a nightly cleaning
crew, Steve was banking on their starting time being
close to midnight, as it was in the building where her
offices were located. Eleven o'clock was chosen as
the best time to move. The last employee should be
gone, the cleaners should not be on-site yet, and the
guard, if any, should be involved in whatever he did

to occupy the long boring hours of the night. Steve's hope was his favorite pastime was sleeping.

At eleven, they gathered their belongings and cracked open the door an inch. All clear. As quickly and quietly as possible, they moved into the stairwell. Thank God, the door barely made a whisper of noise, but it was pitch black. Falcon held onto Steve's arm to lead her. After the first two flights, she memorized how high each stair was, how many there were before a landing, and how many steps she had to take to the next flight. After that, they climbed the many flights to the tenth floor at a rapid pace.

A few ceiling fixtures lit the hallway of the executive floor sufficiently for the guard to be able to see them if he happened to switch to that view. There was no camera in evidence, but Steve knew it was there. She sent up a little prayer and took off at a run for Underwood's office with Falcon right behind her.

There were no lights in Miss Preston's office, but there was no reason to fear turning on a flashlight now. Also, Underwood's wall of glass let in plenty of moonlight and reflections from the street lamps.

Falcon sat down at the secretary's desk and went right to work. Steve was still breathing a little harshly from the run upstairs and sat on another chair to watch him. Once again, it was the telephone that held his rapt attention. After a moment he found a pad and pen, scribbled several numbers, and handed the paper to Steve.

"Miss Preston placed calls to these four numbers in the last twenty-four hours. It is all I can pick up from here. I will try the other office."

Steve studied the numbers. Three were local exchanges. Her intuition told her to forget about anything close by leading them to Underwood. The fourth call was to area code 907. Using her flashlight as a guide, she located a phone book on the credenza behind the desk, and looked up the area-code map. Alaska. Damn. One area code for the entire, enormous state, and it didn't really mean the number had any connection with Underwood's present location.

"Steve?" Falcon called from the other office. She was at his side in seconds. "I have seen something that we might be able to use. Miss Preston placed a small notebook in this safe before she left today. It is very important to her. I believe we should look at it."

"Are you telling me you're a safecracker, too?" Steve shook her head, knowing anything was possible with this man.

"I do not know. But I was able to manipulate the small gears in the machine in Las Vegas. This must be similar."

"You *made* me hit the jackpot? Of course you did. Why should I be surprised to hear that? So go ahead. Show off."

Falcon inspected the numbered dial on the outside of the safe, ran his hands over the outside, and smiled. "I cannot see through the metal to the gears, but Miss Preston cooperated unintentionally. I can see how she opened it to place the book inside." With no effort, Falcon opened the safe, removed the notebook he had envisioned, and handed it to Steve.

She opened the cover and smiled. "Bingo! This is the index of the files in the computer and all the access codes." She quickly scanned the pages looking for a heading that would ring some kind of bell. There it was: "Real Estate Acquisitions" with a long list of subheadings. Steve's gaze halted on "Personal."

"I think this is it." Quickly, she returned to Miss Preston's desk and shined her light on the computer keyboard.

"Do you need assistance?" Falcon asked as he joined her.

She found the power switches, and the area around her glowed from the light of the monitor. "I don't think so. The instructions in the book were written for a novice to follow, and I'm a little better than that."

The main menu for the file came up on the screen. It consisted of a list of states, commencing with Alaska, and continued in alphabetical order with the exception of Alabama. Apparently that state held no interest for Gordon Underwood.

Hoping the Alaskan telephone number was a legitimate lead, Steve punched in the code to call up the Alaska file. Only one description of the location appeared with details of the purchase following it.

"Look at this, Falcon. Underwood bought this huge parcel of real estate near Fairbanks about six months ago. Here's a list of expenses incurred after the property was purchased. Looks like a pretty fancy house for that neck of the woods. What do you think of the timing?"

251

Before he answered, she found the final piece of evidence needed to draw her own conclusion. The phone number was a match. Falcon saw it at the same time and gave her arm a squeeze.

"That must be it. I am filled with certainty."

"Can you zap us there right now? We've got a very detailed description to go by."

Falcon closed his eyes, took a deep breath, and made a difficult decision. "No. I explained the danger to you. We will have to rely on your traditional transportation."

"But, Falcon, this is an emergency. I feel certain, too, and my intuition is usually on target. Underwood could be sitting in that house right now. He'd have no way of anticipating our arrival so fast."

Falcon turned the swivel chair so that she was facing him and framed her face in his hands. "There is nothing in the universe so important that I would endanger your life, Steve. I do not fear the end of my own existence, but I would do my people no good by committing suicide. Now, I believe we should depart while our good fortune continues."

Steve felt the excitement bubbling up as she ran the cursor back up to the description of the location, and quickly copied it beneath the phone number. She turned the computer off while Falcon returned the notebook to the safe.

On the hike downstairs they reviewed the plan for exiting the premises. Again, assuming a guard was at the desk in the lobby, Steve would approach him in her full business attire, and gush out an embarrassed explanation about having fallen asleep in an upstairs lounge. While the guard was distracted by

Steve, Falcon would sneak up behind him, put him quietly to sleep, and make him forget he had ever seen Steve. Simplicity always worked best.

At the bottom of the stairs, Steve whispered, "Now remember, don't move until you hear me thanking him. That will be when I've convinced him to unlock the door and his back is to the lobby. If he's an old geezer, a little eyelash fluttering should hold him long enough for you to move."

They slipped through the doorway into the alcove. Falcon touched Steve's temple. *There is a man out there, but something is wrong. He is highly agitated, anxious.*

Maybe he's just a nervous Nelly. That might help me run this bluff. Here goes. Steve stepped away from Falcon, but not before she heard him tell her to be careful.

The moment she stepped into the lobby area she halted. The guard had been staring at the alcove when she appeared. He bolted up from his chair, sending it crashing into the desk behind him. His elderly, shaking hands gripped his drawn revolver, pointing it directly at Steve.

Falcon's heart fluttered under the onslaught of Steve's panic. He closed his eyes to see what she saw and reached out to her. *Do you want my presence?*

No. Stay there. From the way her heart was racing, Steve had no doubt that he heard her. She carefully set the briefcase down, and let the old man see her hands clearly in front of her and empty. Pasting on a big smile, she took a hesitant step forward.

"Freeze, girlie. I've got a gun."

Steve stared at the wavering weapon. Nervous? The man was scared out of his wits. "Look, I'm sorry I frightened you. You scared me, too, sir. I fell asleep upstairs. I had a terrible migraine, and—"

The guard interrupted her with a grunt and a wave of the gun. "I don't know about you fallin' asleep. I do know you were using the computer in Miss Preston's office, and I know you don't work here, so I figure you're some kind of spy."

Steve felt like kicking herself. She had remembered elevators and flushing toilets and, like a stupid amateur, turned on the computer. All she could do was keep trying to run her play. "You must be mistaken. I was asleep in the women's lounge on the third floor. Maybe Miss Preston is in her office. Why don't you—" She took another two steps before he yelled.

"Stop! It was you. And a man. When the alert came up, I turned on the viewer for her office. You're both on film. Where's the man?" He looked past her to the alcove. "Hey, Mister! You there? You may as well come out where I can keep an eye on you, too."

Steve took advantage of his distraction to move another foot. "There's no man. It was just me. You're right. I am a competitor. But I didn't find anything important." She would try pleading and eyelash fluttering. "Look, you've given me a horrible scare, and taught me a lesson I'll never forget. I swear. This was the first time I tried anything like this, and it will be my last. Just let me get out of here, okay?" She heard a siren in the distance. The guard glanced at the door. He had heard it as well.

"You'll get out of here all right. With the police. I called them right before you came down." His hands were still shaking, but his voice had gained confidence as the sound of the siren grew louder.

Police! Steve tried to keep her breathing normal as she watched the guard moving toward the front door. He was fumbling with his cumbersome key ring, obviously trying to select the appropriate key out of the sizable collection without taking his gun or his gaze off her. *Falcon. Hide! You can't let the police get hold of you.* She heard the beginning of an argument from him and swiftly cut him off. *I'll be fine. Go!*

Steve felt the adrenaline pouring into her veins. The siren was close, maybe a block away. The guard fingered a key and separated it from the bunch. Steve poised. She would count on the man's age to have slowed his reflexes. For one split second he shifted his gaze to insert the key into the deadbolt lock. Steve lunged, aiming a chop at his gun hand.

Falcon stumbled and fell backward under the force that slammed into his stomach. His head cracked against the railing as his body descended the flight of steps he had just run up. The landing stopped his fall a moment before he lost consciousness.

Chapter Fifteen

Fear makes us feel our humanity.
—*Benjamin Disraeli*

Falcon fought against the quicksand that threatened to swallow him up. Gradually, he overcame the devastating pain radiating through his abdomen and sucked a breath of air into his empty lungs. Heart failure? His hand moved to his chest. No, his heart and lungs were returning to their normal level of function. *Steve?* He struggled to his feet, beating down a wave of dizziness caused by his head injury. He had fallen. How? The pain. *Steve?* How long had he been unconscious? Minutes.

Steve! Falcon rationalized that if she were safe, she would not be emotional enough for him to read her. Or was she too far away? He reached out mentally, trying to see through her eyes. Nothing. Perhaps his own distress blinded him now. He had not had time to learn the limitations of these new powers.

Suddenly he sensed the approach of two people. The door below him opened. He stopped breathing and lowered his eyelids. Male voices interrupted the silence.

"To hell with it! This stairway is like a black hole. Get the dog. He'll find the bastard faster than we would anyway."

"I'll get the old guy to switch on the—"

The sentence was cut off by the click of the stairwell door. Falcon heard another whining sound outside, slightly different from the first. Were those men the police the guard had called? What about the dog? He thought of Mr. Spock. Animals held no threat for him. It was only humans carrying antique weapons and the fact that Innerworld's Medical Department was out of reach that fed his fear. Swiftly, he leapt up the next several flights of stairs and exited into a hallway much like the executive floor.

Falcon entered the first open office on the street side and looked down. The scene was a chaotic melee of vehicles of different shapes and sizes, many with spinning red lights on top. Traffic and pedestrians were being headed off by uniformed men. Like the two men who had opened the stairway door, these men were tensed for battle, some anxious, some frightened. The gathering crowd was curious and emanated another hideous emotion Falcon could not register as they vied for positions and craned their necks to see. A group of men in white shirts rolled a stretcher toward one of the larger, box-like vehicles.

At first all he saw between the huddle of men was a glimpse of a white sheet splattered with red. In unison they turned and lifted the stretcher into the rear opening. *Steve*! His mind screamed a denial in spite of what his eyes clearly saw. Her deathly pale face was visible above a sheet so soaked with blood that it clung wetly to her form. The pain had been hers! The severity of it had almost taken him with her into oblivion. His memory replayed the loud report that had occurred simultaneously with the pain.

Why had he obeyed her? He had run like a coward. No! Not true! He trusted her to know what she was doing. Now he was safe, and she was . . . Aggressive barking reminded him he was not safe at all. The stretcher disappeared behind double doors, and a few seconds later, the vehicle's siren started up again. Amidst the screeching noise and whirling red lights, Steve was whisked away.

Falcon had no idea how to deal with such turmoil. He could not even begin to identify all the emotions roiling to the surface at one time. He was furious, angry, frightened, worried, frustrated, and he desperately wanted to sit down and cry—something he had never done in his life. He blinked, and the moisture in his eyes pooled in the corners. A distant voice told him Steve would not approve, and he pressed the heels of his palms against his eyes until he controlled the momentary weakness. The sound of the stairwell door opening brought an end to his vacillating. Falcon's senses read one man, one dog. He felt the animal's excitement and tremendous restraint.

"Duke! Seek!" the man ordered.

Falcon countered. *Duke. Slowly. Come to me.*

Duke came to falcon. Slowly. Then he obeyed the command to mislead his master.

As soon as the man and dog continued to the next floor, Falcon went back down the stairs to wait by the door to the lobby. The lights had been turned on and he was prepared to stop anyone who might enter the stairway, but no one chose that route. Far above him, he heard Duke's frantic barking.

There were four men and a woman milling around the lobby when a distorted voice shouted. "He must be on the roof! Duke's going crazy." Falcon heard amplified barking as the man spoke. There was a horrid crackling sound, then another voice close by answered, "Okay, let him loose. We're coming up. Collins, stay here, and make sure none of those people try to come in." One man left.

Falcon eased out of the stairwell and peeked around the corner of the alcove. The man sat with his hip resting on the edge of the desk, alternately watching the activity in the street and writing on a clipboard. Noiselessly, remaining outside of the officer's line of peripheral vision, Falcon maneuvered into position. The policeman reacted to a blurry movement by his face, but was asleep an instant later. Falcon removed his fingers from the man's temple only after he learned what he required and erased the memory of his touch.

Somewhere on the roof the dog continued his ferocious barking as he led the squad on a search for the intruder. Falcon dragged the sleeping man back into the alcove and exchanged clothes with him. Attired in police regalia, including the man's heavy vest, weapon belt, and helmet, Falcon picked up the clipboard and hand-held communicator, and headed out the door.

From the man's mind he had gleaned where Steve had been taken, how to get there, and which of the officer's many keys operated which vehicle. As Falcon intended, no one thought to question the briskly striding police officer who wore dark sunglasses at night. He got into the car and tuned into the routine the officer performed when he had last been in this seat. Using the key, he turned on the engine, then the lights and siren, and hoped the vehicle was as easy to drive as Steve made it look.

The group of officers in the street moved aside the barricades and people to let him pass. Falcon shifted the stick in front of his right hand, so that the line moved from *P* to *D*, pushed his foot down on the pedal on the right, and gripped the steering mechanism. The car lurched forward with spinning tires and a squealing engine. Hopefully, such a display was valid for an officer in a great hurry.

By the end of the second block, Falcon figured out how much pressure was needed to move the car at a reasonably safe speed. In his experience as Steve's passenger, he had noted that vehicles with sirens and red lights did not need to abide by the various signs and signals along the roadways. He followed their example as he recalled the series of directions that would take him to the hospital.

Falcon knew he had only driven a short distance, but it was the longest minutes of his life. *Hold on, Steve*. He pulled into the area denoted by a large Emergency sign and parked the policeman's car next to the vehicle in which Steve had traveled. With a burst of energy, he ran to the entrance way and then had to wait until the slow-moving glass doors opened for him. He took two steps into the large room beyond and was assailed by a wave of emotions that knocked him back a step before he had a chance to block them.

The enormous room was packed with bodies. Sitting, standing, lying bodies; suffering, tormented bodies. He staggered under the weight of their combined pain and illness. Sorting the emotions bombarding him proved impossible. From every angle came anger, frustration, hostility, fear, but stronger than any other came the awful, limitless pain. And the noise of a thousand voices and the stench of sickness and chemicals.

He had to fight the paralysis setting into his limbs. Steve needed him. He needed Steve. Section by section, he reduced his empathic reactions to the horde of sufferers, blocked out his awareness of the crying and screaming, ignored the horrendous odors. Falcon searched for Steve's aura. She had to be here. The numbers on the vehicle outside matched those of the one she had been in, and he had envisioned the stretcher being removed and brought in here. He could see no further. All of his control was occupied with remaining sane in this room. But why could he not pick up her aura?

His scan stopped at a row of official-looking windows with lines of people standing in front of each one. He trusted the uniform he wore to grant him certain privileges. Walking to the front of one line was all he needed to get the attention of the small Oriental woman behind the window. She smiled up at him.

Falcon did his best to return her smile before impatiently asking, "The injured woman who came in the vehicle marked Rescue 6. Where was she taken?"

"Straight to surgery. Doesn't look good. A major artery was hit."

He paused long enough to get directions, then took off at a run for the stairs. When he reached the surgical area, he had to stop a woman in a white uniform to ask for directions again. His mind was surrounded by a red fog that her answer barely penetrated.

The woman pointed to the door behind him with a strange look on her face. "You're standing in front of it."

Falcon turned abruptly and pushed on the door, but nothing happened.

With a cluck of her tongue, the woman spoke to him again, "You have to push the button to get the doors open, but you can't go in there now. It's sterile. You should know that!"

Falcon looked back at her and made himself relax. She obviously did not trust him to obey the rules. She had crossed her arms over her chest, and her expression had become very stern.

"Of course. I am sorry. I forgot for a moment." He moved away from the door and smiled. Apparently satisfied, the woman went on her way.

Moving back to the door, Falcon placed his hand on the metal. The density meant nothing. He could see into the room quite clearly. People and equipment obstructed his view of the patient. If that was Steve, why could he not get a reading of her?

"She won't make it. Not a gut shot like that."

Falcon jerked his head toward the voice. A man in a uniform like his own stood next to him, holding a paper cup. He crushed the urge to make the officer retract his careless words. Instead he asked, "What happened?"

The officer began running through the details of the call that had brought him here with the woman he referred to as Jane Doe. Falcon could not hear the policeman's words above the blood pounding in his head.

Turning his head back to the door, Falcon realized he could still see the scene inside the room without touching the barrier. The continuous movements of the frenzied medical team allowed him to confirm that the gruesome figure on the table was Steve. Her legs were encased in inflated rubber pants, but what he saw above made him gag. The flesh of her abdomen was severed up to her throat. Tubes and needles connected various parts of her body and head to the machines and bags hanging around the bed. A man had his hands deeply inserted in her torso. The room was chilly, but that man was sweating profusely. A woman wiped his forehead for him.

They were all wearing masks over their lower faces that muffled their words, but Falcon heard them. *Abdominal aorta. Clamp. Sponge. Negative pressure, positive pulse. Losing her. Chest retractors fast!* In spite of his own overwhelming fear, Falcon sensed a mounting desperation coming from the man he assumed was the doctor. The thick tension in the room made it almost impossible for Falcon to concentrate on the proceedings.

The officer next to him was still talking, and Falcon nodded from time to time, but kept his eyes riveted on the barbarism being executed inside. These people were the equivalent to Innerworld's medical team. They *must* know how to heal their own kind.

The doctor inserted what looked like a giant pair of scissors through Steve's rib cage. With a sickening crunch, the bones gave way. Frantically, the doctor massaged the heart muscles. Falcon got the impression the man was trying to will Steve back to health.

Then the doctor stopped working. As one, the people in the room immobilized, looked from the body, to the doctor, to the machines. When the doctor removed his hands and began to suture Steve's chest closed, another man began turning off machines, and a woman removed all the tubes and the strange pant legs. Still, Falcon could not or would not comprehend what it all meant. Until the doctor finished stitching Steve and the woman spread a sheet over Steve's body and pulled one end over her face.

"*No-o-o!*" Falcon roared. He waved his arm and the door crashed open. The shock of his entrance froze the medical personnel for the split second Falcon needed to reach Steve and pick her up. One man yelled at him and grabbed his arm, but Falcon flicked him off as if he were a gnat. The officer tried to prevent his exit from the room, and again Falcon waved his hand and the officer's body hurled backward across the corridor.

Falcon was beyond rational thought. They let her die! He should destroy them all—and he discovered he had the power to do just that. Through his blinding rage, he sensed people moving, preparing to attack. He had no choice. With Steve's lifeless body in his arms, he ran down the hallway and into the first vacant room. Protecting her life was no longer an element to be considered. Nor could he worry about the impression he would leave with these Terrans. In a corner of his mind lingered the fact that he was about to break another serious law of Innerworld.

His fingers moved over his ring.

"Good work, Miss Preston. Keep me advised." Underwood smiled broadly as he hung up the phone. Circumstances could not have worked out better had he arranged them himself. The Barbanell woman was undoubtedly dead by now. The paramedic that had taken her away had bet she would not even last the trip to the hospital. The elderly security guard had shot her by accident, but she *had* tried to burglarize his property. No one could possibly make the connection to him, except the two people who had broken into his offices, and one of them was no longer a threat.

It was that other one whom Underwood thought of now. Falcon and Barbanell had accessed Miss Preston's computer. He had to take the guard's word for the fact that they seemed pleased about whatever they had discovered, for he had ordered Miss Preston to burn the tape of their visit immediately.

Had the two detectives been bright enough to figure out where he was hiding? Where had Falcon gone while Barbanell was getting herself killed? Was he on his way to Alaska at this moment? Underwood knew the aliens had a way of disappearing at will. Perhaps that is what Falcon had done this evening in San Francisco.

Underwood's heart was pumping rapidly, his stomach fluttering excitedly, as he went into the parlor to speak with Delphina. She rose as soon as he entered and held her hands out to him. Without explanation, he yanked her hard against his powerful body and hugged her until he reorganized his thoughts. He backed into an overstuffed chair and pulled her down onto his lap as he captured her mouth in a passionate kiss.

Gradually, his lips softened on hers, and he nibbled his way to her ear. He sucked on her perfect lobe as his large hand moved smoothly up her thigh, caressed her hip, and then her delicate breast. When she breathed, he felt the small, hardened bud rub sensuously against his palm, and he knew she was his alone.

"Delphina?"

"Yes, Gordon?"

"You know I love you above all things. Do you love me just a little?"

"Would that please you to hear the words?"

"More than anything."

"I love you, Gordon, above all things, as well."

He continued his caresses and gentle touches, but his mind was clicking away in a calculated manner that was more familiar to him than tender persuasion. "I may need to rely upon your love in the near future, Delphina. Someone is coming who would do me great harm. A man who would take you away from me. You know I would die if we were separated."

"Gordon, my love, we must not allow this man to do such a thing. Why would he do this? Who is he?"

Underwood sighed and slumped back in the chair, looking as forlorn as possible. "He is from your world, Delphina, and I am afraid he does not understand how much I need you to remain with me."

"Then we will tell him, and he will go away again."

"I'm afraid it won't be that simple. They'll just send someone else until I have lost you." He closed his eyes and grimaced in mock pain.

Delphina kissed his forehead and stroked his smooth head. "There must be something we can do."

Underwood pretended to consider her words, then carefully began outlining his plan to her. "They have so much more power than I, but if I were to possess a small portion of their knowledge, perhaps I would discover how to stop them from coming. I would require only a few of your special skills. Would you be willing to help me?"

"Of course, Gordon."

Chapter Sixteen

Hasten slowly.—Augustus Caesar

Having just finished her shift, Doctor Yeguli was about to head home when a phantom appeared in her path. The shape was humanoid except for the large black globe where the head should have been and the reflective, black shield that wrapped around what might be its eyes. Its arms protectively held a long object wrapped in a blood-soaked shroud. The beast growled and she stepped aside. Bloody fingers shot out from beneath their burden and grasped her arm. The phantom growled again.

Falcon stared at the frightened woman and tried again to communicate his need. What was wrong with him? He could not think beyond the dense, red fog swirling madly around him.

"Falcon! *Falcon!* What's the matter?"

The familiar, deep voice cut through the haze and made him turn toward the sound. *Romulus.* Falcon clung to the name, using it as a focus for his control. Reason found a foothold as he forced himself to remember why, when he had arrived in Innerworld, he had asked for the governor of the colony, and slowly, he defeated the pervasive fog. "Romulus. You once promised me a favor. I must request it at this time."

Romulus closely regarded the man whose gravelly voice confirmed he was his friend. "Of course." He took in Falcon's blood-splattered condition, then appraised the bundle in Falcon's arms. "Are you hurt, Falcon?"

"They killed her, Romulus. I should not have left her. She was protecting me. You will order the doctor to bring her back and repair what the butchers did to her."

Romulus frowned and pulled the sheet back to view the face. As he did so, Falcon clutched the body tighter to him. Whatever happened to Falcon in the last week would have to be explained later. "This is not the female you were sent to track. She's a Terran, isn't she? You brought her here, like this, knowing it's against our laws?"

"Her death is my fault. You promised a favor. Her life is what I ask of you. She has two beautiful, little children, Romulus."

Romulus did not hesitate to make his decision. "Release Doctor Yeguli's arm, Falcon. Let her show you where to put your patient, then we'll talk."

Falcon looked down at his own hand with disgust as he relaxed his fingers. "I apologize, Doctor. I am . . . upset."

She nodded at him hesitantly and, after assuring herself that what she was about to do had the governor's approval, she led Falcon to a treatment room.

When Falcon did not immediately return, Romulus went looking for him. He found him hovering over the patient, holding her hand in one of his and touching her temple with the other. "Falcon. You can't help her. Let Doctor Yeguli do her work, and you come with me. It's time for some explanations." He laid his hand on Falcon's shoulder and waited.

Slowly, Falcon gave in to Romulus's prompting and followed him upstairs to the governor's suite.

"Maybe we should start with an easy question," Romulus prodded. "What the *drek* are you supposed to be dressed for?"

Falcon managed an expression that fell between a grimace and a smile as he removed the helmet and sunglasses and shook his hair loose. "I exchanged clothes with a police officer. They were not acquired in a completely honorable manner, but I had little choice at the time." His gaze scanned the ruined uniform and his bloodstained hands. "I would appreciate the opportunity to improve my appearance before I report."

Romulus offered the use of his shower and a change of clothes in exchange for one more question. "Did you get the ring?"

"No. But I know where it is now. As soon as I am certain Steve will be all right, I will return for it."

"You took a terrible risk using the transmigrator just now, and you want permission to go back out? You were under strict orders—"

Falcon held up a hand. "Please, Romulus, my friend, I can barely hear your words, let alone respond intelligently. Your lecture will be considerably more effective without the smell of her blood in my nostrils." He accepted Romulus's shrug as permission to attend to his needs.

Rom tried in vain to correlate what he had just seen and heard with the Falcon he had met with a little over a week ago. He decided his co-governor's assistance was clearly required, and he sent out his mental call to her. *Aster?*

Hi, darling.

I think we may have a problem and I'd like your input. I'm in my office. I'll fill you in on your way.

All right. What is it? Aster headed to her mate's office as they continued their telepathic communication.

Falcon's here, and, no, he doesn't have the ring. You can hear the update at the same time I do. It's Falcon who has me worried. He brought back a deceased female and demanded she be repaired. But it's more than that. I want you to see him, talk to him. Something is drastically different about our friend.

I'll be there in a few minutes. I love you.

"Say greetings for me, too," Falcon said as he returned. When Rom raised an eyebrow, he went on, "It is not difficult to deduce with whom you were communicating. You reserve that particular expression only for your mate." He smiled easily as he made himself comfortable. Between delivering Steve into capable hands and the hot shower, he had regained control of his overwhelmingly emotional state.

"She'll be here in a moment. Are you feeling better?"

"Yes, thank you. I apologize for my manner earlier. I am not yet accustomed to dealing with my own fears."

"So, it's gotten worse in the last week?"

"Yes and no. I . . ."

Aster's appearance in the doorway stopped Falcon from completing his explanation. She came forward and took both of his hands as he rose. "Hello, Falcon. I'm glad to see you in one piece. You were strictly ordered not to use the transmigrator unless you had retrieved the ring."

Falcon smiled. "The two of you are beginning to sound alike. I hope you will understand why I disobeyed your order when I have completed my report."

Aster squeezed his hands once and went to sit next to Rom. She placed her hand in his open palm and their fingers intertwined. Falcon had seen them touching before. He should not have felt anything unusual when Rom's fingers slid between Aster's. It was an insignificant gesture. Yet his heart trembled, and he found it difficult to take a deep breath. *Steve.* He should have stayed in Medical where he could make sure she was restored, where he could be there when she awakened. Steve would like to have her hand held like that.

"Falcon?" Rom waved his hand in front of him. "Are you sure you're up to this?" He and Aster shared a concerned glance.

Falcon blinked and cleared his thoughts. "I am fine. As I intimated, I am having a few problems adjusting." He caught Aster's slight eye movement and knew she was questioning his meaning. "It is all right, Romulus. I believe if I explain this first, the rest will sound more rational. You see, Aster, before I left, I told Romulus I was experiencing some changes. My human emotions were beginning to surface— emotions I was not even aware I had. I was very disturbed by the belief that if I did not control and suppress these . . . feelings, that I would lose some or all of my felan gifts."

Rom leaned forward. "I gather from what I've seen today, you weren't able to control your reactions."

"I do not believe I ever had a chance of doing that, especially after meeting Steve."

"Steve?" Aster asked quickly.

"Perhaps, after all, it would be better if I simply began at the beginning." For the next hour, Falcon gave his official progress report, peppered with personal asides that involved Steve, her family, his emotional growth, and his subsequent discovery of new and greater powers.

It occurred to Aster that what Falcon did *not* say about Steve told her more than what he *did* say, but it would not be proper for her to mention it. Rom had no such qualms.

"It sounds like Steve may have been a catalyst for this stage of your life, Falcon. Don't forget you are half Noronian, and therefore, subject to the same mating fever I had with Aster." He continued before Falcon could come up with a response. "What about that other little matter we discussed in our last conversation?"

The bronzing on Falcon's cheekbones rose before he could stop it. This was absurd! He was actually embarrassed over a normal physical function. Of course, he did not have any way of knowing whether what he and Steve had shared was normal or not.

"Falcon, you left us again," Rom taunted.

"Oh. Yes. The matter . . . has been resolved."

Rom could not resist. "Satisfactorily?"

Aster glanced from one man to another. There was something male going on here, and Rom was blocking his thoughts from her. Well, she would just have to get it out of him later.

Falcon finally gave in and laughed at Rom's question. If Aster were not present, he might have asked for some further insight on "the matter." Later. "Yes. Very."

"And I believe that brings us to the problem of Steve's presence in Innerworld. What exactly do you plan to do with her?"

"I am responsible. When she is well, I will return her to her family. She is needed."

Rom and Aster both spoke at once, "You can't return her."

"It is against our laws to allow an Outerworlder to return once they are here," Rom added unnecessarily.

Falcon sighed. "She already knows all there is to know. She has not and will never betray us."

"Even so, wouldn't you like to have her stay here?" Aster suggested.

That solution had never entered Falcon's mind, but he felt its seductive appeal immediately and determined to remain logical in the face of such a welcome idea. "There are two small children and her mother to be considered."

Aster opened her mouth, but Rom stopped her. "It is one thing when an Outerworlder is trapped here by accident. There is always the possibility that it was meant to be in the greater scheme of life. What you are considering, Aster, would be a conscious decision that would change the future of two young lives, as well as countless others whom they would have affected. As long as we cannot see what those children's futures hold, I cannot condone interference."

Falcon nodded his understanding. "I have already interfered with their lives. Their mother should be alive and with them in their own world. There are two scientists from your mission who know of our existence. You trusted them not to reveal our secret. I ask you to trust me now. Steve will never speak to anyone of our world. I request permission to return to Outerworld while she is recuperating here. I will return with the ring and Delphina and will then take Steve home." *And never again see her, touch her, love her.* He struggled against the fist tightening around his heart.

Aster was shocked to see his feelings displayed so clearly. Her own romantic heart cried for him. "Falcon, perhaps you could stay out there awhile longer. Rom? Isn't there some way?"

Rom tried to warn her mentally that this was probably not a simple matter of star-crossed lovers, but rather Falcon's inability to blend in with Outerworld humans. Instantly, he realized the futility of such a warning in the face of her feelings for Falcon. "I suppose. We have not yet replaced the emissary we lost in that sector. Falcon?"

Falcon shook his head. "I know you both mean well, but there are too many aspects of Outerworld that rule out such an alternative. My eyes can be disguised, but only with great discomfort to me. Also, my senses are too acute for a world so filled with noise and noxious odors. A more critical problem involves my empathy. I would be forced to live every hour of my life with the guard up against a possible onslaught of emotion from some passing stranger. Now I have to learn to deal with my own emotions as well. I would never find the peace needed to do that if I were out there.

"If all that were not enough, you must know I am proud of my work here, both as a tracker and a trainer in the Arena. Whatever I did out there, my gifts would have to remain hidden. There would always be the fear that someone would discover I was different. I would not be content to deny my capabilities and my felan gifts constantly."

Aster could not refute his convictions, but she also could not stand the thought of an unhappy ending. At least she and Steve should have a chat when the woman awoke before Falcon took her back.

Falcon steered the conversation back to the business at hand by giving Romulus the coordinates of Underwood's Alaskan property. He anticipated being in Outerworld and back within a few hours.

Rom hoped Falcon's optimism would prove to be well-founded. "When you told us about your adventures this past week, it sounded as though having a partner came in handy. Would you like me to assign someone to go with you?"

Falcon tried to smile, but did not quite make it. "No. I fear no one could take my last partner's place." He took a deep breath and got up. "Now, if you will excuse me, I will check on Steve and depart."

After he left, Aster turned to Rom. "Well?"

"Well, what? He's our friend. We both owe him our lives. Do you honestly think I would refuse him anything, simply because it happens to be against the law?"

Aster placed her palm on his cheek and gazed lovingly into his eyes. "You're a wise man, Governor Romulus. That must be why I love you so much."

Rom lowered his mouth to hers to deliver a leisurely promising kiss. "Are there any other reasons, my *shalla*?"

"Hmmm. Maybe one or two." Her tongue tasted his lips, then retreated quickly.

"You know, I think I'll accompany you on your visit to Medical. I'm curious to meet the woman who could create such a disturbance in our unflappable tracker."

Aster laughed. There were still times she was surprised when he knew what she was thinking. "Okay, but then you go away. I want to talk girl talk."

Steve was alive! Doctor Yeguli and her associate were repairing her body, and the monitors showed her heart and lungs functioning normally. The brain activity had not yet returned to the proper level, but Falcon was not concerned. The death process could be reversed any time within eighteen hours.

Only under rare circumstances were the restoration results less than perfect. Work on Steve had begun within one hour of her death. She would be fine.

He had to go. She would undoubtedly be furious when she learned he had gone on without her, but she would be unconscious for another ten to fifteen hours, and he could not be sure Underwood would remain stationary that long. He probably had already been told of the break-in and would have connected it with the two people tracking him. Falcon had to get to him before he moved again.

Although Falcon's mission was to retrieve the ring and Delphina, he made a mental promise to Steve to locate the scientist, Nesterman, and secure Gordon Underwood and any accomplices until Steve could deal with them herself. He decided to try to leave her a message telling her this.

Falcon requested and received permission from the doctor to touch the patient. Her brain activity was so low he picked up nothing of her thoughts, but left his message in her mind anyway, with a promise to return for her soon. His fingers moved from her temple down her pale cheek. Heedless of the doctor's presence, Falcon bent forward and touched his lips to Steve's, then turned and left the room.

On the way to the transmigrator, his mind replayed pieces of the conversation with Romulus and Aster. He would have preferred not to have to think about it at all. There were no choices to make, no options to consider. Last week his human half had been a slight annoyance. Last week there had been no Steve. Tomorrow, again, there would be no Steve. In between she had taught him to appreciate all that being human meant. She had helped him, protected him, given herself to him. She was his first sexual experience. Naturally, he felt strongly about her. It was completely logical that it should sadden him to think of never seeing her again. Aster was his friend and a female. He would be saddened if he could never see her again. But the feeling of loss was not the same as he knew he would suffer over Steve.

There would be other females in his life now. Perhaps he would even be able to find a mate and fulfill the hopes of his felan ancestors by reproducing. But that thought was not accompanied by any feeling of anticipation or joy as he felt just thinking about holding Steve again.

Falcon wondered if Romulus could have been right about the mating fever. Would it happen that way for him in time, or would his felan half alter the symptoms? He did not believe it was possible to experience an attraction stronger than what he felt for Steve. But what did he really know about any of it anyway?

His human half told him he knew more than enough, but he had been wrong before. It was all too new and he lacked sufficient data to make a proper analysis.

"May I be of assistance?"

The question caused Falcon to look around him. He was standing in the Transmigrator Room, daydreaming again. He needed time to sort everything out, time away from people with questions and pending assignments. Perhaps he would return to Emiron for a time.

"Yes. I have special permission from Governor Romulus to transmigrate to these coordinates." He handed the technician a slip of paper and entered the glass cell.

Minutes later Falcon stood in a dark forest and absorbed his surroundings. Holy stars, but it was cold. Steve would have known what climate to expect. She would also have been able to tell him what kind of security systems might be employed to protect the house in the distance.

Remnants of his earlier panic still floated through his mind, threatening to surface and destroy his control once again. Forcefully, he pushed aside all thoughts of Steve and prayed his distracting emotions stayed away as well. All his faculties would be needed for the job ahead, and he could not afford another moment of mental drifting.

He had purposely chosen a location outside of the structure to give him a chance to study the area. The hush of night aided his concentration. There were animals around him and a body of water nearby. He was not close enough to the house to define its inhabitants, but there was a darkness within its walls.

Falcon picked up a subtle vibration coming from the ground. He took a step, then two, and it strengthened. The source seemed to be electrical. Carefully, he moved forward, a step at a time, walking only on those areas where the impulses were weakest. He was certain it was an alarm system, but he had no way of knowing if his zigzagging would prevent his presence from being announced.

The house was set in a small clearing between the edge of the forest and a large lake. Falcon stopped behind a thick tree and opened his mind to whatever was in the house. There were several life forces inside, but their individuality was smothered by the totally black emanations of one individual. It had to be Underwood. He recalled the aura he had picked up from the man named King. Yes, it was there, also. There were no lights on anywhere. Surely they were all asleep. Was Delphina in there?

As if in answer to his question, a tall, slender female with reddish-brown hair stepped out onto the front porch and sat down on a chair. She matched the image he had seen of Delphina. He waited. No one else was moving in the house. The evil force remained somewhere in the rear portion of the building.

Falcon stepped out from behind the tree and approached the house. "Delphina? I am Falcon. I have come to take you back to Innerworld. Are you well?"

Delphina raised her lashes and smiled sweetly. "I am very well, thank you. I did not know if someone would come, but Gordon said I would return home one day."

Falcon frowned. *Gordon?* "Where is he now, Delphina? And who else is in the house?"

"He is asleep as are King and Nesterman. I cannot sleep and I find it very peaceful out here."

"We must hurry. I need your help. Underwood has an Innerworld ring, like this one." He held out his hand for her to see it. "Have you seen it inside?"

"Gordon has a lot of interesting things. He keeps his favorites in one room. Perhaps it is there."

She got up and went back in the house. Falcon followed soundlessly through the front room, down a hallway, to a closed door at the end. He would secure the ring and then go after Karl Nesterman for Steve.

"It is locked," Delphina patiently informed him.

Falcon placed his hand on the door and stared into the room beyond. He could see several glass display cases, shelves bearing trophies, and plaques adorned the walls. His fingers moved to the lock, and he envisioned the mechanism inside. It was a simple exercise to move the pins into place so that the lock opened for him. He pulled Delphina into the room with him and closed the door.

His gaze passed over one wall and stopped on a tall glass cabinet filled with trinkets. The ring sat on a small pillow in the midst of numerous other pieces of jewelry. He touched the cabinet door. He felt no impulses as he had outside. Was it possible Underwood would leave the ring with no security other than a lock on the door? It did not seem right.

"Delphina, do you know anything about this cabinet?"

"No, Falcon, I do not."

Falcon hesitated, unable to pinpoint what was bothering him. He feared he did not have time to be any more cautious. His fingers turned the latch on the cabinet. In its glass front he saw a reflection of Delphina raising something to her face at the same instant he swung open the narrow door.

A puff of blue smoke exploded in his face. He turned to escape the choking fumes, but his knees buckled beneath him. His last sight was a hazy image of Delphina wearing a grotesque mask, slowly backing away from him.

Steve! his mind screamed out to her.

*　　*　　*

"Did you see that, Doctor Yeguli?" the technician asked excitedly.

"What?"

"Look! The patient's brain activity just leapt from subconscious to alert, then settled in the normal range. And the rapid eye movement. Like a dream. How did you do that?"

The doctor rechecked the monitors and shook her head. "I didn't cause it. If I hadn't been standing here, I'd say she was spurred by an outside stimulus. Very odd. Well, whatever caused it, she's coming back to us now."

Chapter Seventeen

The sweetest joy, the wildest woe is love.
—*Philip James Bailey*

"Falcon?" Steve thought she had spoken his name, but her voice sounded unfamiliar. Her parched throat begged for a sip of water before trying to emit another word. For a moment she allowed herself to sink back into the blackness where she had felt none of the searing pain coursing through her body. The sore throat was nothing compared to the knife slashing at her stomach and chest. She tried to raise her eyelids, without success, nor could she move her arms or legs.

Falcon had called her. He needed her . . . for something. Steve's mind leapt at fleeting memories, but they escaped her grasp. This didn't feel like a dream, yet she couldn't make herself come fully awake. If Falcon needed her enough to call to her, he was in serious trouble. She had to go to him . . . somewhere. As her mind started to clear, however, the blackness moved over her again.

"There," Doctor Yeguli stated to her technician as she adjusted the intensity of the light above the patient's head. "She should now return to a level of unconsciousness where she will not suffer so greatly from the pain, but her recovery will not be hindered."

"But look at the brain pattern, Doctor. She's still fighting the tranquilizing effects of the light. It's as if her subconscious is working independently to bring her to." The technician touched several dials beside the bed. "This is incredible. The healing rate of the organs has more than doubled from what it was a few minutes ago. I've never seen anything like it."

"I have—in a felan empath I cared for once. The woman's mental abilities were so great she practically healed herself. I think it's time to speak to the governor about this patient."

When Romulus and Aster arrived, Romulus briefly filled in Doctor Yeguli. Without benefit of a logical explanation, it had to be assumed that the patient's contact with the empath, Falcon, had somehow bound them together. That being the case, Romulus recommended that the doctor allow Steve to regain consciousness without further interference.

Two hours later Doctor Yeguli called the governor back to Medical.

Steve heard hushed voices in the distance. The effort it took to make out specific words acted as a lifeline to drag her out of the dark oblivion. She was certain she had almost awakened before and was determined to succeed this time. Why was she so exhausted? The voices became more distinct, even if the words were still jumbled together.

285

"Steve, can you hear me?"

The question came from a woman, someone who knew her name and sounded genuinely concerned. Steve put all her energy into opening her eyes. She blinked several times before she could focus on the stunning couple standing next to her.

The silver-haired woman took her hand. "I'm Aster, a friend of Falcon's, and this is my mate, or rather my husband, Romulus."

Steve wrinkled her forehead and closed her eyes again. She might have guessed the identity of the two people from Falcon's descriptions. When Falcon had related stories about them, she had thought of them as fictional characters existing in a fantasy world. Did having a conversation with them mean they were real, or had she herself become make-believe?

"Where am I?" Steve finally asked when she reopened her eyes.

Aster glanced at Romulus and, receiving his nod of approval, she explained, "You are in Innerworld in our medical facility. Technically, you should still be unconscious. Are you in any pain?"

"Pain?" Steve tried to keep her confusion hidden until her memory started to function again.

Rom offered her a slight mental prod. "What do you last remember, Steve?"

The first clear recollection she had was of being in a dark closet with Falcon. She felt her cheeks grow warm and forced her thoughts to continue forward from that point. Suddenly it all came back to her, causing her to bolt upright so quickly that she swayed from dizziness. Aster quickly threw an arm around Steve's shoulder to steady her.

"I remember now. I was shot! Oh, my God!" Her gaze darted back and forth between the two strangers. "Where's Falcon? I told him to get away. I really am in Innerworld, aren't I?" She did not need their confirmation to know it was true. "How did he bring me here? He told me he wasn't supposed to use his ring. Where is he?" Her hand moved to her abdomen. "There was awful pain and then nothing. But I'm not injured now. How much time has passed?" Steve finished in a shaky whisper, not at all certain she wanted to hear any of the answers.

Aster continued to brace Steve as Romulus relayed the story Falcon had told them about four hours ago. A few days ago she would have refused to believe such an incredible tale. She had been dead and restored in a futuristic world in the center of the Earth. Now she accepted what she was being told without a single doubt.

"You should have remained asleep under the light for about another ten hours, but, somehow, your mind took over your healing process."

Abruptly, Steve pulled away from Aster and was about to scoot off the bed when she realized she was naked. "May I have something to wear please? I have to go."

Aster touched her hand and smiled. "Wherever you need to go, you will have to wait for Falcon to return for you."

Steve couldn't understand it, but she was filled with anxiety about Falcon. "No, I can't. He called me. I heard him the same way I could hear him when we mind-talked." Steve stopped as she caught the shocked expressions on both their faces.

"You could communicate mentally?" Aster asked slowly. When Steve didn't answer, she reassured her. "There's nothing wrong with that. We're just surprised that Falcon would have formed such a bond with a . . ." Aster paused and turned to her mate. "Darling, would you mind giving us a few minutes alone?"

"Certainly. I need to go over the medical report with Doctor Yeguli anyway." Rom touched Aster's cheek, then sent her a thought. *Ten minutes. We have some decisions to make that can't wait.*

As soon as Governor Romulus left, Steve came to Falcon's defense. "Falcon tried to keep his identity a secret from me. If he has broken any of your laws, it was my fault. I really didn't give him much choice."

Aster laughed. "Hmmm. You say it was your fault, and he says your death was his fault. I suspect you're both to blame, but more than likely neither one of you could have changed a thing."

"I'm afraid I don't get the joke."

Aster grew serious again. "Falcon said he told you about this world. Are you aware that I'm from the United States like you?" Steve nodded. "At first I remained here because I had no choice. Later I was given an opportunity to return to the United States, but by that time I was desperately in love with Romulus and felt at home in his world. Nothing I had left behind could compare to the new life I'd been given here.

"But there was more to it than simple choices for me. Romulus was forbidden by law to fraternize with any Terran. What that law didn't take into account was the remote possibility that he would be drawn to me by a force stronger than the Ruling Tribunal of Norona." At Steve's look of confusion, Aster laughed again. "Sorry. I seem to have forgotten that where we come from Norona and its leaders are still unheard of. Never mind. There really is a point to all this digression.

"Noronians are human, but there are some major differences between our races. One major example is how they select their mates, who are more than spouses as we know them. It's not merely a matter of emotions or personal likes and dislikes. A man and woman may care deeply for each other and yet not be destined to be mates. For Noronians, the term 'soul mate' has a very literal definition. The uncontrollable attraction of the souls of the couple is the determining factor in finding one's true mate. There is a physiological symptom, referred to as the mating fever, which can't be denied, no matter how hard the two people try. And believe me, Romulus and I had extremely strong reasons to fight it. The only cure is for the couple to join, which is a mating of their souls and minds, as well as their bodies.

"The kind of mental bond that you and Falcon have formed sounds like what Romulus and I share, and yet he spoke of returning you to Outerworld. From the look on your face, I gather you are aware that you will be separated from him."

"There's no way he could stay out there. It would cause him too many problems."

"Did you perform a ritual or ceremony of any kind before you were able to communicate tele-pathically?"

Steve wrinkled her brow. "A ritual? No. He was just suddenly able to put thoughts right into my head. It was right after . . ." Her blush finished the sentence for her. "Anyway, it doesn't work both ways. I can only send him thoughts when my emotions are running high or when he touches my temple."

Aster was thoughtful for a moment. "It must be his felan heritage that made it possible, and yet . . . Steve, are you in love with Falcon?"

The very personal question surprised Steve, but she didn't have to contemplate it to know the answer. Telling herself it was impossible wouldn't change the truth. He was an alien; she had only met him a week ago; he felt nothing but gratitude toward toward her. None of those facts altered her feelings. She hedged. "How could a woman not love Falcon?"

Hearing the sadness that crept into Steve's voice encouraged Aster to press further. "I know. I love him, too. As a very dear friend," she added when she saw the reaction she was looking for. "I would miss him if he left here, but I would still be whole. I would not feel as if a part of me went with him. Romulus and I risked everything to be joined, because life was not worth living otherwise. We have a very grave decision to make regarding your future. I need to know your true feelings about Falcon before I make my recommendation."

Steve sighed. Saying it aloud would make no difference. "It's insane. Everything's happened too fast. I love him so much, I don't know how I'll face tomorrow, let alone the rest of my life without him. Is that what you want to hear? Well, it's true. Regardless of my feelings, however, Falcon explained to me how his emotions have just begun to surface. He doesn't know what love is. Even if there was a way for us to be together, he needs time to learn more about this new part of him. I don't want to be around when he realizes that what happened between us was only special to him because it was his first time. Nor would I want to be there when he meets that soul mate you spoke of.

"None of it really matters anyway. I have to go back to my mother and children, and he has to stay here." After a moment's pause, she added softly, "Maybe someday, if I'm very lucky, I'll get used to living without a heart."

Aster squeezed Steve's hand then dabbed at the moisture that had accumulated in her own eyes. Where was the happy ending? "Thank you for being honest with me, Steve. I know what you've said about Falcon is true. You're an incredibly strong woman to accept it like you have. I wish I could make it come out better for both of you, but I don't have that kind of power." Aster held back the thought that, although Falcon may need to test his wings with other women, the overwrought man she had spoken to earlier wouldn't find it so easy to dismiss this woman from his life.

Steve shrugged and offered a weak smile. "There is something you *do* have the power to help me with. Whether it makes sense or not, Falcon called me. I understand your need to trust me, but I'm worried about him. He said you were familiar with Gordon Underwood and his tactics, so you must realize what

291

Marilyn Campbell

danger Falcon might be in. Please. Help me go to him."

"Falcon gave us instructions to keep you here until he returned. You may as well know he's past due. We were preparing to send out another tracker to the coordinates he left us."

"Aster, imagine that it's Romulus out there. I am a trained private investigator, Falcon and I have a mental bond of some kind, and I love him. Who could be a better choice to track him than me?"

It took some effort on Aster's part to convince Romulus that Steve should be the one to go. Minutes after it was decided, however, Steve was dressed and taken to the transmigrator unit. She knew the danger she risked and chose not to dwell on it as Romulus explained how she would be transported. Nor did she bother to advise him that she had already experienced it without any politely phrased warnings.

Aster apologized that she had not been free to show her around, but the less Steve witnessed, and the fewer Innerworlders she came in contact with, the safer it was for everyone. Steve shook their hands, and they wished her luck, almost as if they were acquaintances she might run into again someday. But she knew better.

Being prepared to be transported did not make as much difference as Steve had hoped. The two-minute journey still felt like a roller-coaster ride through the bowels of hell. She didn't open her eyes until she felt the ground beneath her feet, and freezing air blow against her face. She had made it!

292

Standing in the quiet forest, she let her eyes adjust to the predawn light. The house in the clearing ahead had to be Underwood's. She recalled the list of detailed expenses involved in its construction. The security systems were state of the art and began with sensors beneath the ground. She had no way of avoiding detection, but at least she knew that if there was anyone in the house, they would be expecting someone by the time she reached it. What had Falcon done when he had stood in this spot? Where was he now? If he had managed to get a mental call through to her all the way in Innerworld, why couldn't she hear him now? Oh God, please let him be all right.

Steve felt the ache well inside her. If she had to spend the rest of her life without him, she prayed for the chance to be with him one more time.

Steve?

Falcon! Her heart pounded against her ribs. *Where are you?*

I'm confined in Underwood's house in Alaska. Are you near?

Yes. I can see the house from where I'm standing. Are you all right?

I am now. I was unconscious until I heard your thoughts. Thank you for your concern, Steve. I want very much to see you again as well. I understand what you were feeling just then. I experienced it myself when you were injured. I am very curious as to how you came to be here, but I am pleased that you are.

Steve smiled at the pleasure his words gave her. *Got any suggestions about how to get you out of there?*

You must be calming down. I can no longer read you. I assume you can still hear me, however. I am picking up only three human life forces close by—yours and King's I recognize. The third must be Nesterman. I do not know where Underwood and Delphina have gone, but they were here when I arrived. King may or may not be monitoring the security systems.

As I cannot receive your advice, I must request that you accept my direction. King is somewhere in the front of the house. When I tell you, come straight to the front door as fast as you can. I can get out of this room on my own now that I am alert again. Distract King any way you can.

He paused and amended his order. *Correction, Steve, distract King without sustaining injury to yourself please. I cannot tolerate any more trauma this night. Once he sees you, I am certain I will have sufficient time to overpower him.* Another longer pause. *There. I have released the lock on the room I am in. Come now, Steve, quickly. I am ready.*

She took a deep, steadying breath and ran for the house. It took her less than a minute to reach the house, but King was faster yet. The front door opened, a meaty hand grabbed her arm, and yanked her into the house. Before she could defend herself, she was firmly secured against King's hulking body with both her wrists trapped in one of his large hands and his forearm pressed threateningly against her throat.

"Are you part cat, little girl? I understood you were dead."

In a strangled whisper, Steve quipped, "Well, you know how unreliable rumors are." She tested the hold he had on her. Immediately he increased the pressure on her larynx.

"If I snapped your neck right now, would you come back to haunt me again? You and your friend have caused me considerable embarrassment. I am under orders not to touch him, but as far as Mr Underwood is concerned, you are already dead, so it appears that I may deal with you as I please."

King continued to taunt her with his vast knowledge of ways to end a human life with as much suffering as possible, but she heard only Falcon in her mind. *Hold on, Steve. I am in the hallway, but he is turned toward me. If I step out, he will see me and may terminate you quickly in order to confront me. Try to get him to turn around.*

Steve forced out a squeak. King allowed her a slight reprieve, enough to croak out a challenge. "You'd never get a chance to do any of those things if we started out on equal footing."

He laughed at her foolish dare. "All's fair, Miss Barbanell. I have already bested you twice before you could even make your first move."

"I could beat you in a fair fight," she countered self-confidently. "I've taken men your size down before with no more of a weapon than my body."

"Don't be ridiculous."

"Wouldn't it be an interesting exercise, though? I assure you I would do my best to defeat you, but if I lose, at least my death would be honorable."

In the space of a heartbeat, King accepted her terms. He released her and gave her a shove as he took a step back and readied himself. She did not waste time rubbing her bruised throat. A straight-forward attack was out of the question. Regardless of her boast, she knew she didn't stand a chance against him.

"Come, little girl. Show me what you can do." His body was balanced, his hands moving in front of him.

Gracefully, she entered into the dance, performing artistic, professional steps. She took advantage of the seconds he was allowing her to prepare and, keeping just beyond his arm's length, she glided to his left. Another step and a full turn forced him to turn to continue facing her. As she knew he would, his gaze held fast to hers, and she was careful not to look away or to glance toward the hall behind him, as she was so tempted to do.

Abruptly changing her pace, she attacked with a succession of fluid movements of her hands and arms, aimed at the air around him. Confused by her tactic, his gaze followed her hands. What appeared to be a senseless use of energy gave Falcon the seconds he needed to reach King from behind and touch his temple.

King's face went blank. Then like a marionette his huge body folded to the floor.

Steve jumped over him and right into Falcon's arms. He held her so tightly she could barely breathe and couldn't care less. All that mattered was seeing him again. Slowly, he let her slide down his body until she could stand, but he was in no hurry to release her. He placed joyful kisses on her forehead, her eyes, her nose, then angled his mouth over hers for a final confirmation that he was as glad to see her as she was him. This kiss was unlike any they had shared. It was soft and adoring, not passionate and anxious, although she knew it would take very little to make it so. Falcon raised his head and smiled. He knew it, too.

"He should remain asleep for several hours, but it is hard to tell. He has a very disciplined mind. I will secure him in the room where I was held, then I will share with you what I learned from him just now." With little more than a flex of his muscles, Falcon lifted the inert man, slung him over his shoulder, and went back down the hallway.

As soon as he returned, Steve moved toward him, wanting nothing more than to continue their reunion, but she saw that the former, unemotional Falcon had returned to her. Immediately, she halted and lowered the hand she had raised to touch him. He was absolutely right. They still had business to take care of.

Falcon felt her swift mood change and softened his expression. He took both of her hands in his and kissed her fingertips. "No, Steve. Do not try to hold your feelings from me. I welcome your touch, even if I do not show it. I have practiced emotional control for a lifetime. Be patient with me."

She stretched up to offer him a brief kiss of understanding, then stepped back. "And I have always had too little control. So tell me, what's up?"

Keeping her hands in his, he briefly related what had happened to him after he had arrived in Alaska. "The man you seek, Nesterman, is safely secured in a room at the end of that hall." Before she could celebrate the good news, he gave her the bad.

"Underwood and Delphina have transported into Innerworld. They have my ring now as well as the first one."

"Oh, my God." Her mind spun with questions. They had found Nesterman but lost his abductor. "Wouldn't someone have stopped Underwood and Delphina as soon as they arrived?"

"Yesterday, I am certain that is what would have happened. But not many hours ago I surprised the technician on duty by arriving with you, then was given authority to use the transmigrator again. Apparently you were sent off with the governor's permission, also." He paused and Steve nodded. "Whether it is the same tech or not, word would have spread that the travel restrictions have been modified, and the person on duty might not question the arrival of two more people.

"Another advantage they have lies in Delphina's abilities. To have operated the ring successfully, she must have touched my mind while I was unconscious. I have no way of knowing how much she learned or how Underwood could utilize any information gleaned. If nothing else, she would know that mentioning Governor Romulus and the present emergency might abort any questions. After that, almost anything is possible.

"King knew nothing of his employer's plans other than that he was going to Delphina's home and planned to return here. I never touched Underwood, but I felt the blackness of his aura and know he is intelligent and power-hungry—altogether a very dangerous combination."

"If you have no ring, how will we follow him?"

"We?" Falcon asked with raised eyebrows.

"Don't even think about hunting him down without me, buster. I already convinced your friend, Aster, you needed my help. We're wasting valuable time here. Now, what's your plan?"

Falcon released Steve's hands and walked to the window. The sun was rising on a new day, but there was too much turmoil inside him to appreciate it. Taking Steve to Innerworld had been against the law, but he felt justified. Taking her back with him to continue their search would not be viewed with the same leniency. He should leave her here.

"Falcon?" Steve came up behind him and wrapped her arms around his waist. With her cheek against his back, she felt him take a deep breath and hold it for several seconds before releasing it. He was trying to use his formidable control against her. "Don't do this," she begged, holding him tighter. "Not yet. Please. I'm prepared to say good-bye when the case is over. I swear I am. But you have to give me that much time. Let me stay with you awhile longer."

He closed his eyes and let her feelings flow through him. There were some he recognized, but they were altered by a powerful emotion that he had frequently absorbed from other people, but had never had directed at him. This emotion was warm and giving, hungry and possessive. He could feel its tendrils wrapping him in a silken cocoon that could be comforting and confining at the same time.

Love. He felt it strongest when he was with his friends, Aster and Romulus, but he had never completely understood the feeling until this moment. As he examined this emotion, he also knew that it was causing Steve pain because she believed the feeling was not returned. Was he capable of returning her love? Could he allow himself such an experience and remain apart from her? *No. Yes. No!*

Falcon turned in Steve's arms and tenderly stroked her cheek with his fingertips. "Steve, I am appreciative—"

"No!" she interrupted. Her tormented expression was reflected in his unusual eyes, and she knew he was aware of what she was feeling. "Since there is obviously no way I can pretend to feel differently than I do with you, at least spare me the indignity of having to discuss the hopelessness of it. I really do understand, but I also believe you owe me one final consideration. Actually, I want two. Let me finish my job at your side wherever that takes us."

He frowned slightly, knowing he should deny her, but could not. "You have the right to be present when Underwood is stopped. I will take you. And the second thing you wish?"

"One more night." Her throat constricted as she held back the tears that threatened. *With you.*

Falcon crushed her to him, then concentrated on separating her emotions from his own. Impossible. They were much too similar. "I am not certain how 'considerate' it is for me to agree to that request, but since it is something I need as much as my next breath, I do not have the strength to refuse." He inched her away just enough to capture her mouth in a kiss that would have to hold them both until that promised night.

"You never answered my question," Steve managed to remind him when he freed her. "What now?"

"We have an emissary in Fairbanks who can assist us. What do you wish to do with Nesterman?"

"We'll have to take him with us to Fairbanks. If you've got an address where we can leave him, I'll call Lou and tell him to pick Nesterman up there. I'll have him arrange for King's arrest here."

"I assume Nesterman knows about the ring and Delphina. I will have to take away the memories of what he has discovered."

"Can you just take away parts? I would hate for him not to be able to testify against Underwood."

"I will do my best. Then I will put him to sleep as I did King."

"All right. I can't come up with anything better."

Fifteen minutes later Nesterman was peacefully dreaming about being reunited with his wife, his knowledge of the ring revised and the memory of Delphina completely erased. He would remember being rescued by an American investigator and an Interpol agent. After the problem of Nesterman's memory was settled, Steve and Falcon burned his voluminous notes in the fireplace before they left the room.

Satisfied, Steve searched for a telephone only to be frustrated anew. "The line is dead."

Chapter Eighteen

We have scotch'd the snake, not killed it.
—*William Shakespeare*

"I do not understand."

"The telephone line is disconnected," Steve explained with a grimace. "We can't call out."

"Then we must go to Fairbanks."

"Right. Let's see what kind of transportation Underwood left behind."

They found a seaplane anchored on the bank of the lake, and an all-terrain vehicle and a snowmobile in the garage. The decision process was made simple by the facts that Steve could not fly a plane and there was no snow on the ground. After a quick search of the garage and the house, however, they had not found the keys to the ATV.

"I do not believe that is a serious problem, Steve. I had the opportunity to study an automobile when you were in the hospital and my telekenetic ability has continued to strengthen. I should be able to start the motor without the keys. I could drive if you would prefer."

Steve smiled. "I think I'd still like to do the driving, thank you, but I'll leave the magic to you. I saw a map in the glove compartment so we shouldn't get lost. Not that there are too many roads in the Alaskan frontier anyway. I figure we have about a three-hour drive to Fairbanks, maybe a little more."

They delayed their departure only long enough to borrow three warm coats from a closet. Steve was fairly certain it would warm up later in the day, but as they left Underwood's house with Nesterman slumped unconscious over Falcon's shoulder, the weather was quite chilly.

King stretched and tested his muscles before attempting to rise. He could not recall how he came to be in Mr. Underwood's special room. In fact, his mind seemed like a blank sheet of paper. No, not quite blank—erased. Remaining very still, he concentrated as he willed his mind into a meditative state. Ever so slowly, he began to recall images and thoughts, like disappearing ink in reverse.

Barbanell! The woman was somehow responsible for his present situation. She was also the reason Mr. Underwood's opinion of him had lowered so drastically. There was something more to that memory, something that remained just out of reach, but it refused to come again. No matter. Because of her, he had lost face with the man to whom he owed his life.

The years had been good since Mr. Underwood accidentally interrupted the gang that had been intent on taking King's life in Hong Kong. With his broken jaw and bashed teeth, he had barely been able to speak, but he had pledged his loyalty to the American man from that moment on. Mr. Underwood had him taken to a hospital and, when he had healed, had made arrangements for him to be supported and educated. King had accepted his new name along with anything else the eccentric man had wished to gift him with. After all, in the world he came from, he belonged to Mr. Underwood. In return, King had promised to serve him any way he was told for as long as he and his benefactor lived.

And now he had failed again. There would be no forgiveness from Mr. Underwood this time. He would not want to hear that a dead woman came back to life, overpowered a man twice her size, and then locked him in this room. King had been told to do away with her, and, if it was the last thing he did, he would obey that order.

Mr. Underwood planned the room with a fail-safe feature that anticipated the possibility of his being trapped in it. King went to the curio cabinet, its glass door ajar. Staring at the open door for a moment, he tried to recall what significance that should have, but decided it was unimportant. He extracted a fancy pocket watch and pointed the stem at the door to the room, careful not to touch the glass front until he was ready. The heat of his index finger on the required sequence of numbers on the clock's face deactivated the sophisticated lock, and the door opened silently.

As he stepped out of the room, another memory returned. Karl Nesterman—the man he was to guard with his own life. Even before he saw the open door, he had a feeling Nesterman's apartment would be empty. So! Barbanell had helped Nesterman escape. Another black mark on King's record because of her.

A few minutes later he was standing in an empty garage, smiling because of what the missing vehicle signified. There was only one direction the ATV could leave the property. Checking his watch, he knew she could not have gotten too far yet. He had two distinct advantages: He knew where she was headed, and he had faster transportation.

He had already learned the hard way, however, that with the Barbanell woman he could not afford to be cocky. Two advantages might not be enough. Going back in the house, he went into the office and rapidly spun the combination dial on the walk-in safe.

Mr. Underwood had always relished his privacy, but at his Alaskan retreat he was more fanatical than usual. He had refused King's suggestion that they employ several bodyguards, insisting that it was imperative that no one else know about this hideaway. The responsibility of protecting the house and its inhabitants had rested on King's broad shoulders alone.

As in numerous other fields, King was an expert in weaponry. He had stocked the safe with a sufficient variety of modern armaments to ward off an attack by a small army. Up to this moment, there had been no need to remove a single item from the safe. King quickly made his selections and headed for the plane.

* * *

"Thank goodness, a paved road!" Steve applied the brakes a bit too exuberantly, causing the vehicle to fishtail in the gravel. They had been driving for over an hour on what had to be Underwood's private driveway. The expense list on the house had shown a small fortune in road clearing and stone. She assumed the ruts and fallen trees were purposely placed to discourage the curious from following the narrow lane all the way to the house.

Before stepping on the gas again, Steve turned around and checked on their sleeping passenger in the back seat. At least Nesterman had been unbothered by the bone-jarring ride.

The paved road was barely wide enough for two cars to pass one another, but Steve figured that that probably was a rare occurrence. Tall spruce trees crowded in on them from both sides. Every so often a break in the forest would allow them a glimpse of hazy mountains in the distance.

Falcon pointed to a spot on the map. "I believe this X is where we are now. It does not look like we have traveled very far."

"Are we close to the Yukon River? I remember seeing a small town on the other side of it."

"If I am reading this properly, it is about fifty miles from here."

Just as Steve began to relax, anxiety took possession of her body. "Falcon, I . . . I feel really strange."

Without asking permission, his fingers contacted her temples.

"Yes!" she exclaimed. "That's it! Tense and scared,

without any reason for feeling that way. Am I doing that or are you?"

"I believe you are picking up on my emotions this time, Steve. I suddenly have an overwhelming sense of impending danger." He withdrew his hand. "What do you feel now? Don't think about it, just answer."

"It's getting stronger, like something coming closer and closer. I don't understand, Falcon. I don't have any psychic powers. Are you able to put feelings in my head like you do words?"

"I do not know if I am able, but I assure you I am not doing it intentionally."

"Aster talked about a bond between us. Is that what's happening?"

"Perhaps. This is not the time to experiment further. Listen."

Steve cocked her head, but heard only the car's engine and the wind blowing in through the slightly opened windows. She shook her head negatively.

"Do not listen with your ears. Listen with your mind."

She took her eyes off the road for a second to give him a look of disbelief. Then she heard it. "An engine? A plane engine," she said more certainly. Lowering the window further, she leaned her head out to survey the sky. "I don't see anything, but I feel like I know there's a plane up there. This is too weird, Falcon. I'm getting really frightened and I don't like it one bit. Can't you stop it?"

"No. Your fear is justified. Use it to prepare. Do you sense the darkness as well?"

"What? Wait. Yes, I think I understand. What does it mean? Damn! My heart's pounding like crazy, and my stomach's not doing so well, either." She angled the rear-view mirror so that she could keep one eye on the sky behind her.

"Use your inner strength to control your body's reactions. You have the capability, Steve. Command it. We will soon know the source of the danger."

As he said the words, Steve caught sight of a small seaplane coming into view. "Is that Underwood's plane back there?"

"Yes, and King is piloting it. Obviously, I underestimated his abilities to recover and to remember."

Steve pressed the gas pedal to the floor, but the plane continued to reduce the distance between them. A moment later it buzzed the treetops overhead, then climbed back toward the clouds.

"There's no way he can land." Steve concluded reassuringly. "The wingspan's too great. As long as we're in the forest, we should be okay."

The plane circled in the sky in front of them, then returned to skim the tops of the evergreens again. Steve tried to ignore the fact that King was up there and began adjusting to the shock of an emotional onslaught. King's attempts to unnerve her by his presence were feeble compared to this.

"Steve, I am picking up extremely strong emotions from King. There is pride, frustration, and . . ."

"Desperation," Steve said, easily completing his analysis. "He's absolutely desperate about something. I don't understand how I know that, but I do. Here he comes again!"

Rat-a-tat! Rat-a-tat! The gunfire sounded overhead a second before three bullet holes appeared in the hood of their vehicle.

"The man is nuts! He's actually shooting at us. How the hell can he manage an airplane that size and aim a gun at the same time?"

"As you said, he is a desperate man. I recommend some evasive driving, Steve. He returns."

Steve swerved the heavy vehicle to the left and right, but there was little space in which to maneuver, short of driving into a tree. Repeatedly, King performed his death-defying stunt, swooping down and tipping the plane at an angle that allowed him to fire as he soared by. On his fourth pass, another bullet struck the ATV. A quick glance in the mirror told Steve they were laying a thin trail of fluid behind them.

"Damn it anyway! I think he hit the gas tank. I hope you're wearing your hiking shoes. It looks like a slow leak, but I doubt if we'll make it to the river, let alone to that town, before we run out of gas."

"We must concern ourselves with one dilemma at a time. King has not tired of this game as yet." Falcon pointed to the sky, where the seaplane was making another approach. "He is not aiming a gun this time, Steve. He is holding something else out the window."

"What the—"

Her unfinished question was answered by an ear-splitting blast behind them. The reverberations rocked the ATV but caused no damage. Steve swivelled her head around and gaped at the thick cloud of smoke and falling debris. "Oh, geez! The man's got grenades. We're sitting ducks."

"Stop!" Falcon ordered.

Steve slammed on the brakes in time to prevent the car from driving straight into the path of the next grenade. Automatically, they had both ducked their heads, saving themselves from being mutilated by shattering glass.

"It didn't take him long to correct his aim," Steve said wryly. "Be careful. You're covered with glass. Are you okay otherwise?"

"Yes, but it is not over yet. King is feeling very pleased with himself. He probably believes he has disabled us. He comes again, filled with confidence. Get ready to go with as much speed as possible."

Steve brushed splinters of glass off the steering wheel before gripping it again. Keeping one foot on the clutch and one on the gas, she revved the engine in preparation for Falcon's signal.

"Now!"

With tires spinning, Steve pushed the gas pedal to the floor and tore through the smoky residue in front of them. A heartbeat later the third grenade detonated on the spot where they had been idling.

"He's getting too close, and we're just about out of tricks. Look at the gas gauge. The needle shows empty. We'll be running on fumes any minute now," Steve added.

"I do not believe it will matter. That last miss caused King great annoyance. I believe he is preparing to end the game. I feel him drawing in his emotions, gathering all his mental and physical strength into a central core of determination."

Steve watched the seaplane fly on ahead. "Maybe he's going to land in the river and wait for us at the bridge. That's what I would do."

"I do not believe he thinks as you do. Besides, he might be concerned that his actions might be witnessed outside of the forest. Keep driving, but remain alert."

Several minutes passed before the plane re-appeared on the horizon, heading back toward them.

"Slow down, Steve. Gradually. When I tell you, stop and run into the forest."

Steve stiffened but said nothing. She knew better than to question Falcon's wisdom. The plane descended as it came nearer, just as it had several times previously. Suddenly Steve realized what Falcon had somehow already surmised. The nose of the plane was pointing downward at a greater angle and seemed to be coming faster than before.

"*Now!*" Falcon shouted, and threw open his door.

Steve instantly applied the brakes, but before the vehicle came to a stop, Falcon had hauled Nesterman out with him and hefted him over his shoulder again. Glancing back as she ran after Falcon, Steve saw the plane diving straight down toward the ATV.

The explosion hurled them through the air like rag dolls. Steve's breath was knocked from her body as she hit the ground, but she remained conscious. Rising to her knees, she scanned the area and located the two men. Nesterman's totally relaxed state had probably prevented him from being injured, she realized, but Falcon wasn't moving, either. She crawled to where he lay against the trunk of a tree. His groan assured her that he was alive.

Another explosion grabbed her attention. The plane, minus its wings, had hit its mark. Both it and the ATV were ablaze. They had to get away before the whole forest went up in flames!

Marilyn Campbell

"Falcon!" Mindless of any injury he may have suffered, Steve gave his shoulders a shake. His only response was another barely audible groan. She did what she thought he would do. Her fingers made contact with his temple at the same time as she brought his limp hand to her head. *Falcon. Wake up. We have to get out of here. I don't care if your neck's broken, you wake up right this minute!*

Falcon blinked rapidly several times, then grinned at her. *You are improving, Steve.*

She released his hand and gave him a kiss on the nose. "Good! Are you all right? Is anything broken?"

He closed his eyes again, then shook his head and pulled himself upright. "No, nothing broken. But your face is cut, and you still have glass in your hair."

His fingers touched her cheek, but she could not allow herself the pleasure of his concern or his touch. "That doesn't matter. We have to get moving."

His eyes moved past her, growing wide when he saw the flames, and he sprang to his feet. Just then a spark must have found the trail of gasoline, because a line of fire spread rapidly away from the crash site.

There was no need for words. He lifted Nesterman, and they began running as fast as they could toward the river, praying the fire did not entrap them.

Frantic animals scurried through the brush beside them, more frightened by the threat of fire than the strange humans in their midst. Birds screeched and flapped wildly between the trees overhead. The creatures of the forest instinctively headed for the safety of the water. When several deer loped elegantly past at tremendous speed, Steve turned to look behind her. Animals of all sorts and sizes were charging out of the rapidly burning forest—wolves, mountain goats, porcupines—running in terror from the wall of flames stalking them. The wind had joined the flight to the river, carrying the fire along with it. They had to move faster. In minutes they would be devoured by the rolling furnace.

Falcon caught sight of a large bull moose crashing through the trees and held out his hand to it. The monstrous animal slowed, started to pass, then turned and approached his outstretched hand. The moose's hairy sides heaved from the strain of running, his massive hooves pawed at the ground, impatient to be off, but he allowed Falcon to touch him. A few seconds later, he dipped his antlered head in acquiescence.

"He will take us with him." The back of the moose was almost a foot over Falcon's head, but he managed to heave Nesterman onto the animal's hump. Making a hand stirrup, he gave Steve a leg up. With her assistance, he hauled himself up behind her, then leaning them both forward over Nesterman's body, Falcon reached around her to clutch the hair on the moose's hump.

The beast took off with a tremendous lurch that almost threw them off again. The roaring fire was gaining on the herd of exhausted animals, but their lives depended on not giving up the race. A brown grizzly bear rose on his hind legs and growled in objection as they passed.

Steve thought every bone in her body was being

dislocated. She could hear the agonizing cries of slower animals not far behind. The heat of the fire closed in on them; smoke obscured the way ahead. The moose galloped through low-nanging tree limbs and squashed anything foolish enough to be in his path. Several small branches dangled from the fingers of his wide, palm-shaped antlers. Finally, to protect herself from the limbs and pine needles beating at her, she buried her face in Nesterman's back.

Splash! Steve's head jerked up as her feet acknowledged that they had been dunked in icy water. They had escaped! They were in the Yukon River.

Falcon squeezed Steve's waist as the moose paddled leisurely into deeper water. "Look behind us."

Hundreds of animals survived the inferno the same way they had, and Steve smiled when she recognized the big grizzly's head bobbing up and down. Most of the creatures stayed near the shore, seemingly waiting for the fire to give up so they could return to the forest.

Although quick, the fire had been devastating. As it reached the shoreline, it sputtered and died, but left scorched earth and smoldering, blackened trees behind. These animals would have to seek out new habitats, but at least they were alive.

The moose was anxious to be rid of his load as soon as they reached the other side, and bucked several times before Falcon could calm him again. he slid off the animal's back, helped Steve down, then returned Nesterman to his shoulder. He was grateful that his strength and endurance had increased before this part of his mission began. With his free arm, he hugged Steve to his side.

Steve felt numb from the waist down. For several minutes she simply let his body heat seep into her. Finally her toes came back to life, and she was able to stand on her own.

"How c–c–can you p–p–possibly be warm?" she asked through chattering teeth.

"I felt the cold water as you did. I simply did not permit my body to be discomfited by it."

"Of c–c–course. How s–s–silly of me." She knew she had no reason to be annoyed with him, but she couldn't help herself. The sun shone brightly on her face, but the wind blowing against her wet clothes made her so cold it was almost painful.

Falcon took her hand and started walking along the shoreline, adjusting Nesterman over his shoulder. "Come, my lady. Stay by my side and I will keep thee warm."

Steve wrinkled her nose at him, then laughed at the sparkle in his eye. "I didn't realize deadly adventures would put you in such a rare humor."

"Why not? We are alive, are we not?"

She paused to consider that a moment, then laughed again. "You're absolutely right."

A glimpse of rooftops some distance away assured them they were heading in the right direction. As they neared the bridge they had intended to cross originally, it was not surprising to see the area alive with activity. A fire engine, two police cars, and a variety of other vehicles had collected at the edge of town. From the way everyone was milling around, it appeared as though even the authorities were unsure of what needed to be done now that the fire had burned itself out.

Steve abruptly yanked Falcon away from the shoreline, back among the trees where they would be camouflaged. "We can't let them see you."

It took Falcon a moment to comprehend. "Oh, yes. My eyes. Perhaps we could improvise a makeshift bandage and say I was injured."

She shook her head as she scanned him from head to toe, looked down at herself, then at Nesterman. Their coats and pants were torn; dried blood marked their faces and hands where they had been cut by glass and branches. The finishing touch was the layer of black soot clinging to them from the waist up. Below that they were still dripping wet.

"Disguising your eyes wouldn't solve the real problem. We both look like we barely escaped with our lives, to say nothing of the unconscious man you just happen to be lugging around. If we walk up there, they'll know we were involved in the fire in some way, and the questions would begin. Eventually I'll have to supply some of the answers, but now is not the time, and I definitely don't want to explain who you are."

Falcon nodded. "If we can get to a telephone, we will have the assistance we need."

Fighting their way through the tangle of overgrown bushes and fallen tree limbs, they skirted the edge of the small town. The streets were fairly deserted, due either to the fact that it was midday, or that everyone was congregated by the river. Whatever the reason, it served to their advantage when they came out from hiding.

Steve spotted a gas station with a pay telephone, and they hurried toward it. "I hope your friends will accept a collect call. I'm fresh out of change." After she explained her comment to Falcon, she helped him make his call.

Although the other party accepted the charges, Falcon seemed to be having a difficult time convincing that person of their need to be rescued. Steve watched him press a long sequence of numbers on the phone, then hang up.

"I believe I reached an emissary who has been out of touch for too long. The woman's name is Jenny. A baby was crying loudly in the background, and her side of the conversation was very convoluted. I gathered she could not act on her own. Her mate, George, is an executive at an oil company in Fairbanks. She will call his office and tell him our location. They are far from here, she said. It may be quite a wait before he comes."

Steve put off calling Lou until such time as she could give him precise directions to George and Jenny's house so he could pick up Nesterman. Close to two hours passed before George, Jenny, and the baby arrived at the gas station. Other than identifying themselves, they were silent as they began the return trip to Fairbanks.

Falcon saw no need for polite conversation either and came right to the point. "It will be necessary for us to leave this man with you until Steve's employer can arrange to have him picked up. I have been keeping him asleep by suggestion, but if you wish to go along with our story, he could be allowed to awaken once we reach your home. We would also appreciate the loan of some clothing and the opportunity to refresh ourselves. The real problem, however, is that we must return to Innerworld as soon as possible, but my ring was stolen. I will need to borrow yours."

Neither George nor Jenny answered, but a few minutes after they left town, George pulled the car to the side of the road and stopped. Slowly, he turned in the seat and pointed a small pistol at Falcon's head.

"Listen, pal, I don't know who the hell you are, or what you're talking about, so I don't expect we'll be helping you go anywhere."

Chapter Nineteen

I am not now that which I have been.
—*George Gordon, Lord Byron*

Steve gasped, her body instantly tensing at the sight of the weapon.

Calm yourself, Steve. Look at his ring finger, Falcon ordered mentally.

George was wearing an Innerworld ring. Steve sat back against the seat, but could not completely relax, even though she felt no real danger emanating from the man.

"You are wise to be skeptical under the circumstances," Falcon told George. "You have my permission to touch my mind to learn what you need to know."

George nodded at Jenny. Shifting the sleeping baby from one shoulder to the other, she held out two fingers and Falcon leaned forward so she could reach his temple. He returned her gaze steadily, allowing her to see the physical proof of the facts she was absorbing.

"Put away the gun, dear. He's half felan. He knew you were suspicious, but not violent enough to harm them. Falcon is an Innerworld tracker assigned to clear up all these problems we've been having, although he has understandably withheld the exact details of his mission from me." She nodded toward Steve. "She's a Terran, but she's been helping him. He trusts her implicitly, so we should, also."

George looked alarmed. He had lowered the gun but not his guard. "A Terran and an alien empath working together for Innerworld? Jenny, he has mental strength far beyond yours. What if he withheld other important information just now, like he's been exiled? The order that *nobody* was to use the transmigrator still stands. I will not defy that order without more substantial authorization."

Falcon took a deep, slow breath. Steve could actually feel his frustration. She donned her puzzle-solving cap.

"Falcon, I remember you made contact with someone in San Francisco. Couldn't that person confirm who you are?"

Falcon frowned slightly. "He would know even less than Jenny just learned." Looking at George, he ventured, "Are communications with Monitor Control still interrupted?"

George shook his head. "No. As a matter-of-fact they suddenly became fully operational again sometime during the night."

Falcon glanced at Steve and blinked. *About the time Underwood reprogrammed the ring that was jamming the system.* "Time is of extreme essence, but I do not fault you for needing authorization. Please take us to your residence and we will wait while you obtain approval to assist us. I would suggest you address the message directly to Governor Romulus. The mention of my name should get his immediate attention," Falcon stated.

George's eyebrows raised slightly before he nodded his agreement and stepped on the gas.

Steve no longer wondered at the fact that she was picking up on Falcon's emotional state. What she could not figure out was why was he so frustrated? Surely he wasn't worried about getting George's help. Even she could tell the man was already convinced Falcon was on the level and just wanted to get a proper okay. His worry was worrying her.

She reached for his hand and squeezed. When he turned to her, she gave him a quizzical look. *What's wrong?*

His eyes registered his surprise. He had heard her without her touching his temple, and she was hardly worked up. This mental business between them was getting stranger all the time.

Threading his fingers through hers, he let her share the cause of his concern. *I told you I am able to see things that have occurred before. The images fade continually as time passes. After about twenty-four hours, they disappear completely. It works the same way when I am tracking people. I can follow either their brain pattern or their personal aura. Even when I was in Underwood's house, I was not close enough to get a fix on his brainwaves.*

So that you understand the problem we will be facing, you should note that Innerworld is about half the size of the United States and has a population of almost twenty-five million. Since we have no idea where Underwood is headed within the colony, I am counting on the blackness of his aura to lead me to him once we get there. If too much time goes by, my talents will not be of much use.

"Jenny, do you have the time?" Steve asked.

"It's about three. Oh my, you're probably starving! Well, don't worry, we'll be home within the hour and get the both of you fed and cleaned up before you leave." She was anxious to make up for her mate's stubbornness since she had no doubt whatsoever about the integrity of the handsome man in the back seat.

"That would be very nice, thank you." Steve smiled gratefully, then tried sending another thought to Falcon. *How long has it been?*

When I said you were improving, that was a gross understatement. Are you doing anything differently to enable me to hear your thoughts so clearly?

Not that I can tell. It's just happening like the feelings. What about the time?

It is hard to calculate. It was night when I arrived in Alaska, but I do not know the exact time. It has probably been between twelve and fourteen hours already.

Geez! Maybe we'll luck out and someone will have stopped Underwood the second he appeared in Innerworld.

I do not believe we can depend on that any more than the possibility that he crossed Romulus's or Aster's paths. They are the only two who would recognize him on sight. I do not dare send any specific alert about Underwood over the open transmission system, but I

will have George warn Romulus to expect our arrival
with another problem.

So, thought Gordon Underwood as he read the data on the monitor, the alien who had escaped from his Nevada hospital six months ago had since become the leader of his people. "Governor" Romulus, they called him. The big shock though was that his co-governor and mate was the woman who had been with him at the time. It did not sit well with Gordon that he had dismissed her as decoration. She had apparently been instrumental in the man's mysterious disappearance. There was no time today for self-recrimination or righting yesterday's mistakes. Perhaps another time he would find a way to pay them back for the inconveniences they caused him, but not today.

Delphina sat quietly next to him as he perused several more files of Innerworld current events. He found himself chuckling when he realized how drastically Nesterman had disrupted Innerworld's mundane routine with his random fumblings. All things considered, the people here should be grateful to him. It didn't look as though much of anything happened from one year to the next. The change of leadership and surprising pronouncement that the woman, Aster Mackenzie, possessed a drop or two of Noronian blood were the only other big news items recently. He supposed if he researched back into their history he would find upheaval, scientific and medical discoveries, and so forth, but, again, there was insufficient time for such leisurely reading.

He had had no idea what to expect when they had

arrived. The transmigration itself was miraculous. A man stationed at a control panel had merely shaken his head in disgust as he and Delphina exited the glass-walled unit. They hadn't even had to fabricate an explanation. The man had said, "Don't tell me. Emergency. Governor Romulus." Gordon had nodded and the man waved them on. The people here were obviously rather complacent about security, much to his satisfaction.

He had asked Delphina how he might get answers to some of his questions about her world, and she had taken him to a library. He had soon discovered there was very little information he could not access through one of the many computer terminals available there, and he had set to work immediately. His photographic memory automatically stored volumes of facts and formulas. He had only needed to make a few written notations regarding the most complex data.

He had learned how the Noronians traveled across the universe in remarkably short periods of time, and that a gram of the rare dustlike substance, volterrin, which Delphina had mentioned, produced sufficient energy to run New York City for a year.

The cure to cancer and other deadly diseases were child's play compared to some of their other achievements in the field of medicine. Genetic engineering had been outlawed—after they had perfected it, and the dead could be brought back to life.

The human brain held no more mysteries for these people. One mind could communicate with another. With reprogramming, a man's memory could be completely erased and replaced with new thoughts. *That*, Underwood realized, was the secret to their boring, regulated society. Crime did not exist because criminal behavior was not tolerated. The offender was altered to fit the accepted norm. Therefore, Underwood knew he had to return to his own, familiar world. Sooner or later, if he stayed here, he would be found and destroyed like a defective piece of equipment.

He had not located the exact code, but he was certain he had enough information to figure out eventually how to access the Innerworld data banks out of his own home. The ring was the key, and now he had two. He had no doubt that Nesterman would be cooperative once he was given a taste of the fountain of wisdom. If not, he would have King eliminate him. He probably should anyway, considering his ultimate plans.

When he returned to the earth's surface, it would be with a wealth of knowledge that would ensure him the position of power he had always craved. Possessing Delphina was an unexpected bonus.

Another thing he had made note of was the Noronians' use of holography. They were in the inner core of the earth and yet, outside of the buildings, it actually looked like they were outdoors. There was a lavender sky and a huge, bright orange sun with a white ring around it. He would make use of the technique to improve living conditions in his underground facility in Nevada.

He intended to introduce his incredible medical discoveries to the public slowly. Altruism and the betterment of mankind had no place in his scheme, but the citizens of the United States did not need to know that. He would be labeled a hero, as well as a genius, as his foundation revealed one discovery after another. By the time he gifted them with the new energy source, the whole country would be rallied behind him. Anyone who was not could be dealt with by his loyal medical staff, headed by his personal physician, Doctor Quinn, who would soon master the technique of reprogramming such dissidents.

For years he had dreamed of owning his own country, but his plans had never been fully formulated due to the lack of desirable locations remaining in the world. Now he saw his future clearly. What could be better than taking over a modern, well-run country already established as one of the world's leaders? The United States would soon be his for the asking. After that, there would be no more asking, only commanding. The skin of his great bald head tingled as he imagined the forthcoming realization of his dreams.

He smiled at Delphina, and she blushed beautifully. She probably sensed his welling excitement and understood that, under different circumstances, he would have taken her then and there, and without the help of any of her mental tricks.

"I believe I have gathered as much information as I need at this time. Why don't you take me to the mining camp you had told me about—Gladly? I'd like to see where you were going to work." He hoped it would not take long to obtain a few pounds of volterrin from the mine. Since he had no way of knowing if it could be analyzed or reproduced in his world, he wanted to take a large supply of the real thing with him—enough to help his dream come true, without having to return to Innerworld for many years.

The necessary travel time was an unavoidable hindrance. They could reach Gladly instantaneously if they transmigrated there, but, to his annoyance, he had learned that the rings only functioned outside of Innerworld. To transmigrate from within the area, a person had to use the migrator cells and that required a pass. Gordon opted against that method. He wanted to attract as little attention as possible, until they were ready to leave. A bit of forceful persuasion would undoubtedly convince the technician to send them back to Alaska. The fact that these people abhorred violence was definitely in his favor.

In the meantime they had to travel by an alternative mode of transportation. The airbus would take about two hours, but did not require special permission.

This place made him uncomfortable, not only because he was trespassing, but because he, Gordon Underwood, was nobody special here. Also, he was anxious to get back and boast to Nesterman. He was so pleased with himself, he might even forgive King for his recent failures.

As they left the library, he gave a moment's consideration to his captured alien, Falcon. He no longer had any use for him. Perhaps he would give him to Doctor Quinn for one of his experiments. Maybe even his first attempt at reprogramming. That delightful thought made him laugh out loud. It would be the perfect end to the creature who had caused him so much trouble.

Two days without sleep and the last twelve hours without food were beginning to wear him down, but he ignored his body's demands. He could always eat and sleep tomorrow in Alaska.

In spite of the length of time it took to reach Gladly, Gordon was impressed with the airbus. A wheelless vehicle, it silently soared on a cushion of air at an incredible speed. He had not been able to discern the change in scenery until they arrived at the volterrin mining camp. Barren, there were only a handful of small buildings and rows of the metallic structures Gordon had learned were filters, which were each about four stories high and barely three inches wide. What appeared to be metal wires were woven in hexagonal configurations, giving the appearance of a cross section of a robotic beehive. During the day the miners vacuumed and scraped the traps, similar to beekeepers collecting honey. Underwood had learned from the computer files that the Noromians had tried to use machines once, but this was one process that man still performed more efficiently.

Unlike honey however, the volterrin was of no use when taken directly out of its hive. A machine similar to an atom smasher had to be used to separate the element from the useless material surrounding it, and a human was still required to operate the equipment.

It was evening now. No humans buzzed about the filters. Gordon saw two people walking from one building to another where lights had been turned on, but they paid no attention to him or Delphina. Could it be this simple?

He walked toward the filter closest to him and immediately received the answer as his body bumped into an invisible barrier. Instantly, the section of the wall he had come in contact with was glowing with light.

"May I be of assistance?" a man's voice called from behind Gordon.

He turned to see a black-uniformed man swiftly approaching him. Calling upon some of the information he had consumed earlier, he offered what he hoped was a believable explanation. "Yes. I'm a new arrival. This is Delphina. She's my caretaker. I'm considering a career as a miner, but I wanted to see the camp and how it functioned first."

The man frowned, clearly dubious, but when his gaze fell on Delphina he relented. "This is most unusual. She should have known not to come here at night. The protectors are already in place. You may stay in the dormitory tonight. There will be nothing for you to observe until daylight." His eyes never left Delphina as he spoke. His interest in where she would spend the night was completely uninhibited.

Angry frustration curdled in Gordon's stomach. He had not expected to be thwarted so effectively or so easily. The man's leering at Delphina was making it even harder to sound nonchalant. Placing his arm around her, he brought her possessively to his side. "I suppose I have no choice. Tell me, would it be possible for me to see what this stuff they collect here looks like?"

The man was not pleased by the implied message that Delphina was unavailable, nor did he see any need to repeat information he had already given. He pointed to a long structure. "Someone in there will set you up." With that, he turned on his heel and walked away, the light extinguishing as he did so.

The drive to Fairbanks had seemed interminable to Steve. She had tried to doze, but her frazzled nerves wouldn't permit it. Once they reached the house, George immediately went to work on the telecommunicator hidden in the attic. Jenny fussed over Steve and Falcon, helping them get the glass out of their hair, offering clean, dry clothing after their showers, and serving them a hot meal, all of which was enormously appreciated.

Steve called Lou at the office and filled him in as quickly as possible. He was both angry about her long absence without a word and relieved that she and Nesterman were both safe and sound. Since she was still on Underwood's trail, he agreed to make the necessary arrangements for Nesterman's return to California.

As occupied as she was, Steve could not stop herself from looking at the clock every few minutes. George seemed to be taking forever, but then, how long was it supposed to take to contact someone in the center of the earth?

It was after five when the authorization came through and they were thanking Jenny for her hospitality. George handed Falcon his ring, but he could not accustom himself to the idea of a Terran being granted permission to travel to Innerworld, and it showed in his lack of manners.

One minute they were in Jenny's neat living room, the next they were inside a glass booth in

Innerworld's main transmigrator station. Romulus and Aster came forward as they exited. It was clear they were both glad to see Falcon, but the expressions on their faces when they saw Steve were vastly different. Aster's smile grew wider; Romulus's disappeared.

Steve's gaze darted from one to another. So many emotions assailed her at once that all she could feel was confusion.

After a moment, Romulus glanced at the technician, and, noting her interest, informed Falcon that he would listen to his explanations in his office.

"There is insufficient time," Falcon began, but Romulus would hear none of it.

"Ten minutes won't make that much difference. Upstairs. Now." And with those words he stalked off, leaving the three of them to catch up or catch hell.

The instant they had privacy, Romulus turned on Falcon. "I believe I am still the governor of Innerworld and you are still subject to its laws." His gaze flew to Aster, who was looking at him beseechingly. "No. Friendship has nothing to do with this," he responded to a plea only he could hear. The glare in his eyes softened as they stared at one another. A moment later, he sighed and turned back to Falcon. "There are times when sharing a woman's mind can be quite complicated, particularly when you are expected to make sensitive decisions—" A raised eyebrow from Aster cut him off. "All right, Falcon. Explain yourself. Why have you brought her back?"

"Gordon Underwood and Delphina are here in Innerworld." Both Romulus and Aster voiced their shock as Falcon continued, "They have already been here for a considerable number of hours. While we were in the transmigrator, I picked up his aura. It is fading rapidly. If I am to follow him, I must not delay. The only explanation I can offer regarding Steve's presence here is that something most unusual has been happening between us. It may or may not affect my abilities if we are separated, but this is not the time to take that risk. For the present, where I go, she goes. After we have apprehended Underwood, you may render me whatever punishment you see fit. I will give you a complete report of our time in Alaska later. For now I request a change of clothing, a weapon, and permission to finish this mission."

Romulus had no rational choice but to postpone further discussion until later, and offered Falcon and Steve the use of his private quarters to freshen up while he secured the requested weapon.

Falcon held open the door to the adjoining chamber for Steve. She couldn't have said what she expected, but this certainly wasn't it. The outer room had looked like the office of any American executive, and this room was similar to an efficiency apartment, except for the one entire wall done in some kind of silver metal squares. Come to think of it, the medical facility looked familiar to her, also. Somehow she had imagined it would all be more "outer space." Her momentary disappointment vanished when she heard Falcon talking to a computer and it answered him in a very human voice.

She went to his side to observe his actions more closely. Pictures of a variety of men's clothing flashed continually on the monitor until Falcon made several selections. He then gave the computer instructions as to color and material and stepped back from the screen. A beam of light shot out, quickly scanning him from head to toe, then receded again. A minute later the computer informed him his order was complete, and Falcon opened a small panel in the metal wall.

He pulled out a black shirt, slacks, socks, and shoes, exactly like she had seen him wearing before.

Smiling at her wide eyes, he told her, "This is a supply station. Every residence is equipped with one. It provides food and clothing upon request and stores the used items for recycling. The clothing is deposited in another bin after it is worn."

"You mean it's disposable? You never have to do laundry?" Steve thought it sounded like heaven.

"Also, I remember the machine your mother used to clean the dishes and food preparation containers. The station performs all those functions for you. Are you hungry? I could demonstrate."

Steve was astonished. *This* was the kind of marvel she had expected to see. "No cooking? No dishes? No laundry? No wonder they don't want us to find out about this place. Every woman in America would defect. How about cleaning? Has that bothersome little chore been done away with, too?"

Falcon laughed. "Not entirely, but an android can be purchased to do whatever needs to be done. Of course, there is no dust here as you have in Outerworld. Our dust has great value because it contains a rare element, nolterrin, which is filtered from the air before it has a chance to settle. It is needed as an energy source here and on Norona. You would like it here, I am certain."

The words were said without thought to any deeper meaning. Steve understood they did not convey a sincere invitation, nor was a response from her expected, but they brought reality back with a thud and the levity of the moment was lost. She could not sense his emotions or hear his thoughts. He had the ability to shut her out at will, but she did not know how to do that herself. His tender expression told her he read her feelings quite accurately.

"You did not answer, Steve. Are you hungry? Or would you like a change of clothes?" He could not deal with everything she was feeling, he was feeling, *they* were feeling. With each passing hour, it was becoming harder to distinguish between the two. His need to resolve whatever was developing between them was rapidly becoming stronger than his need to complete his assignment.

Steve had heard his questions but hadn't answered. He wouldn't have heard her, she was sure. He was drawn inside himself to a place where she could not go. "No and no."

Falcon blinked.

"I believe you were daydreaming, Falcon," she said lightly to break the tension. "I'm not hungry and Jenny's clothes fit fine."

He nodded distractedly and began unbuttoning George's plaid flannel shirt.

Steve wandered around the small room, then perched on the edge of a chair. She tried to keep her eyes off Falcon, but that was impossible. The more masculine flesh he bared, the more she wanted to see. His unintentional striptease was exactly the kind of distraction her exhausted mind needed.

Falcon knew she watched, but kept his eyes averted. To him, his body was not unique. He had read other females' interest when they saw him, but had never been affected by it. Steve made him feel unique, special, beautiful. His body ignored his order not to be aroused, making the process of closing his slacks somewhat difficult. When he turned to look at her again, his discomfort increased.

He held out his hands, and she drifted into his arms. When he drew her closer, lifting her so that her hips were flush against his, she tilted her head back for his kiss.

We can't, she thought miserably, and moved against his hardness.

We must be off, he thought halfheartedly, and repeated her motion.

His lips pressed to hers, and she held him tighter. Their tongues met, and she sucked his deep within her mouth, causing him to make the purring sound that vibrated all the way down to her toes then settled between her legs.

Neither had the will power to pull away on their own, but combined, they managed to remind themselves of their priorities.

Soon. The word was shared between them.

Falcon released Steve with a sigh. Caressing her lips with his fingertips, he teased, "You look like a woman who has been well-pleasured."

In return, she ran her hand down the center of his chest and over the bulge below. "And you look like a man who was not."

They were perfectly presentable when they rejoined Romulus and Aster, but Steve felt herself blush anyway when Aster smiled a little too knowingly.

Romulus handed Falcon a black box that looked like a remote control for a television. "This weapon is signed out in your name, and you can use my commuter if you need to. It's parked outside. Be careful and keep us advised. It's impossible to guess what Underwood is up to."

"Good luck," Aster added as Falcon and Steve left the office.

"Well," Steve said in the hallway, "we're on your turf now. What's the plan?"

"We return to the transmigrator station, where I sensed Underwood's aura, and go from there."

Throughout the Administration Building, Steve followed a few steps behind Falcon, but she halted abruptly the moment they exited the enormous structure. For a moment she wondered if she had been transported into a fairy kingdom. Knowing she was in the center of the earth didn't matter. Her senses told her she was outdoors.

The delicious fragrance of lilacs filled her nostrils as her eyes devoured the spectacle around her. Stars shining in the clear blue-black sky were complemented by thousands of twinkling lights set in the trees and bushes. Buildings of various sizes and shapes were separated by parks. Whatever the buildings were made of, they reflected everything around them, like giant mirrors.

Falcon realized she was no longer with him and returned to where she was standing. The awestruck

look on her face made him think of her children—
all innocence and wonder. "This is different than
you imagined?"

"Yes. No, not entirely. It's just so . . . beautiful,"
she finally said for lack of a better description of
her surroundings.

"Would it be possible for you to admire the city
and walk with me at the same time? I was tracking
Underwood's aura successfully until you stopped.
Your distraction somehow affected my concentration."

"Oh, I'm sorry, Falcon. I thought that business you
gave Romulus about needing to keep me with you
was an alibi for my being here."

"I thought it was at the time. Now I am not certain." He held out his hand. "If you please."

Steve smiled and placed her hand in his. "I'll try
to think only about Underwood, but that's a pretty
tall order in this setting."

Falcon did not return her smile. His intense expression told her his mind was at work.

"I do not believe the problem was your thoughts."
He held her hand up in front of them. "As soon as
we touched my concentration returned. In fact, the
aura does not seem so faded anymore. Once again,
I am unable to explain why or how, but I would
appreciate it if you would maintain physical contact
with me."

Steve couldn't help but laugh at the serious word-
ing of his request. "My dear sir, it will be my pleasure." She kissed the back of his hand, then gave him
a tug in the direction he had been heading before she
stopped.

Falcon quickly regained the lead, firmly pushing aside the nagging concern of what was happening to him and his talents.

The black aura had begun to disintegrate, but as he held Steve's hand, he was able to track it to the library a few blocks away from the Administration Building. At the door he sensed both the weak traces he had been tracking and a vivid twin. It told him Underwood had gone into the building and remained there throughout the day, then left no more than a few hours ago. By touching the chair Underwood had vacated, Falcon heard a replay of his conversation with Delphina.

"Underwood has no intention of remaining in Innerworld. He came here to steal two things. The first—knowledge—he was able to obtain from the computer files. The second will be much more difficult. They have gone to Gladly, a mining camp some distance away. I assume he will try to pilfer a quantity of volterrin, for he has learned how valuable an energy source it is. He may already be there. Come, we need Romulus's permission to migrate to the camp." He saw Steve's grimace and tapped her nose with his forefinger. "Now you know how I felt on that airplane to Miami!"

Chapter Twenty

Evil often triumphs, but never conquers.
—Joseph Roux

"Yuk!" Steve sneered at the flat, desert-like landscape. "I can't believe this is part of the same world. What're those ugly metal sculptures over there? Fences?"

"Those are the filters that collect the dust. It is necessary to the collection process that the camps be as obstruction-free as possible. Trees, plants, and decorative buildings are a hindrance here. I understand your curiosity, Steve, but perhaps you could curb it slightly. It is most distracting and I do not seem to have the power to close you out as easily as I once did."

"Oh, I'm sorry." She took a deep breath and grasped Falcon's hand. "Okay. Back to work. Is he here?"

"You tell me. Remember the sensation of darkness when King was approaching? Underwood's aura is much stronger, blacker."

Steve hesitated, surprised to discover she had

unconsciously been blocking it out. She *could* stop something from entering her head and let it in when and if she chose. How simple it really was, like opening and closing a window. Only days ago she thought of mental telepathy as little more than an interesting topic of conversation. Now, she was not only communicating with her mind, she was reading other people's emotions as if they were her own, and had even picked up an aura of someone she couldn't see.

There was no doubt Falcon was responsible for these changes, but her easy acceptance of these skills and innate knowledge of how to utilize them was bewildering. Rather than being shocked as she supposed she should be, it all seemed perfectly natural. She had the oddest feeling that the ability to use her mind in these ways had always been there, but had never been exercised.

Testing this newest awareness, she pictured herself opening that mental window.

Anger, hatred, blackest evil assailed her from every angle, poking, prodding, tearing at her flesh. She cried out in fear and revulsion. The evil took a human form but not entirely. Its golden cat's eyes were sly and wicked. Its wild mane of hair became a nest of hissing snakes that struck and coiled around her, imprisoning her securely in the demon's trap. Her fists beating against her captor, she frantically struggled to break its hold. Tongues of white-hot fire licked at her feet, enveloped her ankles, her legs. In a moment she would be consumed and become a part of the evil.

"Steve! Stop it. Stop the fear!" Falcon shook her,

gripping her so hard he knew she would be bruised, but she fought to escape him as one demented, as if he were death itself. He invaded her mind, careful to keep his own protected from whatever images tortured her.

Break away, Steve. Not with your body. It is your mind that is being held. Close the window. You can do it.

But she couldn't—not alone. Falcon joined his strength to hers, and together they banished the overwhelming darkness.

Steve's body wilted in Falcon's arms. Trembling from head to toe, it was all she could do not to cry. She had never been so terrified in her life. She sniffed and pulled herself together. "I guess I haven't got the hang of it yet." Her attempt at a smile didn't quite make it.

Falcon took a shaky breath and hugged her gently. Rotating his thumbs over her upper arms, he withdrew the discomfort he had caused. "Please forgive my error in judgment. I should not have suggested you reach out for something that powerful when this is so new to you. It seems so natural for you to share my abilities, I did not consider how it would affect you."

Steve tilted her head back. "That's strange. Just before it happened I was thinking how *natural* it felt to do these things. I guess I got cocky. What I felt, or saw, or whatever, was that Underwood's aura?"

"It is his essence, what motivates him. I perceived it in a different form than you. Each person's fear comes in an individual package. Because I knew what to expect, I could view it without giving it

341

access to my mind. I had assumed you would only sense it through me and feel only what I feel. What happened is . . .improbable."

Steve accepted his warmth for a few more heartbeats before she gave into the anxiety nagging at her. Hers? His? It didn't matter. She eased away from Falcon and straightened her shoulders.

"Okay. What now?"

"He is in that building. We will request the assistance of the guards to ensure he does not slip away again."

Steve felt her system's adrenaline replenishing itself. She forced herself to stand by patiently during Falcon's explanations to the two black-uniformed men. One guard recognized Falcon, which sped the matter up considerably. Both men removed a small black box from their belts as they strode away. Steve wondered what sort of weapon it was, and whether she would see it used in the next few minutes.

When the guards disappeared around the rear of the building, Falcon nodded to Steve. "It is time to bring the hunt to an end."

"Just tell me what you want me to do."

"I believe you have an appropriate, but illogical, expression to fit the occasion: *'Play it by ear'*."

Steve winked at him. "Gotcha."

In spite of the way they casually approached the entrance of the dormitory, Steve's heart thudded in her chest. Falcon stepped in front of her and cautiously opened the door.

Several faces turned their way as they entered. Only one distorted in fury.

Gordon Underwood jackknifed up from the chair

in which he had been lounging next to Delphina. "You! How . . ." His gaze darted wildly from Falcon to Steve. "You're dead! This isn't possible!" He took a step sideward and groped for Delphina's hand, urging her to stand beside him without taking his eyes off Falcon.

Steve had witnessed other men in similar situations. At this point they were sweating bullets, but this was not an average man. Although momentarily flustered, he quickly regained his cool, sophisticated facade. He puffed out his chest and lifted his chin, daring any inferior being to touch him.

The other inhabitants of the room scrambled away from the four participants, remaining close enough to watch the drama without risk of becoming a player. It reminded Steve of a saloon scene in a bad western, but instead of brandishing six-shooters, Falcon had his weapon neatly concealed in the palm of his hand. He didn't need to wave a gun to look threatening. His expression, his stance, his entire being bespoke of leashed danger and confident power.

Steve remained stationed in the entranceway, as Falcon inched closer to Underwood.

"I'm quite curious," Underwood ventured conversationally. "Perhaps you would be considerate enough to explain how the two of you managed to follow me."

"No." Falcon advanced another foot.

The big man narrowed his brows. "I see. But at least tell me what you did with King and Mr. Nesterman. I had grown somewhat fond of them both."

"Nesterman is free. King is dead."

343

"Dead?" He looked surprised, then turned to Steve. "I've studied these aliens. They are opposed to violence. Did you kill King?"

Falcon answered for her. "He ended his own life."

"Tch–tch. How very Oriental of him. I suppose he thought it was what he deserved for failing his master. So now, what is it you think *I* deserve?"

"You will be punished for your crimes against the people of Innerworld. More than a thousand innocents died because of your interference."

Underwood chuckled lightly. "Yes, I read about that. A shame, but it *was* accidental. I have also read about your ideas of punishment. Reprogramming is so much more civilized than execution. However, I'm afraid I can't oblige your sense of righteousness. I have some pressing business matters to attend to back home."

With a vicious jerk, Underwood positioned Delphina in front of him, twisting her arm up her back and circling her throat with his other hand. He started backing up to the rear door of the building, when Falcon moved again. "Don't take another step. You may not believe in violence, but I do, and I will not hesitate to hurt this pretty lady if I have to. I could break her neck with one snap, but I won't— yet. I'll just tighten my fingers, little by little, slowly shutting off her breath. An agonizing way to go I assure you, and her pain would be your doing. Ah, but there's the rub, isn't it? You're not permitted to cause another person pain. Too bad. Well, we must be going now. Say good-bye, Delphina."

"Good-bye," she whispered obediently.

Steve wanted to do something, stop him herself if

she had to. But Falcon was ordering her to wait, to be still. She did not dare open herself to Underwood's emotions, but through Falcon she knew the man was not as calm as he appeared. He was grasping for straws. There was nowhere in either world he could go where they would not follow.

Falcon's wrist moved imperceptibly. His finger twitched. A bolt of lightning flashed out of the black box, streaked across the room, and blasted Delphina between the eyes.

"No!" Underwood roared as she went limp in his arms. He'd been deceived! He dropped her to the floor, flew to the back door, and yanked it open, but his path was blocked by two guards pointing those strange weapons at him. Raising his hands over his head in surrender, he cautiously made his way back into the room. Logic told him it was better to be captured and alive than dead.

Dead. Delphina, *his* Delphina, was dead. He stared at her lifeless body, her beautiful auburn hair fanning over her face and down her back. The woman who had made him feel like a man again, the woman he loved with all his heart, was taken from him. He would never again . . . Tears of grief clogged his throat and he swallowed hard. Lowering his hands and glaring stonily at Falcon, he demanded, "Why? She had nothing to do with any crime you believe I committed. Why did you have to kill her?"

"I did not kill her."

Falcon sent a mental command to one guard, who brought his weapon up and touched Underwood's neck, paralyzing him instantly. Underwood's eyes were wide, his mouth open in shock. He could see and hear but not move or respond. Falcon's fingers shifted on his weapon, and a small knife extended from one end.

Steve came up beside him, not understanding everything she was hearing and seeing, and yet *feeling* that Falcon had it all under control.

Falcon nudged his foot under Delphina and flipped her onto her back. A black hole smoldered in the middle of her forehead. Bending over her still form, he brought the knife point down to the base of her throat. In one swift motion he slashed a line to her stomach. Steve gasped and covered her mouth with her hand, afraid she would be sick. Then her brain registered what her eyes perceived. *There's no blood!*

His fingers pushed aside Delphina's dress, then dipped into the slit his knife had made. He tugged at her flesh, peeling it back as if it were another layer of clothing. Beneath the skin, where Steve expected to see ribs and bloody organs, lay a circuit board and a mass of silver disks. Delphina was an android!

Rising again, Falcon delivered part of Underwood's punishment. "You need not concern yourself with Delphina. As a reactive computer specializing in fantasies, she is extremely valuable. Her body will be repaired and her memory of you will be erased. She will be programmed to pleasure her next owner as well as she served you."

Underwood was still rendered immobile, but as Steve regarded him, a tear oozed out of the corner of one eye and trickled down his cheek. The man had feelings after all.

He is a murderer, Falcon reminded her.

Yes, I know, and a kidnapper, also. Will he—

Falcon interrupted her thought by speaking aloud to the guards. "We would appreciate your assistance in bringing these two to the migrator for transport back to Administration. His fate must be determined immediately."

As soon as their prisoner was taken into custody and the rings retrieved, and Delphina was shipped to Creative Services, Falcon and Steve met with Romulus and Aster. Once they brought the governors completely up to date, they exchanged ideas of how to deal with Gordon Underwood.

Total reprogramming was the standard sentence of Innerworld's justice system, but in Outerworld, only Steve would know what had happened to the billionaire. There was no way Mr. and Mrs. Nesterman would be satisfied with the notion that Underwood had simply vanished into thin air. Steve tried not to think about how foolish she would look if that was the only explanation she could offer.

Aster touched Rom's hand. "Remember how you handled that wretched man, Victor? Surely you can think of something equally brilliant to satisfy everyone involved."

After considerable discussion, that is precisely what they came up with.

"Let me see if I understand this." Steve paused to organize her thoughts. "When you touched King's mind in Alaska, he was able to bring his memory back because technically everything was still there but buried. With reprogramming, Underwood's memory would be permanently altered to whatever you chose for him to remember."

Falcon nodded. "As I mentioned at the time, King had a very disciplined mind. There is no question that a mind-touch would not be an adequate method of controlling Underwood's future activities."

"We have the rings back," Romulus said, "and as far as Innerworld is concerned, after reprogramming, Underwood will no longer present a threat. In the morning we will give him to you. He will be subdued sufficiently for you to return to Outerworld and deliver him to your authorities."

Steve was still not certain she understood everything. "But to anyone who knows him will he look and act as he always did before? It would be a waste if no one believed he was really Gordon Underwood."

Romulus leaned forward as he summarized the plan. "In a total reprogramming, the human is drastically changed and often ends up being little better than an android. That's why we're going for a very limited adjustment here. Underwood will have all his previous memories and knowledge, including the fact that he kidnapped Nesterman to study a unique ring. He will not remember, however, how he came to be in possession of this ring. Too many other people are aware of the fact that you and Falcon were searching for him, so it would serve little purpose to eliminate his memory of the two of you.

"All of the technical knowledge he acquired while he was here will be erased, but not his memory of being here. He will always believe there is a world in the center of the earth, where he could acquire all the power he hungers for, but it will always be out of his reach. Considering how skeptical most Outerworlders are, it is doubtful that anyone of consequence will take him seriously if he chooses to relate his incredible story.

"Nor will he forget his relationship with Delphina and the fact that she was an android. Instead, his love for her and the humiliation he experienced when he realized his mistake in loving a machine will be intensified to ensure his silence about her and a lifetime of frustration and unhappiness. It may sound like an unusual punishment, but after the misery he caused our people, it's justified."

Falcon had one more factor to add. "Before we left Alaska, I touched Nesterman's mind. I am certain he will not recall ever seeing Delphina. He will only remember his kidnapping, and Underwood's obsession about an opal ring. King was the only other witness Underwood had."

"And what do I say happened to Falcon? Surely someone will ask."

"His false identity was well established," Rom answered, "The Interpol file on him will remain open for the time being, but his next assignment will be listed as top secret, thereby explaining his disappearance if anyone investigates that far."

Steve nodded, suddenly too tired to think about any more details. It was not the events of the past days weighing her down, but the one, final event yet to come.

Falcon acknowledged her thoughts by taking her hand in his and pulling her up from her chair. "Please excuse us for tonight. We are both fatigued."

Rom and Aster saw them to the door, assuring

them they would not be needed again until morning.

Steve felt Aster's romantic heart reach out to her, but she dared not meet the other woman's gaze, for fear her own resolve would falter.

Chapter Twenty-one

The only victory over love is flight.
—*Napoleon Bonaparte*

"Where are we going?" Steve asked once they were outside.

"My residence. It is not as large as yours, but I believe you will be able to spend a comfortable night there."

She lowered her lashes, feeling oddly shy when she caught the glow in his eyes. He was giving her the night she had so boldly requested.

Falcon stopped and turned her toward him. Cupping her chin, he raised her face and studied her intently. "I do not understand this emotion you are feeling. Please explain."

Steve's cheeks pinkened. "I—I don't know if I can. I know it's silly, you know, to be embarrassed about it, but, I mean, I'm not really much more experienced than you, and well, first I seduced you, then I asked you for another night—"

Falcon hushed her rambling by placing his thumb on her lips. "It is not important." His thumb traced the outline of her mouth. "Do you want me?"

His gravelly voice raked through her, rendering her mute. *You know I do.* His hand moved to the back of her neck and held her as his mouth lowered to hers. Softly, he caressed her until she eased her body closer to his.

He raised his head and smiled approvingly. "That is much better. Now we will go."

A vehicle that looked like a small bus, but floated above the roadway on a cushion of air, delivered them to Falcon's apartment. Again Steve noted that the building had a futuristic appearance, but the interior of the one-bedroom apartment looked very familiar. She was about to ask where the soft lighting originated when Falcon pulled her into his arms. He had discarded his unemotional mask the moment they were alone.

He kissed her hard, once, twice. His mouth left hers for only a second when he returned for more. Steve felt as though she were being devoured and wanted desperately to feed his hunger while satisfying her own. His hands roamed her body, urgently kneading her flesh through her clothes. She arched against him, pressing her hips to his to relay her desire to skip the preliminaries.

He tugged at her shirt. She tore open the waist of his pants. They stumbled toward the bedroom, dropping a trail of clothing along the way.

At the edge of the bed the high-speed action abruptly slowed. They each paused and stepped apart. The sound of their strained breathing echoed through the room, but neither responded to the erotic call.

Steve wanted each moment to last, to make the night last forever, and Falcon seemed to understand. Or did he have the same need to savor every touch?

Simultaneously, their hands moved to the other's shoulders, then they began a thorough exploration. His palms grazed her breasts. Her fingers trickled down his sides. Their gazes held fast, wordlessly revealing the pleasure they were giving and receiving.

When their hands moved lower, intimately stoking each other's passion, their sighs were a shared sound, announcing the end of their temporary patience.

Falcon lowered Steve to the bed and positioned himself on his knees between her parted thighs. His fingers teased her sensitive flesh.

"Falcon, *please*," she begged, and reached for what she wanted.

He nudged her hand aside. "Not yet. Allow me to have my way with you first. I want to observe you as you enjoy your pleasure. I wish to feel what you feel in this manner."

She was tempted to deny him, to demand he be swept away with her, but the music his fingers played on her body reached a crescendo so swiftly she could hold nothing back from him.

Her release washed over him in waves of heat and shudders. The intensity of it was so strong that his shaft began to throb, and with one swift plunge, he embedded himself deep inside her.

When he had climaxed and her heartbeat slowed a bit, Steve murmured into Falcon's ear, "And now do I get to have my way with you?"

His answer was a purring sound and a movement within her body that indicated he was not yet finished having *his* way.

The night became a blend of endless ecstasy and unspoken wishes. No matter how sincere those private wishes, however, they could not hold back the dawn.

Falcon lifted Steve's hand and kissed her fingertips. Placing her palm over his heart, he said, "Steve, I know what you know and I feel what you feel, yet I believe there are words to be spoken between us." He hushed her attempt to interrupt with a mental gift of comfort. "You cannot stay."

"And you can't go with me. I understand. But . . ." She closed her eyes to hold back the tears that immediately surfaced. "It still hurts."

"You say you understand. I do not. Perhaps I will in the future, when I am more accustomed to all the emotions I have only recently come to possess. I have no understanding of the bond that has formed between us. The physical aspect is like touching the heavens. The mental companionship has filled a lonely void I was unaware I had. I have always believed my life would be a solitary one."

"Now you know differently. I'm so happy you came into my life, Falcon. I was lonely, but, unlike you, I knew it. For the rest of time, whenever I feel alone, I'll remember you and what we have shared. There's a part of me that you'll keep, but I believe I'll also have a part of you with me. There is so much more you're going to experience, and if I feel a little jealous when I think of you with other women, I'll just remind myself that I was first. Because of that, I'll know you haven't forgotten me. And that will have to be enough."

Falcon remained silent for several minutes before speaking again. "I have decided to return to my home planet, Emiron. I am not satisfied with this uncertainty. I must find out if what has happened to me has happened with others of my kind, and what else I might expect in the future. There is something else I must go back for, also. When I was conceived, it was part of an attempt by my people to strengthen their race, with the hope that a mixed breed would be able to repopulate the planet. I had not given that reason for my existence much thought until recently. I feel no desire to return for such a purpose, and yet it is my duty. Perhaps I will father children such as Vince and Mary Ann." He smiled, hoping she would, too.

She failed at first, then chuckled as she picked up his train of thought. "No, I could not be pregnant. Fortunately, I had that taken care of years ago. Good heavens. Keeping up with normal children is hard enough. I can't imagine what it would be like with one who had your talents. It would be a nightmare!" They laughed together at the kind of mischief such a child could get into, and the levity helped somewhat, until Falcon brought them back to reality.

"It is uncomfortable for me to consider never seeing your children. But the thought of never being with you again cuts me with very real pain. It is not possible. After I have done what needs to be done on Emiron, I will return to see you. I may not be able to remain in your world, but I could easily visit for short periods."

"God, Falcon. Don't say that. You don't realize what you're suggesting. I'd be on an emotional roller coaster—always on edge, waiting for that elusive someday when you would appear at my door. Then, when you did, I would be counting the days until you left again. I'd be going through this heartache over and over. And what if you never came back from Emiron? Would you have me live the rest of my days based on the possibility that I might see you one more time?

"You can't imagine how hard it is for me to say this. I'm terribly close to begging for one more day with you. The irrational part of my brain is ready to give up everything—my family, my career—if you asked me to stay with you. This time, the rational side will win, but if you came back another time, I'm not sure I would be so brave.

"I love you, Falcon. I'll always love you. But I don't want you popping in and out of my life. I hope someday you learn firsthand what love is, then you'll understand what I mean."

"Define love."

Steve shrugged. "That's what everyone would like to know, I guess. Aster said something to me that sounded pretty good. You know you're in love when you are no longer whole without the other person at your side."

"Like two halves of a circle. Only together do they make a whole. Yes, I see that. I also know that I have put thoughts and feelings into your head which were not your own. Perhaps once we are apart, you will discover that our attraction was not so much your doing, but more the fulfillment of my desires imposed on you."

She sighed and kissed him until their passion reawakened. "Believe whatever you'd like. It won't change the truth."

"One thing is certain. If you are ever in need of me, call my name. Somehow I will hear and attend you."

Steve didn't answer, for she knew another certainty. She would never make that call.

Chapter Twenty-two

And her yes, once said to you, Shall be Yes for evermore. —Elizabeth Barrett Browning

Steve swallowed her eighth aspirin of the day. The doctor had written her a prescription for a stronger medication—a drug that offered marginal relief to migraine sufferers. The slip of paper was still in her desk drawer, where it had been stuffed six months ago. She couldn't tell the doctor what she thought was the true cause of her headaches. He would probably have her committed.

A smirk twisted her mouth. Hell, they'd probably put her in the same "rest home" where Gordon Underwood had been permanently incarcerated. Of course, no one would suggest she was criminally insane as he had been judged. That decision had been the one bright spot during these past dismal months. The Nesterman kidnapping case never went to trial, for Gordon Underwood's ravings about a world in the center of the earth and the wicked tricks the aliens played on him immediately assured him a place in the psychiatric hall of fame. For weeks, every newspaper carried stories of the great man's downfall. A man of his genius and financial power being openly declared insane was the kind of divine retribution that made the world go round. The commoners loved every minute of it, laughed at his ludicrous claims, and promptly forgot about him a few weeks later.

But Steve couldn't forget the man who retained possession of her heart. What she had not known that last day in Innerworld was that he left something of himself with her—something completely unwelcome.

It had not occurred to either of them that the various psychic abilities she had acquired would remain with her. They had both assumed that he was triggering her expanded mental powers and that they would return to normal once they were separated. They had been mistaken, and it wasn't the least bit pleasant.

Seven months after they had said good-bye, Steve was still picking up on other people's emotional states, occasionally even hearing their exact thoughts. She didn't want to know what people were thinking or feeling, particularly those people who cared about her. Their smothering concern was driving her crazy. To make matters worse, she couldn't figure out how to shut out everyone else's feelings. It had seemed remarkably effortless when she was with Falcon, but without him, the so-called gifts were controlling her. At first she had cried, partly for her lost love and partly out of pure frustration. But when the tears had dried up, the headaches had taken over.

Then it took weeks for the children to stop asking about him. Her mother didn't ask, but she had followed Steve around with a Mother's-here-if-you-want-to-talk expression on her face. Her mom recognized a broken heart when she saw one, but her feelings were still hurt because Steve wouldn't open up to her.

At work the situation was equally stressful. Lou and her coworkers knew she was disturbed and went out of their way to help. First Lou had taken work away from her, then he had piled it on. She simply couldn't get interested in any of it and she knew that worried him most of all. His patience with her indifference was wearing thin.

The guys had razzed her with their best shots and got upset when they failed to get a rise out of her. Soon their concern had turned to irritation. She realized that they didn't care what her personal problem was anymore. After seven months of moping around, they thought she should straighten up and get on with her life.

Sometimes she wished she could scream at all of them. They didn't know what a true mess her brain was in. She couldn't concentrate unless she worked in her bedroom in the middle of the night. Even then, one of Vince's nightmares could unexpectedly burst into her thoughts.

What did you do to me? She tried not to think of him at all. When she did, she was careful not to say his name. She had no idea what would constitute "calling" him, but she wasn't taking any chances. Sooner or later this problem she had would go away on its own. It *had* to.

"Daydreaming again, Steve?" Lou teased as he stepped into her office and dropped a file on her desk.

She glanced from him to the file, then back to his face. Not only was he smiling, his eyes twinkled mischievously. The file obviously contained a pip of a case; his excitement was barely contained.

"A good one?" She massaged her temples in an attempt to quiet the pounding enough to hear his answer.

"Could be just what the doctor ordered. It's time for you to hit the road for Florida again, kiddo. There's a little town near Daytona called Cassadaga. It's a gathering place for psychic types. Everything from religious spiritualists to Tarot card readers. There are a few newspaper articles about the place in the file.

"Anyway, a few weeks ago, a card reader was found dead, apparently bitten by a very rare, poisonous snake while she was asleep. The police wrote it off as accidental, but another psychic in the neighborhood is insisting it was murder. She's hiring us to find the killer before he strikes again."

"He?"

"Figure of speech, I'm sure."

"Let me guess. She saw the murder in a dream and she'll be sure to get lots of publicity out of our investigation."

"Spoken like a true skeptic."

"Well, what other reason would she have to give us her hard-earned cash to find her competition's alleged murderer?"

"She's convinced it was not a singular murder, and she might be the next victim."

Steve whistled. The woman either had a great flair for melodrama or she had some genuine talent. What Lou couldn't know was that it would only take Steve a moment in the woman's presence to discern the truth. That was why she lost interest in the cases she handled in the last few months. Half of them were solved five minutes after she began her first interview. Maybe this one would be different.

It occurred to her that she was looking forward to meeting this woman. A legitimate psychic might even be able to help her live with her own unwanted powers.

"All right. I'll take it. When am I supposed to be there?"

"I promised the day after tomorrow. There's a few background checks we can make from here before you go."

Disappointment stabbed at her. She was ready to go right now.

Lou started out the door, then stopped and slapped his forehead. "What's wrong with me? I almost forgot the other reason I had to talk to you."

Steve angled her head and waited for the other shoe to drop.

"You'll be taking a partner with you."

"A partner?" Steve's voice rose several decibels. She almost sounded like her old self. "You know damn well I work alone, Lou. What are you trying to pull?"

"Hey, it was out of my hands," he said, showing her his squeaky-clean palms. "Senator Irven put the pressure on. What could I do? Our license comes up for renewal next year."

"Lou . . ." Steve warned, "what *are* you babbling about?"

Incredibly, Lou maintained an innocent expression, but Steve could feel him suppressing his mirth.

"It's an international exchange program being conducted between law enforcement agencies, both public and private—a way of sharing information and know-how through routine, hands-on experience."

"Please tell me you're working up to spitting out one clear sentence here."

"Okay, okay. Here's the deal. Interpol is exchanging one of their agents for one of our investigators, and I'm assigning him to you."

Steve's heart stopped and started again with a jolt. *Interpol?*

Lou backed out of the doorway, grinning like an idiot.

She recognized his aura the moment he allowed her to sense it. "Falcon?" she whispered, knowing he was there, yet not accepting it.

He moved into her office and closed the door behind him. "You once told me a simple thank you was not enough." He produced a bouquet of pastel roses from behind his back. "I was to give you flowers, also. I did not forget."

Steve sat frozen in her chair, still half-believing she was imagining him. He looked different. Perhaps he'd lost a few pounds. His hair was shorter, tamer; his eyes perfectly normal, a medium brown color without any golden lights. When she didn't reach for the flowers, he laid them on her desk and came around to her side. She stared at the blossoms, terrified that the slightest movement on her part might cause him to vanish. Seeing him again was worse than she had expected. When he left her this time, she would surely die.

"Steve?" His fingertips touched her cheek, turning her face toward him, but she did not raise her eyes. "Why did you not call me? I would have heard you. I feel your need, your confusion. Let me help."

She stood up and backed away from his touch. "I told you before I wouldn't be able to handle you coming in and out of my life. That hasn't changed." A gasping sob escaped her, and she hugged her sides to hold herself together. "Why are you here?"

"I need you. Even though you did not call me, I have felt your need of me as well. You were never out of my thoughts. I have been to Emiron and learned what I needed to know. I cannot make it without you."

Steve gave up the struggle. Opening her arms, she met him halfway. Oh, dear God, she was alive again. Falcon was with her, holding her, taking away her pain. It didn't matter how temporary it was.

"Are you not curious to hear about my journey?"

She shook her head no, then yes, and they both laughed. He sat down on the chair and urged her onto his lap.

"The planet, Emiron, is much as I remember it, but the people are not. Their hopelessness has been reversed. The experiment to save the population from extinction was a success. Children have been born to the generation of mixed breeds. You would probably find them most peculiar. They consist of a wide variety of species, but they *are* gifted felan children, and there are thousands of them. I was welcomed, though my presence there was not required. I have been released from my duty to them.

"I spoke to many others, like myself, who had undergone all the transformations I did. Had I remained there all these years I would have known what to expect. The changes for each began when it was time to mate. The personal emotions surfaced, the mental and physical powers increased, and, suddenly, reproduction was a possibility. Do you remember our first encounter?"

Steve wrinkled her nose at him. "I thought you were a gorgeous pervert. You *sniffed* me."

Falcon closed his eyes and inhaled deeply. "Mmmm. Like no other female. If only I had known then what I know now, I could have spared us both the pain of these last months. I opened myself to desire whenever I was near other females, but I had no wish to take pleasure with them. I was as I always was before—indifferent. Then I would think of you and ache with need.

"Yet I still could not comprehend that you were meant to be my mate. It was not until I found myself losing control of my talents that I understood the rest of the cycle. You recall that your abilities strengthened, but toward the end of our time together I was having trouble focusing unless we were touching. That was because you were already a part of me. My skills are practically useless without you."

"You've just explained what's been happening to me. I still have the abilities, but I can't seem to sort them out the way I did when I was with you. It's been driving me nuts. What does all this mean, though? What can we do?"

"It is not complicated. As Lou Dokes informed you, I am now your partner."

"Not complicated? The list of complications is a yard long."

Falcon shifted her to a more comfortable position on his lap and nuzzled her neck. In between tiny kisses he eliminated her list. "I had considerable guidance while on Emiron. With your help I will be able to cope with anything your world throws at me. With my help, you will reaccustom yourself to using your mind as you did with me before.

"New lenses were designed for my eyes. I hardly know they're in place, and every night, when we're alone, I can remove them. As your partner, I will be able to do the work I enjoy and not have to hide my special skills from you. And last, Romulus has appointed me as an official emissary here in San Francisco. From time to time we will return to Innerworld to report to him together."

"This is more than a little awesome, Falcon. But you seem to have forgotten one major point. I have two children and a mother to take care of. I certainly can't let them know who you really are."

He frowned at her. "Of course I have not forgotten. I will take precautions around them. My identity will remain a secret from them as long as you feel it is necessary."

"You missed my point. There is nothing I'd love more than knowing you'd be sleeping in my bed tonight, but you can't. I mean, I can't. It wouldn't be right."

"You are making no sense, Steve."

"My mother would never approve, and it wouldn't be proper for the kids to see their mother in bed with a man she isn't married to."

"Then we must marry."

"*What?*"

"Can we take care of this matter today? I have an urgent need to be in that bed tonight." He let his body confirm that statement.

"Falcon! That's crazy. What would everybody say? There's the license, and Mom would be furious if we didn't tell her first and—"

His mouth pressed against hers, ending all protests as he worked his wonderful magic on her senses.

She surrendered. *We could get married in Nevada in a few hours.*

He stopped kissing her immediately. "Nevada? Yes, that is a place of beginnings for me. We will go there, right after I tell you the most important thing I learned while we were apart."

"And what might that be? Some new mental trick?"

"No, not a trick, a new emotion—at least for me." He brought her closer for another long caress. *I love you, Steve. We belong together.*

She trembled as the truth of his words filled her soul, and she in turn poured all her love into his. *Forever.*

Marilyn Campbell loves to hear from her readers. Send S.A.S.E. for reply. P.O. Box 840002, Pembroke Pines, Florida 33084.